Damned Pretty Things

To Jexi,
I hope you enjoy
the trip!
Cheers,
Holly Wade Matter

Damned Pretty Things

by

Holly Wade Matter

Aqueduct Press
PO Box 95787
Seattle, Washington 98145-2787
www.aqueductpress.com

Library of Congress Control Number: 2020943635

ISBN: 978-1-61976-185-8

First Edition, First Printing, November 2020

10 9 8 7 6 5 4 3 2 1

Cover Illustration Courtesy Delaney Alonso

Quote from Knut Hamsun's Pan, translated by
W. W. Worster (p. 226).

Printed in the USA by McNaughton & Gunn

Acknowledgments

I'd like to thank the National Endowment for the Arts and the Seattle Office of Arts and Culture for their generous support during earlier incarnations of this book.

I'd also like to thank Nora Lee, Jean Anne Matter, Jim Comer, Elizabeth Finan, L. Timmel Duchamp, Kath Wilham, Dylan Eakin, and Nisi Shawl for encouragement, advice, critiques, editing, and inspiration.

Above all, I'd like to thank to Brad Matter for all his love and support.

In loving memory of Farley and Jane Wade

"F" is for Fortune in Fingerless Gloves

There were times when I would step into the Bel Air, the only interior space I can say belongs to me, and a soft scent would brush past my nose, subtle and teasing because I didn't know whose it was. The scent was old-fashioned. It could have been that of pale violet, powdery sachet wafers that ladies used to slip into their underwear drawers, or it could have been something else. Sometimes I stopped and asked aloud, "Whose is this?" Was it mine from an unre-membered past when there were grandmothers in my life, or from my far future, when my skin is soft and wrinkled, and I have (I hope) a fixed address and an underwear drawer to call my own?

When I was feeling blue, I imagined it was the perfume the Devil's girlfriend wore the night I sold my soul.

Would you like to hear that story?

(I always ask. As I've learned from hard experience, the Devil plays better in some towns than in others.)

I imagine it probably happened like this: one night, I hiked out into the silent country and waited in the cross-roads with my steel-string guitar on my back and my thumb stuck out. You might think I was being overly optimistic, trying to hitch a ride at that lonely hour, but if there's one thing I know about the psychology of the spirits, it's that they like you to ask for help in ways that are both gaudy and embarrassing. At midnight, the Devil drove up in his 1956 Chevy Bel Air two-door hardtop, Matador Red and Onyx Black (and yes, I do know the factory never made one in that particular color combination). He stopped an inch short from hitting me in the knee with the gleaming chrome bumper.

His girlfriend was with him. The dress she wore probably came from the shop in a heavy gold-foil box with three layers of coral tissue paper and a gold seal. Pumpkin-colored silk chiffon with a pattern of coral chrysanthemums. "Oh, baby!" I see her throwing her arms around the Devil's neck and giving him a kiss after she opened the box. She wiggled into that dress, which was barely able to contain her curves, smoothed on her seamed silk stockings, stepped into her gold ankle-strap sandals, and sprayed on some of that perfume. They got in the Bel Air to drive into town for a big night of drinking and dancing. Except there I was, standing in the crossroads, blocking their way.

"Oh, baby, don't be working on our night out."

He didn't listen. Like many a salesman, the Devil has a hard time distinguishing between the professional and the personal. He is always ready with a handshake and a pitch.

Have you met him? I didn't think so. Well, let me tell you what he looked like that night. Tall, dark, and handsome doesn't even begin to touch it. Heavy-lidded eyes that seemed black, except for gleaming pinpoints of garnet red. Skin so dark and flawlessly smooth that you wanted to reach up and brush your fingers against his cheekbones to make sure he was solid. Lips made for persuasions of all kinds. He was dressed in a black suit and shirt, a blood-red silk tie, a black snap-brim Fedora. He held a lit cigarillo gracefully between the knuckles of his middle and ring fingers...maybe to draw attention to the gold seal ring he wore, with a bas-relief rooster upon it.

"Well, hello there, young lady." His voice was smooth but with a subtle bite to it that reminded me of the taste of iron in blood. "And what is a fine young lady like yourself doing out at the crossroads at this hour, with that guitar on your back and that thumb sticking out? Are you attempting what I think you're attempting?"

"I don't know. I can't claim to be a mind-reader," I said, "though I do have some skill at reading palms."

"Do you, now? Well, then, have a look at mine and tell me what they say."

He secured his cigarillo between his teeth and presented his hands. I held them, palms up, in my own, where I could see them in the headlight beams. His skin was every bit as soft as I'd imagined, and hot, and buzzing with low-voltage electricity. What I read in the many lines and creases was a list of goods and services offered, complete with corresponding price... "One Soul."

"It says nothing I want to hear," I replied. I imagine I had a smart mouth in those days.

The girlfriend sighed and shifted her weight from one hip to the other. With an impatient flick of her wrist, she snapped open a gold fan and commenced to cool her cleavage.

"Ahem...."

"Just hold it, Sweet Honey," the Devil told her. And to me, he said, "What were you looking to find?"

"A certain ability with the guitar, bordering on genius," I said.

"Only bordering?"

"I'm modest."

"I can see that. A rare and precious quality in these troubled times. Guitar's easy enough. I've done that one before. Ever hear of Tommy Johnson? Of course you have."

"Robert," I said. "It was Robert Johnson."

His eyes flashed. "Look who thinks she knows everything. Maybe she already knows how to play that guitar, too. Maybe I'll be on my way."

"I always heard it was Robert Johnson."

"And you always heard wrong. It was Tommy, sure as I'm standing here. Wasn't it Tommy Johnson, Sweet Honey?"

His girlfriend huffed out a sigh. "Tommy Johnson."

"You see? Tommy."

Just like the Devil, to give you what you want and still let you fade into obscurity. I almost told him, *Considering I've never even heard of Tommy Johnson, maybe you didn't do him any favors.* But I held my tongue.

"Skill with the guitar…. Don't know why you couldn't find it. I know it's on here somewhere. Guitar, guitar, guitar…ha! Here it is."

"But," I added, "with that Bel Air of yours thrown into the bargain."

That brought him up short. "You want my car."

"Yes."

"Why?"

"Because I hiked all the way out here, and I'm pretty tired, and I don't feel like hiking all the way back."

"You couldn't just ask for a lift, could you?"

I shook my head. I imagine I was pretty stubborn in those days, too. "Besides," I said, "it's damned pretty, and I happen to like damned pretty things."

He thought a little bit, and then, as if he had somehow missed the last few seconds of our conversation, he said, "So you want my car."

"Yes."

"And a certain ability with the guitar, bordering on genius."

"Yes."

"Both."

"Uh-huh."

"Tell me something," he said. "What do you have written in the lines and the creases of your own palms?"

"I have my history," I said. "I have my identity. My name, and my family, who I will love, how I have lived, and how long I can expect to live."

"Tell you what I'm going to do," he said. "I'll give you the things you've asked for, in exchange for your soul…and for the lines and creases of your palms."

"What do you want those for?"

"Oh, I don't know. Just want 'em."

Well, it seemed like a strange thing to want. But it also seemed like a strange thing to want to keep—especially seeing as I was bartering my soul, which you might say ranked higher in importance.

"Mister, you've got yourself a deal," I said.

"Let's shake on it."

First he shook my right hand, and then he shook my left, and I found the ignition key in my right hand and the trunk key in my left.

"Now hand over that guitar of yours," he said. I put the car keys in my pocket, unslung the guitar from my back, and handed it to him. He sat down on the bumper, patted his pockets, and came out with a set of strings, ordinary-looking ones, too. I wondered about that, while I watched him restring my guitar. He spent some time tuning it afterward, leaning in close, eyes narrowed with concentration. He'd hum a note, pluck a string, twiddle the tuning peg, hum again, pluck, twiddle, until he got it right where he wanted it. He had a perfectionist streak in him; and he, like most men, could futz his womenfolk into the grave. His girlfriend and I both let out sighs of relief when he finally handed the guitar back to me.

"Now then, young lady, how's about you give us a tune?"

When my fingertips touched the strings, they buzzed with the same low-voltage electricity as the Devil's own hands, and I understood. It wasn't me that had changed.

Maybe it would never really be me. It was the strings. They spoke to my fingers, instructing, guiding, and my fingers spoke back, translating the language of the strings so that my head and my heart and my hips could be in on the conversation, too. I couldn't tell you what I played. The song had no words, no name that I knew of; and I have never played it since. But it made me feel so glad at heart that I didn't much care that things hadn't worked out as I'd imagined they would.

When, at last, my fingers stilled, and I could trust my voice to speak, I asked the Devil, "What happens when a string breaks?"

He smiled. "You'll have to wait and see." His voice made me think of sugar and sulfur. "Now won't you?"

I didn't know what to reply.

"I bid you goodnight," he said. He snapped his fingers and there appeared, a little ways down the road, a red 1959 Cadillac convertible with a black top.

"Least you got rid of that old grandma Bel Air," the girlfriend muttered, as the Devil went to inspect his new vehicle. She took a gold compact out of her handbag and refreshed her lipstick. Then she glanced up and, for the first time, seemed to really see me. We eyed each other suspiciously.

There are women whose beauty lies in symmetry, and there are women whose beauty lies in incongruity. The Devil's girlfriend was an incongruous beauty of the first water. She'd got a girlish, almost innocent face, framed by straightened hair that had been cut into a shingle, with two spit curls like little arrows pointing to her dimples; but her body was a topography of deadly curves that filled the dress to capacity and spilled out the front. She'd got that rich, burnt umber-toned skin I, too fair for my taste, had always envied, and yet her eyes were bluer than the waters of a Caribbean lagoon.

"Well, aren't you a mess," she said.

I looked down at myself: wrinkled black skirt, sweat-stained white T-shirt, and an enormous pair of hiking boots coated with road dust. I guess she'd assessed me pretty well.

"Never mind." She stepped nearer. "I'll give you a little something, too, if you ask me real nice." She nodded back toward the Devil, who was leaning back in the driver's seat of the Caddy, enjoying his cigarillo and ignoring us completely. "He cheated you, anyway."

She raised her left arm. A heavy gold charm bracelet, chiming with the tiny bells on it, slid to the middle of her forearm. Among the other charms, I saw a peacock, a hand mirror in the shape of a scallop shell, a turkey vulture (of all things), and a gold champagne bottle.

"Pretty, isn't it? This one's yours, is what I'm thinking." She unhooked a charm and held it out to me on the palm of her hand. It was a miniature bee skep, woven out of plaits of gold wire. It was the cleverest little thing I'd ever seen. I could all but hear it buzzing with tiny gold bees. When I made to touch it, she drew her hand back.

"Ask me nice, Miss Mess."

"You don't really want to give that to me, do you?"

One eyebrow went up, one scrunched down, and her mouth tightened into a rosebud.

"Guess somebody else might want it," she said to the sky.

Quickly, I said, "May I please have that charm?"

She smiled sweetly. "You most certainly may."

Even back then, I wore my hair in micro braids. She took hold of one, unraveled it, and then plaited the charm in. "Don't ever take it out, and don't ever cut off that braid. May come a time when you want some help. May be nobody but Sweet Honey will be able to help you. When that time comes, you just tell the bees."

"Thank you." That didn't feel like enough. "Thank you very much."

She kissed her fingertips and pressed them to my forehead. "You're most welcome." Then she walked, sensual and swaying, to the Caddy. She turned once and pointed at me with an imperious forefinger. "About telling the bees? Make sure it's really important, you hear? Some folks have made the mistake of wasting my time." She smiled in a way that made me shiver. "And didn't I make them sorry."

"Wait!" I took a step forward, then stopped. "Don't you want anything in return?"

"Why, yes, I do. First money you make from that guitar?"

I nodded and waited.

She looked me up and down. "You take that money and buy yourself a pretty dress."

She got in, the engine roared, the lights flashed on, and the Devil and his girlfriend drove away.

Well, it could have happened that way.

It could have.

Anything's possible, isn't it? If I chose to, and I frequently do, I could change my story in each town, and each time the story would be neither more nor less true than the last. These are the core facts: that I play the steel-string guitar exceptionally well, that not one of my strings has ever broken, and that I am searching.

I am searching for my history, my identity, my name, and my family. I am searching for the one I will love. I am searching for how I have lived, and how long I can expect to live.

And I always wear fingerless gloves because my palms are smooth, without a single line or crease.

I could see the question in Maud's eyes. I've seen it more times than I can count (at least on my fingers and my toes): *But what* really *happened?*

In reply, I wanted to ask her a question of my own: *What is your definition of* real?

Instead, I picked a desultory tune on my guitar and said, "Did you ever hear a lie you knew was a lie but you wanted to pretend, just for a little while, that it wasn't? Did you ever hear a whole flock of lies, one after another, and wonder if maybe, somewhere among them, there flew a story that was real? And did you wonder which one? Did you think you'd be able to tell? Would there be something about the teller's face that would show you? Would her eyes shift, or blink, look at you differently or just look away? Would her words feel different to you, lighter, able to fly higher? Would you feel something sliding up your backbone, soft as a feather, that would tell you true from not-true?

"And did you ever wonder if it even mattered in the end?"

As I played, and as I spoke, I looked right at Maud, who leaned so far forward that it was a wonder she didn't fall out of her chair. The way she held her hand over her mouth, I wondered if she were afraid it would give her away to me before she was ready to be given away.

If that were true, she should have covered her eyes, too.

But I'm getting ahead of my own story.

What I remember of the night I (may or may not have) sold my soul to the Devil, is finding myself standing in a crossroads, with a guitar in hand and a couple of car keys in my pocket. The Bel Air was at my back, engine ticking and snapping as it cooled. The headlights flanked me, illuminating motes of dust that had been scuffed up from the dirt road. I looked up into a sky so big and dark, with so many stars, that I knew I had been transported to a different world. I was certain that where I came from, the sky was never that dark, the stars that absurdly abundant. Crackling sounds came from the woods, and strange scents that I didn't know. There were animals out here. I had a sense of bears and cougars and things with sharp antlers and no friendliness for me. What about splintercats? What about Sasquatch?

Did I drive myself out here? Was this really my car? Why couldn't I remember? Why couldn't I remember *anything*?

I felt tipsy, wanted to sink down right there in the middle of the dirt road, but that desire scared me in its own right, so I opened the car door and sat down inside. I watched my scared eyes in the rearview mirror, hoping they'd tell me something.

Then I caught sight of the single charm braided into my hair. When I touched it, it shocked me; and the impression of a man and a woman like ghosts, like gods, like carnival creatures, played hide-and-seek in my mind.

Some people have told me, in so many words, that a girl who could lose her name and her past must be pretty careless and basically untrustworthy.

If it makes me mad to hear it, it's only because I know they're right.

I'd been on the road for 'round about a year since that fateful night, traveling from town to town, from campground to campground, playing in cafes, taverns, farmers' markets, wherever anybody would let me. A story, a song, and palm-reading on the side kept me alive. Taste in music varies but never, I've found, the desire to know the future. Some days I could make a decent chunk of change telling fortunes at one of the rest stops along the interstate. Then I'd treat myself to an inexpensive motel, with a real bed and a real shower, and have a poached egg with my pancakes for breakfast.

If anybody asked me where I was headed, I'd tell them I was working my way toward the city. No matter how much folk and blues I played, anybody could tell, just by looking at me, that I was an urban child. But the city might as well have been the center of a maze, with no direct road to lead me to it, since every time I got within twenty miles, something else enticed me away...an intriguing road, an invitation to play, and sometimes, just my own pitiful sense of direction.

It was a direct commission that brought me to the red bridge to Sky. Whether something more than chance and a bent nail caused my right rear tire to blow out before I could cross the bridge, I leave to your discretion.

Fate or chance, the fact remained that I was stranded on the shoulder of a narrow, two-lane highway, on what had to be the hottest July day the west side of the mountains had ever known, with a spare tire that gave like bread dough when I poked it, and the knowledge that I hadn't passed a single vehicle, filling station, farm house, or trailer since I first turned onto this highway. When I opened the map and found it was another five miles to Sky, I strongly questioned the wisdom of having accepted that commission.

I boosted myself up to sit on the trunk, my feet on the bumper, and fanned myself with the road map. I'd had a headache since morning; now my head felt stuffed to the splitting point. Hunger had a lot to do with it. At noon, I'd held my nose and eaten the bruised and half-fermented peach floating in the warm melted ice in the cooler. The only food I had left was a random assortment of cellophane-wrapped crackers and bull's-eye mints from diners all over the state. But my head throbbed, too, from a coming storm. The overcast made me think of an iron lid clamped down on a near-boiling sky, pressure building until it was enough to send the lid rattling and clattering and the sky boiling over.

I shielded my eyes from the glare and squinted at my surroundings. Grassland lay on one side of the highway, a sprawling thicket of hazel, red alder, and big leaf maple on the other, and the valley itself lay cozy between foothills that didn't look recently logged. All around me, the countryside made its usual summer racket: grasshoppers springing in the dry grass, a garter snake slithering into the salmonberry bushes, bees hovering and darting, mosquitoes whining, and a couple of jays squawking from a lone Douglas fir in the meadow. A hawk, deceptively lazy, glided on the air.

All the while, the brick-red, WPA-era steel bridge seemed to mock my predicament. I hopped down and went to visit it. It spanned a shallow ravine and a shallower creek. The pitted macadam road on the other side continued straight for a space, then gently curved to the right and disappeared behind the trees. Wild grass and asters grew in the cracked macadam along the railings. The red paint was peeling, and there wasn't any graffiti.

I ran my palms over the painted steel, the bumpy rivets, of the nearest truss. It was hot even through my fingerless gloves. I peeled off a patch of red paint and let it fall.

My temples throbbed. My feet ached, hot and swollen in my boots. Sweat trickled down the back of my neck. Not even a baby breeze stirred my skirt. The subtle creek music enticed me. The bank was steep but not high…it should be easy enough to climb down.

"That five miles to Sky isn't going to walk itself," I said with authority in my voice.

But the child in me…that child wanted the creek.

I climbed down the bank, holding on to vine maples and alders along the way, pausing partway down to pee discreetly among some sword ferns.

I took off my shoes and stockings and tender-footed my way across the dry creek pebbles to the edge of the water. Then I dropped my boots on a boulder, tied my hair back with one braid, and knelt down. I didn't take off my fingerless gloves (I almost never do), just splashed water, cool and soothing, on my face. A little ways downstream, I found a good boulder for sitting, with a cushion of dry moss, and dangled my feet in the water.

Every day, two or three times a day, I'd touch each of the charms woven into my hair, counting them, naming the places where I'd chosen them and the circumstances of the choosing. I did it to reassure myself that I could remember the past year, at least.

I tapped the bee skep charm and said, "Hey, bees! I've got no money, I've got no food, I've got no friends, and I've got no spare tire." I almost asked for help. Almost. But even in those straits, I wasn't far gone enough to actually believe my own stories.

The scent reached me first—the intoxicant of petrichor rising from hot macadam. Then the desultory patter of rain on alder leaves, the pop and ripple of drops on the surface of the water. I looked up at the sky and got a raindrop square in my right eye. The first sound of thunder came, distant and blunt, as if it had been dumped from a rusting wheelbarrow on the other side of the mountains.

It occurred to me that if lightning chose to strike me at that very moment, it would not be out of place with the current tenor of my life.

It also occurred to me that I'd left the Bel Air's windows rolled down.

I snatched up my boots, hopped across the dry rocks, scrambled up the bank, and made it to the road while parts of it were still gray and dry. I threw my boots into the car and rolled up the windows, then stood on the shoulder and watched the road grow black and steam, as if the pavement were bound with spirits that only rain could release. The scent was delicious, like nothing else on earth. If it had been a perfume, I would have sprayed it all over me, every single blessed morning.

The iron lid above me shifted with an ear-cracking roar and a crooked vein of pure electrical passion, and more water than I'd thought existed rattled down upon me. It drummed on the roof of the Bel Air and ran off it in sheets, washing away weeks of road dust and bug corpses. It filled the potholes to overflowing and rippled across the road. I danced in the rain, my bare feet smacking down on the warm, wet road and sending up spray. I laughed, and leapt, and shook my braids. I stumbled a bit once my skirt got soaked and clung to my legs, but I didn't care. Didn't I have monsoon in my blood? And wasn't I, above all things, a shameless exhibitionist?

When the old green Ford pickup drove up and stopped, for one wild moment I believed I'd conjured it by dancing. The driver's window rolled down and a real, live human being leaned out and shouted, "You need some help?"

"More than you could possibly imagine," I shouted back. I think I was giddy from sheer relief.

The driver seemed taken aback and squinted up into the sky as if asking for an explanation (or a favor). He didn't even flinch at the next lightning bolt, which seemed to find a home about half a foot away from the far end of the bridge.

"You want me to," he shouted, "I'll change your tire now, but it might be better to go into town and wait it out."

"That's okay. My spare is flat, too."

"What do you want to do?"

"Not die, for one thing," I shouted. "Please don't take offense, but I don't know you, and for all I know, you might be a killer maniac."

He tilted his head a bit to one side and looked at me, considering. "For all I know, you might be one, yourself. And I'm not much looking forward to dying, either."

I laughed. I knew he'd be all right. I might not know my name or my birth date, but I did know to trust my instincts. "Wait. I need to get something." I fetched my boots and stockings and my guitar out of the car, and locked up.

He leaned across the seat and opened the passenger door for me. I got in and arranged myself and my guitar so that neither of us were on his lap.

"This isn't a high car-prowl area," he said, amused. It surprised me to hear him use a city term like that.

"I'm a hayseed for only part of the year," he explained.

"Did I say anything?"

"You didn't have to. You have an expressive face."

"Oh." I gazed at the water running off me and onto the seat. "Sorry about the water."

"It's just a little rain."

When he drove onto the bridge, the hairs rose on my nape and my arms. I couldn't tell you why—maybe I was just lightheaded from hunger—but it seemed to me that I was leaving the ordinary world behind and entering a world where the spirits weren't strangers.

I looked him over. He seemed human enough. He was a tall man, with a strong, slender build and a baked-in tan that made me think of cowboys. His hair, which had recently been cut, was mostly brown, with uneven chunks that had been bleached out by the sun. He was clearly a working man; the backs of his hands were marred by all kinds of little wounds and scars, some still pink and healing. The sleeves of his chambray shirt were rolled up past the elbow. The hairs on his forearms were golden. He smelled good, like cedar and pitch and coffee. His eyes were pilot-light blue, he was probably close to thirty, and he wore no wedding ring.

"Thank you for picking me up."

"Pleased to be of service."

"What's your name?" I asked him.

"Everybody in town calls me Lightning," he said.

I blinked at him, and then I laughed. "That's a powerful nickname. Funny, me meeting you during a storm like this. My name's Fortune."

He glanced at me sideways. "I always hoped I'd run into you someday."

"Any puns on my name that you might be thinking of springing, let me assure you I've already heard them. All of them. About two thousand times apiece."

"So much for conversation," he said. I liked his smile. "Do you carry that guitar everywhere you go?"

"Most everywhere. I can stand to lose just about everything else but this."

"Must be one special guitar."

We lapsed into a friendly silence, and I all but pressed my nose against the window. Since I'm never a passenger, I don't get much chance to look at the scenery.

The lonely country gradually gave way to human habitation...first a few isolated houses with pastures out front, and horses standing around looking miserable as only rained-on horses can manage. Then a dairy farm with a big barn and silo. The windows of the farmhouse were warm with light that cut through the gray, pelting rain and the storm darkness. It seemed to me that it would be the nicest thing in the world to be inside and cozy during the storm. My sodden clothes had gotten cold. I had goosebumps all over and was trying hard to keep my teeth from chattering.

16

We passed more houses, with smaller pastures and fewer horses, and then houses nearer together with no pasture at all but tidy, little front yards. Then the speed limit changed to 25 mph, and we were in town.

I liked little foothills towns like this, too far from the city to be suburbs and too far from the ski slopes to be resorts, kept tidy and archaic with their false fronts, their cast-iron street lights, their grocery stores that looked like converted airplane hangars. This town was true to type. Railroad tracks ran parallel to the main street (called Main Street, of course). Older model cars parked along the curb. Bicycles leaned against the street lamps. There were even piles of horse manure in the road here and there.

We stopped at a seemingly unnecessary stop sign in front of the Diamond Dress Shoppe. The plaster mannequin in the window was wearing an enormous, 1970s Afro wig, was missing one hand, and had part of its nose busted off. To add insult to injury, it was displaying a pink dress with an elastic waistband, patch pockets, and a ruffled front. In a flash, I apprehended the mannequin's sad history...a decade or two forgotten in the stock room of one of the big city department stores, removed and then sold cheap when the department store went bankrupt.

We passed a tiny white stucco church with the name Nazareth Temple in bas relief over the red door. I craned my neck to make out the details of the carved wooden sculpture in front of the Tribal Cultural Center. There was another, similar sculpture in front of City Hall.

Off to the left, on a little hill, higher than the rest of the town, stood a three-story brick building with a cupola that I later learned was the high school and had been since before the first World War.

When we came to the movie house, Lightning put the truck into park but didn't turn off the engine. The vertical neon theater sign, intricate and deco, spelled out BLUE MOUSE THEATRE. An animated blue mouse ran up one side and down the other. According to the marquee, the theater was currently showing a movie called "Marmots in the Family."

Lightning laughed. "I wonder if they've really got it this time. They've been trying to show it for years but they always get sent some other movie by mistake. Once it was a Bollywood musical. Half the girls in town went saree-crazy that summer. Maud says she went to every single showing." Something brought him up short, and he turned and looked at me funny. "She was dancing, too, the first time I saw her. Up at the very top of Wolf's House."

When he said the name "Maud," the hairs stood up on my arms, as they had when we crossed the red bridge. "Maud," he said, just like that. Just as if I'd never heard her name before that moment. Just as if I hadn't come looking.

Maud dancing at the very top of Wolf's House. I had a sudden, vivid vision of her as a circus girl in pink, with a parasol for balance, spinning and teetering on the apex of a steep roof to the anxiety of the gasping audience below. Wolf, I knew, would have to be the local lumber baron, complete with a villain mustache, a 1920s tuxedo, and wicked designs on Maud: *Whatever you ask me, I will give you, even half of my kingdom.*

"Where is Wolf's house? Are we going to go past it?"

"Wolf's House is that mountain up ahead."

"Oh. Is Maud your girlfriend?"

He blushed to the tips of his ears. "No," he said emphatically.

I smiled and sang, "Long Maud, Long Maud is neat of foot, Long Maud is soft of tread..."

His hands twitched on the steering wheel, as if he'd gotten a shock of static electricity. The windshield wipers slapped back and forth, back and forth. "She's long enough, Maud is. She's nearly as tall as I am." Then, irrelevantly, "It's her birthday today."

"How old?"

"Eighteen."

"Old enough at last. If you like, I'll read your palm and tell you what your chances are."

"I don't need my palm read to know that."

"Aw, let me. It's the least I could do," I said. "Payment for the ride."

"No need to pay me."

I thought for a while. "Maud," I said. "Tall. Eighteen. Astrological sign of Leo. Runs the filling station?"

"Waits tables at the Sky Cafe."

"I wonder...is that the type of place where I could sing for a sandwich and a cup of coffee?"

He gave me another funny look. "I've never heard that particular question before."

"Well, to be brutally honest, I don't have enough for a sandwich, let alone a new tire." My stomach growled like a mean dog. I couldn't have timed it better if I'd tried. I sighed. "No matter. Even in a barter economy, the artist is always the first to get stiffed."

"You think so?"

"I have been a grasshopper in this world for as far back as I can remember. Believe me, I know. It's a value perception problem."

"Tell you what. I'll buy you a sandwich, just for the fun of it."

"I won't say no."

He drove on about a block and pulled up in front of the aforementioned Sky Cafe, which was sandwiched between an antique shop on one side and the Avery Photography

Studio on the other. "Go on in. I'll be along as soon as I park the truck."

"I can't go in barefoot."

"Sure you can."

So I got out, toting my boots and my guitar with me, and made a run for it, through the pelting rain, to the Sky Cafe.

I didn't so much walk into the cafe as I was blown inside. The door sucked shut behind me with a bang and the hysterical tinkling of the bell.

When you enter the Sky Cafe, the first thing you see is yourself. Even when you're expecting it, it startles the hell out of you. The front doors open into a foyer, where a massive oval mirror, probably seven feet tall at its highest point, hangs in an ornate, blackened silver frame. It's quite an old mirror, speckled, tinted a murky, grayish-blue, and rippled in a way that makes you want to believe that glass, over time, flows like ice. The tinted glass leeches all the warm tones out of your skin and hair and clothes, and the overall effect is that of seeing yourself in a tintype, as if you had become your own ancestor.

I started when I found myself looking into the eyes of a weirdly familiar girl. It took me a moment to understand that she was me; but even after my brain straightened it out, I continued to stare, examining myself from head to toe as if I were a stranger. She was an odd one, this light-skinned, barefoot black girl, with her hair all done up in fine plaits, and the plaits braided and woven with charms, and beads, and things from gumball machines; ribbons and wire; tiny bits of bone and polished wood. Odd, again, dressed in an antique chocolate-brown skirt that clung to her legs and a white armistice blouse made nearly transparent with rain. She had on a pair of tatty leather fingerless gloves that had nothing stylistically in common with either her hair or her clothes, and she held her Edwardian boots by the knotted-together laces.

She was pretty—damned pretty, even—despite the anxious expression on her face and the fact that she was wet as paint. She held her guitar with negligent ease, like a child holding her doll by the ankle. She looked like somebody I'd like to know but who was certain to have one or more annoying habits and was probably outrageously dishonest. I dropped my boots and stepped toward her, cautiously, and touched my fingers to hers. The mirror misted around our fingertips.

Somebody cleared his throat and said, "It's a miracle anybody ever makes it past that mirror. Cover it up, Robin, or all your customers are going to starve to death."

"John, you know Eddy would never let me do that."

I broke out of my trance and turned. A small group were gathered at the window, as if they had been watching the storm (they had). Now they watched me, instead.

I felt like a little kid who might or might not be on the verge of a bawling-out. I smiled and raised my hand in a feeble wave. "Hi." Then, hoping this would make a positive difference in my reception, I picked up my boots and added, "Lightning brought me."

"Well, come on in and make yourself comfortable." This was Robin Avery, the owner and chef. She was maybe forty, maybe older and not showing it (black, as they say, don't crack), dressed in chef's whites, with her hair done up in a white headscarf. Her figure showed that she enjoyed her own good cooking, and her confident air that she did so without remorse. She had on a pair of gold, wire-rimmed glasses that looked distinctly Edwardian, and when she smiled, she showed a chipped front tooth she hadn't found time to get fixed yet. "No matter what anybody here says, I was not, I repeat, not opening beer bottles with my teeth," she told me later.

The power had gone out, and it was dark enough that Robin had lit the candles on all the tables. One table held the remains of a sheet cake—Maud's birthday cake. That, and the scents of sausage, tomatoes, rice, caramelized onion, and coffee, made my mouth water and my stomach grumble.

Let me tell you a little bit about the people who were there.

John Jordan Caldecote, Maud's father, edited the newspaper and did all the printing in town. He was a tall, shy white man with wavy, wiry, gold hair, a flushed face, fingers permanently stained with printer's ink, his eyes wary behind black, horn-rimmed glasses. The whole time he was in the cafe, he seemed just seconds away from leaving, jingling his keys and pacing. I later came to learn that this was just his normal restless style.

Pat Burnett was the director of the Tribal Cultural Center, and was collaborating with Mr. Caldecote on an ever-expanding book about the valley's history. A streak of iron-gray hair ran from his forehead to the end of his braid, and allegedly had since the time he was hit in the head with a baseball in junior high school. From the strength of his neck and shoulders, he looked like he might have been a member of his college wrestling team twenty years earlier. He'd just quit smoking the week before, but kept patting his shirt pocket out of reflex, and started at any unexpected sounds. The thunderstorm made a miserable man of him.

Mrs. Diamond owned the dress shop with the sad mannequin. She'd come down for a coffee break and got stranded by the storm. She was about fifty, petite, dressed in a peach polyester pantsuit. She wore a frosted, girl-group-era wig the color of almond butter. She was light-skinned, like me but afflicted with freckles all over her face and hands. Her fingers were loaded with rhinestone knuckle-dusters that flashed menacingly in the candlelight with every movement of her hands—and she moved them a lot, ostentatiously chain-smoking in front of poor Mr. Burnett. I learned later that they had a bet on as to whether he could make it thirteen days without taking a puff.

Mrs. Diamond and Robin were first cousins, and neither could much stand the other, but Robin felt obliged to give Mrs. Diamond free coffee whenever she wanted it, and Mrs. Diamond reciprocated with a standing offer of a 10 percent discount on clothes Robin would never in a million years have bought.

The prep cook, a white boy slouching by the window with his fists jammed in his pockets, was one of the most unpleasant-looking people I'd ever seen. His body language screamed "juvenile detention alumnus." He had shaved his dirty brown hair down to a stubble that showed all the scabbed places where he'd nicked his scalp. His cheeks and chin were likewise nicked, his lips chewed, and his face, when it wasn't animated, looked both dumb and mean. He never called anybody by name, only said "she" and "he" as if he expected you to know exactly who he was referring to. He was probably twenty-one or twenty-two at the most. Everybody called him Low, which might have been his last name or might have been a reference to his character. His full name, his history, and the source of his bizarre accent—he spoke as if the inside of his mouth had been stung by hornets—were mysteries...he'd shown up in town about a year before, claiming to be a friend of Eddy Avery, one of Robin's many nephews. Robin had hired him and let him rent the studio apartment above the cafe. Whatever Robin knew about him, she wasn't sharing.

An elderly white woman sat at a corner table, away from everybody else, and picked at a slice of cake. She was dressed like a well-to-do woman in a black cashmere cardigan, black creased slacks, and a strand of pearls in the style of the 1950s. She seemed frail, shoulders bent, eyes faraway and sad. Nobody introduced her, and she didn't introduce herself. But every time I caught her eye, she smiled at me.

And then there was Maud.

I knew her immediately. She was, indeed, long—probably six foot two in her cowboy boots—with an air of cool self-possession that I hadn't seen in many tall women, or many women her age, for that matter. Her movements were so flexible and unstudied that when I learned that her middle name was Poplar, I thought her parents must have possessed second sight. She'd inherited her height and her long, narrow face from her father. Her eyes were big and dark as blackthorn plums, her eyebrows heavy, her mouth cautious. Her sable-brown hair she wore in a stick-straight ponytail that ended just past her shoulder blades. That afternoon, she had on a knee-length black skirt, a sleeveless white blouse, and the previously mentioned cowboy boots. The only make-up she wore was lipstick in a shade I always thought of as "dime-store whore red." It actually looked good on her.

As an object, Maud wasn't especially good-looking. I imagined she wouldn't photograph well—that her face would show too long, too bony. But Maud in motion was a damned pretty thing.

When I spoke Lightning's name, she flushed up to the roots of her hair, and her gaze flickered past me. Her hand went up to cover her mouth and didn't come down until I said, "I got a flat tire just before the bridge. If your resident Good Samaritan hadn't come along and offered me a ride, I might have been out there forever." Then she relaxed and was able to look at me again.

"You must be freezing in this air conditioning," she said. The huskiness of her voice startled me. It reminded me of blackstrap molasses because it was more bitter than sweet.

"Just set your guitar down and come back with me," Robin said. She took me to the women's restroom

"Your clothes are pure World War I vintage. Where did you get them?"

"They were given to me by an old lady I met, who told me I was the spitting image of her older sister, who'd died in 1918 of the Spanish Flu."

"Let's make sure you don't die of flu your own self." She left and came back with a Black Watch plaid rain coat lined with fake fur.

"Somebody left this here about two years ago and never came back for it. It'll be big on you but better than going around in sopping-wet clothes."

I stripped off my blouse and skirt and buttoned up the raincoat. It was too big but the fake fur lining was nice and dry. As I put on my stockings and boots, Robin hung up my clothes to drip, drip, drip on the bathroom floor. She glanced curiously at my fingerless gloves but said nothing, and we went back out.

"What I want to know is, what's she doing with all that trash in her hair?" Mrs. Diamond was saying as we came out. Maud closed her eyes with an embarrassed sigh, and Mr. Burnett cleared his throat.

Low surprised me by looking me in the eye and saying, "It's like them girls in Africa. Them Fulani girls."

"What do you know about Africa?" Mrs. Diamond demanded. Under her breath, she added, "Or girls, for that matter."

"Oh, he was probably a highly decorated hero in the French Foreign Legion before he came here to chop parsley for Robin," Maud said. "Weren't you, Low?"

He brushed near her, hissed "French *you*," at her, and stalked away to the kitchen.

"Leave poor Low alone," Mr. Caldecote said to his daughter.

"Poor Low my eye," she said. "He's revolting."

"All the more reason to show some kindness."

Maud's mouth gave a skeptical twist. Then Lightning came in, holding his jeans jacket over his head like a tent, and she forgot about everybody else. She stood at anxious attention, looking like a child about to get a present, before she recollected herself and adopted a blasé stance.

Lightning hung his jacket on the coat rack near the mirror and joined us. Everybody was pleased to see him, even Mrs. Diamond, and he shook hands with them all. He even shook my hand, with formal courtesy, since we hadn't really had a chance before. But to Maud, he just nodded and said her name with a complete lack of enthusiasm. He didn't wish her a happy birthday, even though he'd mentioned it to me himself. He intrigued me.

Low came back with two cups of coffee and gave one to me and one to Lightning. "Still hot."

"Thank you," I said.

He didn't meet my gaze. "Sure, whatever." Then he gazed sidelong at Maud, his eyes narrowed to slits, and said, "Somebody's gotta take care of things around here."

Lightning said, "Thanks, Low. Good to see you again. Doing all right?"

"Yeah, sure," he replied. To Robin, he said, "I'm goin' on break."

"That's fine, Low," Robin said. Low stalked off again, and slammed the back door behind him.

"Break from what?" Maud said, looking after him with disgust. "He brought out coffee. How exhausting."

"She is merciless, isn't she?" laughed Mr. Burnett. "Got to be hell to be single and smitten when Maud's around, isn't that right, Lightning?"

I had never before seen two people so quickly and so diligently look at anything but each other. Lightning frowned and drank his coffee. Maud covered her mouth and stared at one of the portraits on the wall, as if trying to remember if she owed that person money.

These portraits—big, framed, enlarged tintypes of Native Americans, of black folks, of white folks and Asian—covered the walls. There was that quality in their faces, in the way they held themselves, in their old-timey clothes, but especially in their eyes, and the way their eyes met the camera, that you don't see any more. There wasn't a face among them that you would ever expect to see in the modern world. But when you got up close, you realized they weren't photos at all but photorealistic drawings, down to the scratches and specks and haze. I later learned they'd been drawn by Robin's nephew Eddy, and that each one was of townsfolk still alive, including Mr. Burnett, Maud's mother, and Robin.

"I still want to know about that hair." Mrs. Diamond got up and came over to me. "Got to get a better look at these." She reached for my hair. Faster than I could think, I shoved her hand away.

"*Don't.*" My heartbeat gave a kick, and for a moment, my blood felt fizzy in the veins of my forearms. Mrs. Diamond looked at me in narrow-eyed outrage and nursed her wrist as if I'd hit her. I took a few deep breaths to settle down. Trying to keep my voice calm, making each word distinct, I said, "I am not a mannequin."

"Well, I never in my life," she said. "Pardon me for coming too close to the Queen of Sheba."

Robin rubbed her hands across her eyes. "Carla, for heaven's sake, just sit down and shut up."

Mr. Burnett snorted, and Mr. Caldecote quickly turned and looked out the window. And Maud looked ready to cry from mortification.

"It's all right," I said to her, and smiled. I tried to take a sip of coffee but my hands trembled so badly that I had to put the cup back down. I couldn't make them stop.

"She's about to faint from hunger," Lightning said to Robin. "Did you have anything ready in the kitchen before you lost your power?"

"I did, and I'm glad I've got somebody here to eat it up for me." Robin made for the kitchen, and Maud, with a glance like she couldn't stand to leave, turned and followed her.

Maud brought me a big bowl of vegetable soup, and a roast chicken sandwich bursting with butter lettuce besides, and the same for Lightning. I fell to. It's no disrespect to Robin's culinary skill to say just about anything would have tasted heavenly to me at that point.

Mr. Burnett and Mr. Caldecote left us to eat in peace while they discussed plumbing challenges and golf, while Robin went back to the window to watch the storm and occasionally comment on a particularly flamboyant lightning strike. Maud divided her attention between Lightning and me.

"Where have you been all these weeks?" she asked him.

"Around."

"Not that it matters to me," she said quickly. "But Gabriel was asking about going up to the Anvil this summer…"

"You know that's always fine with me, Maud," he said.

"It wasn't once. And anyway, sometimes people change their minds." She looked at her folded hands with a gaze so artlessly woeful that I wanted to take Lightning aside and tell him "Guess what? She's crazy about you."

But that was not my business.

In the meantime, Mrs. Diamond scrutinized me, even forgetting to torment Mr. Burnett by smoking. I could tell I'd come up against a champion grudge-holder. Her expression seemed to say, *You've got a dirty little secret, and I'm going to find out what it is.* I think it must have been her clothes. Peach polyester is enough to make anybody mean.

"You'd better call your folks," she said at last, when I'd licked the crumbs from my fingers and wiped my mouth. "They might be worried about you."

"I can't," I said.

"Why not?" She actually sneered. I'd never seen a sneer before. "Did they kick you out?"

"Jesus, Carla...." Robin groaned.

"Worse," I said. "I don't even know who they are."

Then I pulled my guitar up on my lap and picked out a tune, slow and bluesy, while I told them my soul-selling story.

I did say I was an exhibitionist, didn't I?

The truth is that in all the towns I've been, nobody has ever seen the likes of me before. I am used to being a one-woman freak show, and as far as matters of survival go, it would be to my disadvantage not to be. But in the Sky Cafe, none of them, except Mrs. Diamond, looked at me as if I were a freak. Robin didn't blink at my soul-selling tale; she even looked as if she'd like to maybe correct me on a few details I'd gotten wrong.

Maud, leaning forward, seemingly afraid of missing a single word, a single pause or breath, listened to me like I were someone she'd waited for all her life, and now that I was here, she could hardly believe I'd finally come. I felt as if I were speaking to her from within her own dreams.

I said, "I see prophecies on billboards, and cereal boxes, and shop signs. When I look twice, the words resolve into something quite ordinary and expected, but the hidden messages remain: 'facial torch.' 'Hat potatoes.' They prove the truth that we live in a world of wonder, where magic is camouflaged in every ordinary thing.

29

"Imagine living a life motivated by the love of wonders. Our world is full of them, absolutely bursting with them. Rainforests. Fifty-foot-long squid. Shrubberies that are 12,000 years old. Fungus! Just think of fungus! Think of the Missouri River flowing backward in 1815, just as if the earthquake that caused it made time itself flow in reverse. Think of dogs in Cairo struck dead by meteorites from Mars."

Mr. Burnett said, kindly, "How can you know all that and not know your real name?"

"I don't know. Every day, I find myself knowing things but not knowing how I know them. When and where did I learn to waltz? How do I know to order white wine with poultry? Or that Amos Tutuola wrote *My Life in the Bush of Ghosts*? And yet, I can't find the straight path back to myself. Sometimes I remember flashes of things. Army tanks in my neighborhood, on the street the next over from mine. Selling kola nuts for cowrie shells in a hot outdoor market. Pushing up my sunglasses and hugging my books to my chest as I walk through a crowd of screaming white people. I know these memories can't be mine, not directly mine. It's more like they're from an exhibit I walked through once, at the Museum of Mystery and Industry."

"The what?" Maud breathed.

"The Museum of Mystery and Industry. Haven't you ever heard of it?"

She shook her head.

"It's what I'm looking for," I said. The lie came so easily it nearly took my breath away. "Why I'm trying to get back to the city. If I could find it again, I'd learn who I was, and who I am, and where I belong."

"How do you know?" Lightning asked.

"Because I'm a mystery," I said. "They'd have to know how to solve me."

The elderly woman laughed out loud. It was a friendly laugh. I nodded to her and smiled.

But Mrs. Diamond, skeptical, screwed up her mouth. "Why don't you just admit you're a liar and a vagabond?"

I laughed. "All right. I'm a liar and a vagabond. But I still don't know who I am. These," I said, touching one ornament after another, "are my memories. You know the saying, He wears his heart on his sleeve? Well, I wear my memories in my hair. I add a bit of something from everywhere I've been. It's my history."

Mrs. Diamond made a disparaging sound. "Most people just collect spoons, honey."

"Most people don't have to invent themselves from scratch."

"Poetic," Mr. Caldecote said, wryly approving, "but you could surely start with your name and address and work from there. What does it say on your driver's license?"

That cracked me up. It was just the kind of dry joke I'd expect from a shy, intelligent man like him. Then I realized that nobody else was laughing. Nobody was even smiling.

It occurred to me that maybe he was testing me, trying to catch me out. "There's no such thing," I said. "Nobody needs a license just to drive."

Low, who had returned from his break, whistled. He looked happier than I'd ever have figured he could. Mr. Caldecote, Mr. Burnett, and Lightning reached into their pockets, Mrs. Diamond into her purse, and they brought out their wallets. Each had a card with their photo on it, an outline of the state, and the inexplicable phrase "Driver's License."

"I have one, too," said Maud. I glanced at Robin, and she nodded.

My feeling on the bridge had been right. I had entered another world.

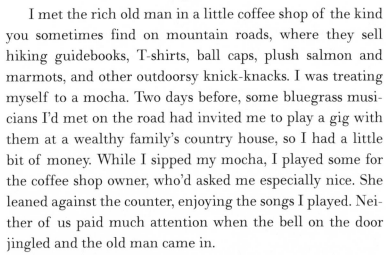

After I lay my guitar aside, Maud cut me a big piece of her birthday cake and all but crouched at my feet while I ate it.

I wished that I could understand what it was about her that made me want to both engage her and protect her from myself. What a lonely sort of life she must live in this little town. Why did she stay here? What was she waiting for? If she left, if she wanted, she could even engage in a spot of world conquest.

I had been commissioned to find her. I had been commissioned to bring her back with me. In that respect, she really had been waiting for me.

Sometimes you just need a catalyst.

I met the rich old man in a little coffee shop of the kind you sometimes find on mountain roads, where they sell hiking guidebooks, T-shirts, ball caps, plush salmon and marmots, and other outdoorsy knick-knacks. I was treating myself to a mocha. Two days before, some bluegrass musicians I'd met on the road had invited me to play a gig with them at a wealthy family's country house, so I had a little bit of money. While I sipped my mocha, I played some for the coffee shop owner, who'd asked me especially nice. She leaned against the counter, enjoying the songs I played. Neither of us paid much attention when the bell on the door jingled and the old man came in.

I sang for her a song I'd only just learned from a couple of buskers, a boy on guitar and a girl on hammered dulcimer. They'd learned it at a campsite a year or two ago but hadn't known its provenance. It had been prettier on the hammered dulcimer than on my guitar, but I gave it my best.

Long Maud, Long Maud, is neat of foot.
Long Maud is soft of tread.
In a gossamer gown
with a lily crown
atop her noble head.

Long Maud, Long Maud, come drink with me.
Long Maud, my hand to take.
By your gossamer gown
and your lily crown
your heart I mean to break.

Now he has thrown the blood-red wine
into her face so white.
Her gossamer gown
and her lily crown
are running red from spite.

Long Maud, Long Maud, she throws her curse.
Your heart will bleed for me.
By my gossamer gown
and my lily crown
I'll hate no man but thee.

I became aware that my audience had doubled. The old man stood a yard away from me, watching me intently. The coffee shop owner clapped, but the old man just stared.

"Can I help you, sir?" the coffee shop owner asked.

He ignored her, and said to me, "I would like to speak to you, young lady. In my car."

"I beg your pardon?" It wasn't just the request. In fact, it wasn't a request at all. I wasn't used to being told to do something. The rich old man had the air of somebody who always got his way, and that put my back up.

"You'll be quite safe."

I read him quickly. "I don't doubt you. But I have to wonder what you want with me, and why you think I ought to jump when you tell me to."

"Young and arrogant. I say to you, I have something important to discuss with you. Come along. I don't have time to waste."

Well, I came along, not because he told me to but because I was curious, and also feeling mercenary. What could he have to discuss with me but a possible gig? He took me to a new model Lincoln Continental with heated leather seats. The interior smelled of money and comfort. He sent his driver inside so that he could speak to me in private.

"Who are you? What is your name?"

"I go by Fortune."

"Fortune. Yes. I heard about you from a friend. You performed at a country house a few days ago, didn't you? You told a story about selling your soul. Where did you hear that song? Where did you learn it?"

I told him. I also told him that the other night was the first time I'd ever performed it.

"That song is about my family," he said. "My name is—" And he named a name that even I knew. I whistled long and low. That only seemed to annoy him.

Quickly, I said, "Is it very old? The song?"

"The melody is old. The lyrics were written two years ago. There's another version."

> Long Maud, Long Maud, her foot is neat
> And gentle is her tread.
> Her blood-red lips are sugar sweet,
> And lilies crown her head.

"She sounds like a vampire," I said.

"She's worse than a vampire. She's a spiteful little girl who cursed my grandson."

Well, that was something I didn't hear every day. "I don't believe in curses."

"A girl who sold her soul and her memory doesn't believe in curses?"

"My credulity does have limits."

"You ought to believe in them. They're real. This one certainly is."

I didn't have to ask him to tell me his story.

"In the song she's called Long Maud, sometimes Witch Maud, sometimes Fairy Maud, but always Maud. She fell in love with my grandson. She *dared* to fall in love with him. He accidentally spilled pomegranate wine over the front of her ludicrous white ball gown, and she cursed him for it. She cursed him to love only her for all of his days. She cursed him to love her until the day she should love him back."

"I thought you said she already loved him."

"Apparently she loved her ball gown more. She swore she would hate no man in the world but him. She swore that every word he spoke to her would only make her hate him more. So you see how it is. My grandson is pining for the love of a girl who hates him. Until she loves him back, he'll pine for her. But he has no way to *make* her love him."

"That's an elegant curse but a bit extreme for ruining a dress."

"Exactly. That's why I want you to find her."

"Excuse me?"

"I want you to find her and bring her back to me. I will make her take off that curse if it's the last thing I do. At my age, it very well may be."

"Why haven't you gone looking for her yourself?"

"You will perhaps think this fantastic—"

I laughed out loud at that. His whole story was fantastic.

Offended, he said, "—but it seems I am not allowed to look. My chauffeur cannot find the turnoff to Sky—"

"Sky?"

"That's the town where Maud allegedly lives. My chauffeur cannot find the turnoff, and when I take the train, the train doesn't stop. Letters I have written, addressed to her poste restante, are all returned unopened. The curse, or some *thing*, won't let me near her. Imagine it as a membrane between my world and hers that I cannot permeate."

"What makes you think I can? Permeate the membrane, I mean. Why me?"

"Because I was told to look for you. I was told by a reliable source that fortune would help free my grandson. At first I thought he meant money. As you must know, I've certainly plenty of it, and there's not much that money can't do. But here you are, singing the song about my grandson, and you call yourself Fortune."

I shrugged. "That's all very interesting. But why should I find this girl for you? Why should I even care?"

"Because I'm a very rich man, and I would pay a great deal to have this curse broken. What would you say if I told you I could buy your soul back for you? Or that I could give you enough that you could buy it back yourself?"

"If you have such an in with the Devil, why not ask him to bring you this Maud?"

He laughed. It wasn't a nice sound. "I did. And then he told me about you."

Of course, the idea of Maud cursing somebody was, now that I'd met her, absurd. The only person she seemed to genuinely dislike was Low, and I couldn't see her mustering enough energy to do more than pick at him when she couldn't outright ignore him. If she was what the rich old man said she was, why would she have such a hungry fascination for me? A fairy or witch, if such things actually existed, could see through a con artist like me like a flashlight through paper. No, she was a dreamer who lived on stories. A girl who could throw a proper curse was surely a story in her own right, with no need to feed on the stories of others.

I finished my piece of Maud's cake and headed for the restroom to fish a dime out of the pocket of my sodden dress. The rich old man had given me his business card. He'd written his address and private number on it, and I'd memorized them, since I have a bad habit of losing things. I found the pay phone. The rich old man answered after the third ring.

"Who is this?" he demanded.

"I think I've found your Maud," I answered.

"You think or you have?"

"All right. I have."

"Good," he said.

"What am I supposed to—"

The line went dead.

When I came back, everybody but Robin, Maud, and Mr. Caldecote had braved the storm and left the cafe for their own varied destinations. Low stood outside smoking, his arms wrapped around his ribcage. Even the old woman had vanished.

"Where's Lightning?" I asked.

"Gone," said Maud. "Not even a 'happy birthday,'" she added quietly. She stared at the entryway, her face dejected.

"Why is he called Lightning, anyway?"

"I don't know," she said. But I could tell she hadn't even heard me.

"I would have liked to thank him. He bought me soup and a sandwich. At least, I hope he did."

"He did," said Robin. "He also made noise about buying you a tire tomorrow morning. You made quite an impression on him. Maud, you might as well go home with your dad. The power could be out all night. And you," she said to me, "are going to need a place to stay."

"Oh!" Maud exclaimed, her dejection falling away. "Come stay with us! She can, can't she, Papa?"

"I have no objections," Mr. Caldecote said. "Call your mother and ask her."

Maud sprinted off in the direction of the pay phone. Mr. Caldecote paced to the entryway, jingling his keys, clearly ready to be gone. Robin gazed at me as if thinking a number of unflattering things. At last, she said, "We're all very protective of Maud."

"Why does Maud need protecting?"

"You can see. You must see. She's excessively naive and excessively impressionable. You mesmerized her with your stories."

I smiled. "I like a good audience."

"Make sure you treat her like one," Robin said.

"As opposed to?"

"As opposed to a mark. She doesn't have two nickels to rub together. Believe me, I know. I write her paycheck every two weeks. And her family doesn't have much, either."

"Whatever it is you think I am, I'm probably not. I'm not interested in anybody's money unless I play for it."

"Does that mean you're going to reimburse Lightning?"

"Yeah. Sure. Sandwich, soup, tire, ride into town. No problem."

"And how are you going to do that?"

"I'll set up somewhere and play for coin, just like I always do. Maybe right across the street at the train depot. You do still get trains, don't you?"

"Hmm." Robin gave a single nod. "Good luck with that."

Maud came back. "Mama says it's fine," she called to her father.

"Then let's go."

"Leave your wet things here. You can pick them up tomorrow when they're dry. Good night, John. Good night, Maud. Good night, Fortune."

So it came to pass that I entered the Caldecote household with nothing but my guitar, my shoes, and a borrowed raincoat. The storm had cooled the air to a more manageable 80 degrees. The Caldecotes didn't have air conditioning, so all the windows were open, as was the top of the dutch door in the kitchen.

Nothing could have prepared me for the chaos of the household. Cole, sixteen, had commandeered the kitchen and, despite the heat, was busy baking chocolate chip cookies. He was not a neat baker. Flour drifted across counters and dusted the floor, showing footprints of varying sizes. He was a tow-headed kid, tall as his father but with the build of a high school football player. Aida Kay, age fourteen and a half, was pale and slender, with a ragged mop of strawberry blonde hair and eyes bright blue behind her glasses. She was playing a loud game of Monopoly at the kitchen table with Dandy, age nine, a snub-nosed girl covered in freckles; Gabriel, age five, with a serious expression and a head of golden curls; and the nine-year-old neighbor twins, Candy and Cindy Chang, whose precise bob haircuts contrasted strongly with the chocolate smeared around their mouths.

Mrs. Caldecote sat on the floor against the refrigerator door, reading Shirley Jackson's *We Have Always Lived in the Castle* with apparent total concentration and drinking Shasta diet cola straight out of the can. Her broad cheekbones and deep-set brown eyes, I later learned, were the envy of her daughters, who had not inherited them.

And somewhere in the basement, Sophie, age twenty, feelingly played the Third Movement from *Scheherazade* on a slightly out-of-tune piano.

Mr. Caldecote kissed his wife, then disappeared. Apparently even his own family could be too much for him.

With the exception of Sophie's playing, all activity paused when I came in. Mrs. Caldecote got up to welcome me with some self-deprecating words about the mess. Maud introduced me to her brothers and sisters and the neighbor children with a mixed air of embarrassment and protectiveness. She seemed to want me to think well of them, or at least not mind them too much. Gabriel and the three little girls crowded around me immediately, wanting to know about all the charms woven into my hair. They each took turns listening for bees in the bee skep. I could tell they wanted to touch all the objects but they were too polite. Even if they'd asked I'd have told them no. I couldn't stand the thought of all those little fingers, tugging this way and that.

Mr. Caldecote had warned me in the car that the Devil wouldn't play well in Mollie McBride Caldecote's house, so when the children asked me about the charms and other objects, I simply said they were reminders of places I'd been and things I'd done. I could tell that the little girls thought this was the greatest thing they'd heard in a while. They went in search of little things to braid into their own hair.

Maud went to change the sheets on her bed. Cole invited me to eat cookies, and Aida Kay offered to pour me a glass of milk. Downstairs, Sophie tired of *Scheherazade* and switched to Beethoven's "Moonlight Sonata." Mrs. Caldecote asked me if I could eat spaghetti and meatballs, which was apparently Maud's favorite food. I assured her I could, and asked if I could help.

"Sit. Eat your cookies and tell me about yourself."

Of all the phrases in the English language "tell me about yourself" is one of my least favorite, especially if I can't pull out my Devil story.

"There's not much to tell," I said. "I'm basically an itinerant musician. I drive from town to town, play where I can, earn what coin I can, and just keep going."

"That sounds fun," Mrs. Caldecote said. "You must meet so many people and see so many interesting places."

"It does have its moments."

"What does your mother think, you being on the road like this?"

"Fortune has amnesia," Maud announced, coming back into the kitchen. She'd changed into a pair of Levis and a T-shirt.

"Goodness!" said Mrs. Caldecote. "That's not something you hear every day. So you don't even know who your own mother is?" There was something teasing to her tone. She must have thought Maud was woofing her.

"Hand to God, I don't."

Startled, Mrs. Caldecote said, "Well, I am sorry."

"I'm used to it," I said, feeling foolish.

"Why don't you play something?" Mrs. Caldecote's tone was apologetic. "If you're not too tired, that is."

I settled my guitar on my lap and picked out "Barbara Allen." Everybody knows it, or some version of it, and I sang the version I favored, the one Jean Ritchie recorded. At the third stanza, Maud sang with me in harmony.

> So slowly, slowly she got up
> and slowly she came a-nigh him,
> and all she said when she got there,
> young man I believe you're dying.

The timbre of her singing voice was lonely, like something lost and wandering. For the third time that day, the hairs on my arms rose, as did the hairs on the back of my neck, from the pure uncanny sound of it. My heart thumped. My fingers stilled on the strings.

Maud looked instantly abashed. "I'm sorry," she said. "I shouldn't have interrupted."

"Yes you most certainly should," I said. "Let's continue, and you'd better sing."

> Oh yes, I'm low, I'm very low
> and death is on me dwelling.
> No better, no better I'll never be
> if I can't get Barbara Allen.

> Oh yes, you're low and very low
> and death is on you dwelling.
> No better, no better you'll never be
> for you can't get Barbara Allen.

> For don't you remember in Yonder's town
> in Yonder's town a drinkin',
> you passed your glass all around and around
> and you slighted Barbara Allen?

We sang the song to its finish. Sometimes Maud stumbled over the words, being used to a slightly different version than the one I sang. But always her voice wove with mine something beautiful, something rare. It was a marriage of her bitter to my sweet, of my smooth to her rough. My voice was the rose, Maud's, the briar.

We finished, looking at each other as if we'd each discovered buried treasure.

"Wow," said Mrs. Caldecote. Mr. Caldecote and Sophie had come in to hear us, too.

"That was deeply creepy," Sophie said. Then, to me, "No offense. That song gives me the willies."

"Very nice, girls," said Mr. Caldecote. I got the impression he didn't usually throw compliments around like confetti.

Then the little girls came back in with various plastic toys and the music was forgotten as Maud and Aida Kay and I braided them into their hair. There was no more singing that night, or speaking of singing, but both of us were thinking. I was thinking, *this is how I get her*. Maud, it soon became obvious, was thinking, *this is how I get out*.

After supper, Mrs. Caldecote brought out Maud's birthday cake, an angel food with pink seven-minute frosting. The flames of eighteen birthday candles flickered and smoked, as birthday candles always seem to do. We all sang the happy birthday song. Maud looked at me, closed her eyes, and blew out all the candles in one breath.

After dinner, Maud took me down to her room and showed me her birthday present—a vintage-looking black dress with flutter sleeves.

"My first little black dress!" she said, elated. "Mama sewed it. She wouldn't let me have one until I turned eighteen."

I borrowed a nightgown from Aida Kay, who was nearer my size (though not by much) and lay down on Maud's bed. When had I last lain in a bed? It was still too hot to lie under the covers, or even a sheet. Maud lay on the floor beside me on a heavy old sleeping bag.

"Is the floor hard?" I asked.

"Yes. It's okay, though."

"You really don't mind my taking your bed?"

43

"I really don't mind."

"The ground is hard, when I sleep on the ground. I usually sleep in the back seat of my car. It's a good thing I'm short."

"Do you like what you do?"

Truthfully, I answered, "I can't imagine doing anything else."

"What's the worst part about it? Sleeping on the ground?"

"No. The worst part about it is that I'm never *entirely* certain I'll be able to play. What if it's all taken away from me? What if I'm not able to pluck a single note? It's a mystery to me, my music. I always *do* play, and once I do, once I'm there in the song, it's almost like being in a trance. It's a feeling like nothing else."

Then I asked, "Do you like what you do?"

Maud sighed impatiently. "I suppose. Some of the time. I love Robin, and I like most of the people who come in. Sometimes a train passenger will be a jerk, but mostly everybody's just glad to be there."

"What's the worst part?"

"Seeing people get back on the train and not being able to go with them. It's the same when Sophie goes back to college after holidays and summer. She goes away, and I'm left here."

"Don't you want to go to college?"

"Papa wants me to, but I have no idea what I'd study if I did," Maud said. "Sophie's different. She knows exactly what she wants to do. She's going to be a doctor. The only thing I know I want to do is travel, and you don't go to college for that. So I work full-time at the Sky Cafe and save my money. Someday I'll just go to Bombay and London and Paris."

"Why not start smaller and take the train to the city?"

"Huh. I guess I could. I haven't been to the city since I was fifteen."

"Yeah? What did you do then?"

"I stayed a month with my great-aunt Helena. She used to work for a very rich family. Well, not work exactly. She advised them. She was associated with them and had been for almost all her life. Anyway, their son was turning eighteen, and they were going to throw a big party for him. Helena wanted to take me. She said it would be good for me to get to know the family. I borrowed Mama's old prom dress. Oh, it was so gorgeous. I wish you could have seen it. It was layers and layers of white tulle with a skirt out to here. Mama bought me a pair of white satin shoes to go with it—you know, the kind you can dye. But I got sick the day of the party and had to stay at home in bed."

"That sucks," I said. I was wondering about the rich old man. His story and Maud's didn't add up at all.

"I was sick for three days. Fever and delirium and everything. Non-stop nightmares. It was awful. Helena nearly took me to the hospital. When I got better she called Mama and had her come get me and take me home, and I haven't been to the city since."

"Did you ever get to wear the dress?"

"Not except to try it on."

"Maybe you can wear it when you go to Paris."

She shook her head. "This is so gross. When I was sick I puked pomegranate juice all over it. The cleaners couldn't get the stains out."

"That's too bad," I said. I wondered about that. What if somebody other than Maud had worn the dress to the party, somebody other than Maud had thrown the alleged curse? Maud didn't seem to know anything at all about it. She had no reason to lie to me about being sick. She had no reason to lie to me about missing the party.

"Mama was able to salvage a few yards of the tulle. She's got it in her cedar chest, to use for wedding veils if any of us ever get married."

"Well, that's something, at least. But I think you should go back to the city."

"To the Museum of Mystery and Industry," she said, smiling.

"To the Museum of Mystery and Industry."

The next morning Maud and I rode into town with her father, and I collected my clothes. I felt better once I was dressed in my vintage rags. I gave the raincoat back to Robin and thanked her for the use of it.

Then Mr. Caldecote drove us to where my car was parked. Lightning was already there, changing my tire. The sunlight brought out the gold in his brown hair, the vivid blue of his eyes. He was wearing a T-shirt that showed off his strong arms, and a pair of Levis that hung, just barely, on his hips. Watching him work, which I did without shyness or remorse, was a pure pleasure. I could see why Maud was crazy about him.

"I am paying you back," I told him. "Just as soon as I have the money."

"No rush," he said, smiling. "I understand from Robin you intend to stick around for a while and play for the train passengers who come through. I hope you won't mind if I sneak into your audience from time to time."

"Why would I mind?" I laughed. "I am an exhibitionist, after all. The more the merrier. If you're really lucky I'll get Maud to sing with me."

"Wait, what?" Maud said. She looked surprised, then gratified, and blushed.

Lightning didn't seem to have heard her. Looking at me, he said, "I haven't heard you sing yet. I'm looking forward to that." That was my first inkling of what was beginning to happen.

The passenger train came through Sky at noon heading east and at 5:00 PM heading west. The trains stopped for an hour going both ways, which had something to do with the freight train schedules and nothing to do with Sky as a destination. And yet the town had turned those two hours to a good accounting. The cafes did brisk business for lunch and early dinner for those passengers who didn't feel like eating in the dining car. Those were the busiest times at the Sky Cafe. The Avery Photography Studio pulled in tourist business with novelty old-timey sepia photographs. Passengers could go next door and shop for antiques, if they felt like it, or step into Mrs. Diamond's sad boutique (which primarily catered to the oldest of Sky's female population). At the drug store they could buy an ice cream cone, or fresh fudge, or a box of the tribe's alder-smoked salmon. Or they could hit the tavern for a beer.

"If Maud's going to sing for the passengers, she's going to have to do it in here," Robin said. "I can't spare her."

I'd driven Maud back to the cafe. Today was a work day for her.

"Do you really want me to sing with you?" Maud asked, hesitant and hopeful.

"Didn't you hear the way we sounded last night? That was...I don't even know what that was. Amazing? Eerie? Perfect?"

"I have a weird voice."

"You have a *fantastically* weird voice. You aren't afraid of performing, are you?"

"Not exactly," she said. "I used to sing in the school choir but always as part of the ensemble. I've never sung a duet before, except with Sophie at home."

"But you're always singing, Maud," Robin said.

"To songs on the jukebox," Maud said, as if that invalidated it.

"It's true, you don't have what I'd call a pretty voice," Robin said. "But pretty isn't everything. Your voice has got character. It's strong, and you sing in tune."

"What do *you* think of Maud's voice?" I asked Low, who had just slouched through the door.

"Oh, lord. Don't ask him," Maud said. "He wouldn't have a good thing to say about me if you paid him a hundred million dollars in advance."

Low hesitated, his eyes shifting between Maud and me. One corner of his mouth raised. "It's pure whorehouse," he said. Then he slouched off to the kitchen.

"Gross!" Maud exclaimed. She shuddered. "The thought of him even...gross!"

"I think I know what he means," Robin said kindly. "It's a bit boozy and smoky. I'm not saying you drink or smoke, Maud, so don't get all upset."

"Do you suppose he's ever even been in a...gross!"

"You take things far too literally, young lady," Robin said.

Low came back out with a cup of coffee and handed it to me with a grin. I got the impression he'd taken a liking to me. "She sings about death and disaster," he said. "You sing about death and disaster?"

"I have done. Murder ballads are real crowd-pleasers."

"You write songs?"

"Not good ones," I admitted. "Not yet, anyway."

"Maybe write a song about me. I want to hear her sing it in her whorehouse voice."

"You are the most revolting human being on the whole entire planet," Maud said.

"Children, don't fight," Robin said.

"What's your story?" I asked Low.

He looked momentarily taken aback. Then he scowled at the ground. He took a Swiss Army knife out of his pocket and opened the largest blade.

"See this?" he said. "My family didn't like me. They didn't like the way I talked. So I killed them with this knife. Anybody got a problem with the way I talk? I cut out their tongues. Then I cut their throats."

Maud stared at him, horrified into speechlessness. He held up the knife, turned it in the light, rubbed the pad of one thumb against the blade. A drop of blood, crimson and sinister in its perfection, welled from the cut.

"Then I slip away," he said. "Come to little towns like Sky. They been chasing me, the cops, but they'll never catch me. So what do you say? You gonna make a song about me?"

"I'll take it under consideration," I said.

Surprisingly, he winked at me. Then he put the knife away and slouched back to the kitchen.

"How can you even stand to talk to him?" Maud demanded.

I said, "I like him. He's kinda funny, in a deranged sort of way."

She stared at me in flat incredulity.

A few customers had drifted in, and Maud got to work. Robin and Low were already in the kitchen, making wonderful smells. I went to the pay phone and called the rich old man.

"Who is this?"

"It's me again. Fortune."

"What do you want?"

Well, that was a laugh, since he was the one who wanted something from me.

"She wasn't there," I said. "Maud. She wasn't at that party."

"Who told you that?"

"She did."

Outraged, he said, "Have you told her that I'm looking for her? Have you told her why?"

"No," I said. "Of course not. But I'm telling you, she wasn't at that party."

"And I'm telling you that she was."

"I know you want to see her. Maybe you ought to be straight with me and tell my why. I mean, *really* why."

"How dare you speak to me in this way! I told you. She cursed my grandson."

"I don't believe she could curse a housefly that was bothering her."

"You don't know what they are. Those McBrides. You don't know what they can do."

"Her name is Caldecote."

"Her name is Caldecote, but she's a McBride through and through. I don't have time to explain this to you. I don't have *time*. Bring her to me. Bring her to me *soon*. That's all you need to know."

He hung up.

"Well, to hell with you, too," I told the dial tone, and hung up.

I set up my pitch on the curb outside the train depot. I had my guitar, and I had my collapsible nylon camp sink to collect any money folks wanted to toss. I guessed buskers weren't thick on the ground in Sky; I got some curious looks from passersby.

I played "Darlin' Corey" sad and slow, my sweet voice turning it into a macabre children's song.

> Dig a hole, dig a hole in the meadow,
> dig a hole in the cold, cold ground.
> Dig a hole, dig a hole in the meadow,
> we gonna lay darlin' Corey down.

I played "Where Did You Sleep Last Night" when the train pulled up. I played "500 Miles." An audience gathered. Coins landed in my camp sink. I nodded my thanks. I played "Henry Lee." Some folks put folded bills in my camp sink. I played "I Want to Be Evil." That one always gets the laughs. I played "Shake Sugaree," to which I'd added my own verse:

> Have a little secret I ain't gonna tell
> I even pawned my soul and now I'm going to hell.

I had run through half my repertoire by the time the train pulled away from the station. My audience, by that time, consisted of a couple of townsfolk and Lightning. I hadn't seen him come up.

I beckoned to him. "Let's count the loot." My total for the hour was $22.75. Not too bad at all. I was finally able to pry from Lightning that the tire had cost $80. He wouldn't hear of my paying him back for the soup and sandwich. "Take your first installment, mister," I said, and he reluctantly did so.

"I'm collecting stories today," I said. "So far, I've heard Low's, and a gruesome story it was. I emphasize the word 'story' because I'm sure it was a lie told for Maud's express benefit. Now I want to hear your story. Truth optional but preferred. Buy me lunch?"

He grinned. "Only if you promise you won't pay me back for it."

"I promise."

We went to the Sky Cafe, which still had a few lunch-time customers. Maud waited on us with friendly efficiency but clearly wished she could join us.

"You sure you want my story?" Lightning asked me. "It's nothing as interesting as yours."

"No mayhem and murder, like Low?"

"I'm afraid not. I'm my family's prodigal. Instead of go-ing to law school like my father and my sister, I dropped out and became a carpenter. They don't have anything to do with me these days."

"I'm sorry."

"Don't be. We never got along much in the first place. I work jobs all over, and I've got a place at the top of Wolf's House. If you ever hear tell of the Mansion, that's my place. It was my grandfather's. He left it to me when he died."

"Is it really a mansion?"

He laughed. "Hardly. It's a nice, rustic stone house. It was supposed to be the family's summer retreat, but my grand-mother wouldn't consent to live there. It sat empty from the moment it was completed. A few years back, right after I inherited it, I caught Maud and her sisters trespassing, and made Maud work it off by scrubbing the stone walls. Need-less to say, she's never forgiven me."

"Are you sure about that?" I marveled at how unobserv-ant a grown man could be.

"What do you mean?"

"Seems to me she's got a crush on you."

"Oh?" he said. Then, dismayed, "Oh."

I leaned in close and whispered, "Are you telling me it's not mutual?"

He shook his head and shrugged. "She's a kid."

"Eighteen as of yesterday," I reminded him.

"A kid plus one day is still a kid in my books. Crap. What do I do about this?"

"*I* don't know. I've got zero experience in matters of love. The one time I was ready to kiss a boy, a bee came and stung me right on the upper lip."

Lightning shouted with laughter.

"It's not funny. It hurt like hell."

"Maybe it was one of those magical bees of yours, making you wait for the right man."

At that moment, Maud came up with the coffee carafe and topped off Lightning's cup. "Can I get you another iced tea?" she asked me.

"No, thanks. Can you sit down for a minute or two?"

Maud glanced around the cafe. "Sure." She sat, looking expectant. "What's up?"

"Sing with me. 'Barbara Allen,' just like last night. I want Lightning to hear."

"Oh." Maud blushed. "You mean right now?"

"Exactly right now." I pulled my guitar up on my lap. We sang, as we had the night before. Our voices married as they had, strange to sweet. Robin came out to listen. Even Low emerged partially from the shadows. When we finished, the few other patrons in the cafe applauded, as did Lightning and Robin. Low disappeared back into the kitchen with an unreadable expression on his face.

"What do you think of Maud's voice?" I asked.

"Oh, I've heard Maud sing plenty of times," he said. "I will say your two voices work well together. They're both so different."

Maud, still blushing, got up quickly on the pretext of making her rounds with the coffee pot.

"Should we take our act on the road?"

He looked startled. "I thought you were going to stick around Sky for a while."

"I don't stick around anywhere," I said truthfully. "As soon as I've paid you for the tire, I'll be off. What do you think...should I take Maud with me?"

"I don't know," he said slowly. "She's awfully young, and she doesn't have much experience in the wide world."

"In that case, it might be good for her to travel with an old hand like me."

"How old are you, anyway? Twenty? Twenty-one?"

"Beats me," I said. "No memory, right?"

"Oh. Right. Sorry. Where are you staying tonight?"

"Hmm. I don't want to impose on Maud's parents again. If there's a campsite nearby, that'll do. I've got a tent and a sleeping bag in the car."

"There's plenty of room at the Mansion," he said, looking into his cup of coffee. He glanced up. "Both for you and your protective bees."

I felt my face grow hot.

"Not a killer maniac," he said. "Remember?"

"I don't intend to get stung on the lip again," I said.

"Maybe you won't."

"Maybe this isn't the right time to try it."

He smiled. "Maybe you're right. But you are welcome to my spare room, if you don't feel like sleeping in a tent."

"I'll take it under advisement," I said.

"Well, I've got to get to work," he said, getting up from the table. "Thanks for the company." He put down a five-dollar bill for Maud's tip.

"Thank you for lunch. And thanks for your story. We'll have to figure out some way to spice it up."

"I wouldn't mind," he said. He left me with the dregs of my iced tea. I watched him pay, I watched him go, and I thought about that spare room. And then I thought about

Maud, whom he saw as just a kid plus a day. I was pretty confident he saw me as something else entirely. The thought made me smile, but I touched the center of my upper lip, right where the bee had stung me, and my smile faded, and I sighed.

I grew more keenly conscious of the weight in my head, which hadn't lifted from the day before. Maud came to my table. She'd taken off her waitressing apron.

"I've got a few hours before my next shift," she said. "A few hours before the evening train. Let's go down to the creek."

The railroad bridge spanned a section of the creek that the town kids had dammed with rocks to make a swimming hole. The hot air was thick with the smell of creosote. A dull glare came off the rails. Our feet crunched in the chunks of gravel. Maud helped me to forget, for a time, the weight in my head. We sat on a big boulder, our feet in the water, and sang like a pair of sirens. I taught her "Where Did You Sleep Last Night?" She taught me "Dark as a Dungeon." The blend of our voices soothed and intoxicated me. I suspect it intoxicated her, as well.

Tipsy, we sat in silence and let the water wash over our feet.

"Water is the most pleasant thing," Maud said at last. "Flowing water."

"My head is so heavy. I wish I could just cut off all my hair and throw it into the creek, and let your flowing water wash it far away from me."

"Don't do that," Maud said, distressed. "It's so beautiful."

I smiled at her. "You are something else, Maud Caldecote. I mean that literally. You are...something."

"Not like you."

"No. Like *you*."

"Do you really think you sold your soul?" she asked abruptly. I wondered if she'd been worrying over it since yesterday.

"I don't know. If I sold it for my music, that seems to have worked out pretty well. Doesn't the Devil always find some way to trick you so that your bargain never comes out the way you wanted? Doesn't he spoil everything, eventually?"

"Your memory."

"Yeah. My memory."

"Is the Museum of Mystery and Industry just a story?"

"I don't know."

"Let's go to the city and find out. We can play some music to get money for gasoline and food, just like you've been doing."

There it was, at last. Maud was doing my work for me. I'd had a feeling she would.

"I'll drive," she promised. "I'll do anything."

"Don't you see what you've got here?" I asked her. "Don't you even care?"

"It's too quiet. It's so quiet, sometimes I think my head's going to explode."

"What do you want?"

"Freedom," she said.

"Freedom from a loving family?"

She blew out her breath. "You don't understand," she said. "I've lived here all my life. Everybody thinks I'm the same person now that I was five years ago, or fifteen years ago, or eighteen years ago. I'm not a child, and I don't want to live like a child. I want—I want to drink champagne. I want to take lovers."

I laughed at the simplicity of her ambitions, which she thought daring. "Champagne and lovers aren't exactly thick on the ground I tread," I said.

She waved that away and continued with eighteen years' worth of small-town impatience. "I want to live my life without everybody looking over my shoulder, ready to tell Mama and Papa what I'm up to. I can't even go to the grocery store without somebody asking Papa if I remembered to buy milk."

"What about Lightning?" I asked.

She blushed and looked genuinely vexed. "You want to know something stupid? I was certain that on my eighteenth birthday he'd come into the cafe and kiss me. I thought about it for weeks. I *counted* on it. And he didn't even so much as wish me a happy birthday. Isn't that the stupidest thing you ever heard? Me, waiting around for somebody to kiss me who thinks I'm still fifteen years old."

Abruptly, I asked, "Would you sell your soul for that kiss?"

She laughed. "I hadn't thought of that."

"I'm serious. Would you?"

She looked at me a good long while. "I don't know. I might have done. Before you came here, I thought that kiss was exactly what I wanted. And now I don't want it at all anymore."

"Are you sure about that?"

"Well…yeah."

"What *do* you want?"

"The chance to do something extraordinary. I want to travel with you, and sing with you, and see the world."

"You can travel. You can sing. You can see the world. Just not with me." Every word might have been a petal that I tugged from a flower and dropped into the creek. Except my words sank to the bottom and stayed there. She tried so hard, I could tell, not to look disappointed. She blinked rapidly and stared off into the distance, her hand over her mouth so that it wouldn't give her away. And I wondered what the hell I was doing. She was giving herself to me. I could take her to the city, take her to the rich old man, and get my reward—a soul, or memory, or enough money not to miss either too terribly much.

"It's nothing personal," I insisted. But it was. I liked her too much. And suddenly I realized that I wanted her company too much. It was a hard life. It would be easier with two.

"I was just thinking that shared things are more fun," Maud said quietly, still not looking at me.

"Shared hunger? Shared uncertainty? I never know where my next meal is coming from, or the next tank of gas, or the next real bed. And if something happens to me, nobody will know. I'll be buried without a name, and nobody will know, and it will be as if I never existed in the first place."

"Not if I'm with you," Maud said.

"Well, that's a comfort," I said. My tone was sarcastic. I instantly regretted it. More gently, I said, "The thing is, Maud, I'm a freak wherever I go. I don't fit in anywhere. Here, right here, is the first time I haven't felt so lonely and alone. And now you want me to leave and take you with me? Out there?"

"The Museum of Mystery and Industry," Maud said. "We can try to find it and come right back."

"One of us would," I said, "at any rate. You might decide to stay out there in the world, with your champagne and your lovers."

"And you might come back here and marry Lightning, and then people will ask him if you remembered to buy milk."

"It honestly doesn't have to be one thing or the other."

Bitterly, she said, "It's nothing, then. It's being bored and having to work with that troll and seeing the same people I've seen every day of my life."

Trying to sound cheerful, I said, "Speaking of work, we've both got to get back to it."

We left the stream with mutual reluctance and a mutual sense of dissatisfaction.

I ended up going home with Maud again after all. The children were all outside playing…. Aida Kay and Cole had gone riding on Nut and Mab, the Caldecote's mares. Dandy and the neighbor twins were setting up a camp somewhere in the woods between the house and the abandoned logging road. Sophie was at her summer job in the next town over. She was a nurse's aide in a convalescent home. I went downstairs to luxuriate in the shower. After I'd changed, I started upstairs but stopped when I heard Maud and her parents talking in the kitchen.

I have to admit it. I eavesdropped. Perhaps I'm conceited, but I figured the conversation might be at least partially about me, so it seemed only fair I'd know what they were saying.

Maud, it appeared, was more stubborn than I'd imagined. She still entertained the idea that I might be persuaded to take her with me when I left.

"I can't say I'd be happy about you going," said Mrs. Caldecote. "Fortune has said it herself that she can barely survive on what money she makes. How are two people going to survive? You very likely won't make any more money as two people singing than Fortune makes as one."

"I've got my own money," Maud said.

"You'd best leave your savings alone," her father said. "That's for college."

"If I ever go to college," she muttered. "Don't worry. I'm leaving my savings alone."

"Does Fortune know you've got money?"

"I haven't said anything about it. She's not using me for money, if that's what you're worried about."

"That's not what I'm worried about. It's only right that you should pay for half the gas and other expenses and buy your own food," her father said. "Now, hold your horses. I have to say, I'm not happy about this, either. But I'm *really* unhappy about you going without giving Robin two weeks' notice. You can't leave her in the lurch like that. And if you do, don't expect her to ever give you a job again."

"I already talked to her about it."

I smiled at this. I didn't know if Maud's stubborn faith was more endearing or annoying.

"What did she say?"

"She said they'd make do, and that Regina would be glad for the extra hours since she's *actually* going to college in the fall, and that when I was tired of being a hippie I could come back and be a waitress again."

"Robin's far more forgiving than I'd be," her father said. "Don't take advantage of it."

"Honey, I understand you want to get out into the world and have adventures but the last time you left Sky you got so sick."

"I'm not going to get sick again," Maud insisted. "Why would I get sick again? Look at me! I'm healthy as a horse. I'm as healthy as Nut and Mab combined. Can't I just go with her for a while and come right back?"

Mrs. Caldecote sighed. "We can't tell you no. You're an adult. You've been an adult for two days now. You've got to make your own choices. But I'd feel better if we knew anything at all about Fortune."

At that point I was tired of listening. I didn't want to hear my character dissected. I crept down the stairs and then came back up, singing as I came. Mr. and Mrs. Caldecote got up when I came into the kitchen. Their smiles were strained. Maud's eyes were red from tears, and she looked sullen.

"You'd better change out of your work clothes," Mrs. Caldecote said. "Fortune, how would you like to help me weed my herb garden?"

"I would love to."

In the garden, I recognized rose, rosemary, and lavender. Mrs. Caldecote introduced me to borage, rue, and a plant that smelled like a cross between grapefruit and armpit which she said was clary sage.

"Show me what to weed," I said, and we fell to working together. She asked me about my day, and I told her about my pitch in front of the train depot and how much money I'd made (and paid back to Lightning).

"Why is he called Lightning?" I asked.

"You know, I don't know. I suppose I should ask him one day."

I knew I ought to have asked him when he told me his incredibly abbreviated life story.

"Is he a good man?"

"I think he is. I don't understand why he's still single. He confessed to me once that he first came here because of a disappointed love affair."

"Does everybody come to you with their confessions?" I asked.

"Eventually," she said.

"I thought they might. You have that air about you. I've got a confession to make to you."

"All right."

"I like Lightning."

Mrs. Caldecote looked surprised. She'd clearly been expecting a different sort of confession.

"I'd like to get to know him better. Especially if Maud is over him."

"Is she over him? I'd be thankful if she were. I really don't think she and Lightning would do well together. If you like him, why not stick around and get to know him better?"

I just smiled and shook my head. "I've thought about it. But I understand he comes and goes."

"That's true. He comes and goes. By the way, Jordan told me about you. He told me about your stories."

"Oh. Uh-oh. Am I no longer welcome in your house?"

She waved that away. "I can see why you would hold a glamor for Maud. You're a bit of a damsel in distress, aren't you?"

"I never thought of myself that way before."

"You have to understand one thing: Maud never wanted to be the princess. Maybe it was because the princess role was already taken by Sophie. No. Maud always wanted to be the good witch."

"She wants to come with me," I said. "When I leave here, she wants to come with me. She wants to sing with me. She wants to live my kind of life. I told her no, but she seems so dead set about it that I'm thinking about changing my mind."

"The other thing you need to understand about Maud is that she's got a temper. I don't mean that she gets angry from time to time, as people do. She flies into rages, blind rages."

"There's a lot out there to rage against," I said.

"That's very true. But when Maud rages, she hurts herself. She literally makes herself sick."

"Maybe spending time with a cool head like mine would do her good."

"Maybe. She clearly idolizes you. I don't think I've seen her this fascinated since—since I don't know when. And I haven't seen her this eager to leave.... Jordan and I were both relieved when she decided not to go to college right away. We knew she'd do better here than out there."

We fell silent, each working to uproot small interlopers to Mrs. Caldecote's tidy garden. Then Maud came out, freshly showered and changed. Before Maud was in earshot, Mrs. Caldecote said, "If you decide to take her with you, I hope she can help you find what you're looking for."

The next day I made enough money that I could pay off Lightning and still have a bit left over for gas. It was time for me to go. Maud begged me to come home with her one more time for dinner. Mr. Caldecote barbecued hamburgers and hot dogs while everybody else, even Sophie, played "Green Light, Red Light" and "Mother May I?" on the grass. The Caldecotes were fond of making up absurd steps: "Mother, may I take three helicopter steps?" "Mother, may I take seven Rudolphs?" We played up until dinner, and played again after dinner, until the sky grew deep blue with twilight. Over the coals of the barbecue we toasted marshmallows. Maud liked to burn hers. Mrs. Caldecote toasted hers patiently, getting them perfectly, evenly brown. Gabriel tired of marshmallows and attempted to toast grapes.

Maud and Sophie looked at the sky and simultaneously chanted, "Star light, star bright, the first star I see tonight. I wish I may, I wish I might, have the wish I wish tonight." Maud closed her eyes and wished silently, her second wish in as many days. Her face expressed the strength of her wish.

In full mother mode, Mrs. Caldecote said to me, "You're not actually leaving tonight, are you? Stay the night and go in the morning."

It was a relief to me. I was tired. My head still felt heavy. One more day of sleeping in Maud's bed, one more luxuriant shower...it sounded awfully good.

I couldn't sleep that night, thinking about Maud lying down there on the floor, thinking about Lightning not far away in his Mansion atop the mountain, thinking about the rich old man. I thought about my own loneliness. If this past year had been spent wandering from town to town, campground to campground, in search of home, then maybe I had finally found it here in Sky.

I got up and dressed quickly and quietly, thankful that Maud appeared to be a sound sleeper. I snuck out of the house to my car, and I drove down off the mountain, on out of town, to the red bridge that would take me across the creek and away from Sky. But before I crossed the bridge, I pulled over and got out. I walked out onto the bridge. The moon was extraordinarily bright that night, so bright it was difficult to see the stars around it.

Without thinking about it too long or too hard, I touched the bee skep charm and said, clearly and distinctly, "All right. I admit it. I am in sore need of help."

And just like that, sitting on the big boulder I had sat on the afternoon I arrived, was Sweet Honey.

She was dressed and posed like a 1920s bathing beauty, complete with slippers with ribbons that crisscrossed up her calves, stockings up to her knees, and a bathing cap like a tight-fitting cloche, everything soft gold. She twirled a Japanese parasol against her shoulder. Her bathing outfit was wet and gleamed like gold silk lame. Creek water beaded on her skin, dazzling as diamonds in the moonlight. I had to squint and shield my eyes.

She called out, "Well, don't you look like Miss Ada Despair."

"I thought I made you up," I said.

"Then how come you sent the bees to fetch me?"

"*Because* I thought I made you up."

"What's wrong, Miss Maybe-Not-Such-A-Mess-Anymore?"

I suddenly found I had no words. I only had a pressure inside my head that hurt, that grew stronger with every shallow breath, that I couldn't find a way to let out. What was wrong? Everything, everything. I didn't know where to start. There was too much, crowding and pressing to get out, things I hadn't even known were there, some things that I couldn't even name. All the fear and loneliness and uncertainty, all the questions about my identity, longing for a family I may or may not have ever had, a world I may or may not have invented because if I hadn't, the void would have killed me.

She closed her parasol, laid it down beside her, and held out both hands to me. I climbed down the bank and waded across the stream to her, not caring about the water rushing into my boots or weighing down the hem of my skirt, and knelt beside her, the water now up to my belly and cold.

She stroked my head. Cool water ran across my crown. Instantly, the painful weight lifted from my head. My heart was another matter.

"Help me." The words felt like a stone in my throat.

"Say it."

"What do I say?"

"You say, first, the thing that comes first."

"I don't want to be alone anymore."

She smiled. "Then don't be."

"But I still want to be myself. I don't want to lose myself."

"It seems to me that you've already lost yourself."

"Then I don't want to lose myself again." I struggled for the right words. "I don't...don't want to be subsumed, or overshadowed, or devoured."

"Do you love him?"

"Huh?"

"The man they call Lightning. Do you love him?"

"How can I love somebody I've only just met?"

"Who you talking about, then?"

"Maud."

"Oh. Child, does a postal carrier fall in love with the package she's delivering?"

"I just want to travel with her a bit. Before I deliver her to the rich old man. Isn't that all right?"

"Depends on how soon you want answers. Depends on how soon you want to get paid."

"What's he going to do with her, once he's got her?"

"That all depends on if she can break her own curse."

"What is she, that she can curse somebody?"

"Damned," Sweet Honey said with a smile. "Just like you."

I awoke to the sound of Maud snoring. I was still in my borrowed nightgown. But even through the sound of Maud's snores, I could hear the steady drip, drip, drip of water from my dress, where it hung from a hook on the door.

After a huge breakfast of pancakes and bacon, Mrs. Caldecote loaded me down with presents of food: bread, cheese, peaches, tomatoes. The children were anxious to see what I would weave into my hair to remind me of them. They offered various toys and hair ornaments, but none of them felt right to me, and I didn't want to deprive them.

Maud came to hug me goodbye. Despite my heels, the top of my head didn't come any higher than the bottom of her chin. I had a brief impression that we were two pieces of a puzzle, as seemingly separate as South America and Africa, until you fitted them together and wondered how you could have ever not seen it.

And then the scent came to me from her freshly-washed hair…the soft, old-fashioned scent I would smell sometimes in the Bel Air.

I pulled away from her.

"Are you wearing perfume?"

"Mm-hm," she said. "It's L'Heure Bleue. My great-aunt Helena gave me a bottle the summer I stayed at her house. Robin won't let me wear perfume to work so I only wear it on my days off."

So the scent was from my future, after all. Whether I betrayed her to the rich old man or kept her by my side as the first real friend I could remember, Maud was my future. I heard, or imagined, faint buzzing near my ear, the humming of the bees. I remembered the way that Sweet Honey smiled at me.

"Maud, do you really want to come with me?"

"More than anything," she said.

"Are you certain? Listen…I eat lots of ramen I cook on my camp stove. Sometimes I don't have money for propane so I eat the ramen dry. If it's a choice between fuel and quarters for the shower, I choose the shower. Fresh fruits and veggies are a luxury.

"In the wintertime I have to fill up a thermos with hot water so I'll have something hot to drink first thing in the morning. Even though my sleeping bag is rated 0, I sleep with a hot water bottle. If I'm at a campsite without showers I use that water to wash with in the morning. I know all the year-round campsites, and some are mighty primitive."

"I'm not particular," Maud promised.

"You'll need your own sleeping bag and sleeping pad and hot water bottle."

"There's a sporting goods store in town."

I had run out of arguments, and Maud had run out of opportunities to back out.

"In that case..." I took a hank of her hair. "Mother, may I?" I asked.

She bit her lower lip and said, as if she were afraid I was only joking, "Yes, you may."

She bent her head down and I wove her hair into my own. I would give Maud an adventure before I took her to the rich old man. Give her her money's worth. Give her her hair's worth.

So we stood, hair to hair, head to head, two damned pretty things.

Maud of Sky

The Caldecotes—John Jordan and Mollie McBride—built their house midway up the west face of Wolf's House. Far to the south rose the Mountain, broad and beautiful and white, with a child mountain tucked neatly to one side; to the west, lower hills, and sunsets. Below Wolf's House lay the town of Sky, in a valley where spookies stretched high and diaphanous on days of rain and fog. At the top of Wolf's House stood a radio antenna with blinking red lights, an abandoned mansion, and a house-sized granite erratic called the Anvil.

The Caldecotes built their house beneath the place where the narrow dirt road, made adventurous with its washboards and potholes, ended. They fed a gravel driveway, ornamental as a dry riverbed in a Japanese garden, down from the end of the road to a brief and natural plateau. The foundation was built on solid rock, a mountain bone close to the skin. The land beneath the house was steep and wooded, falling away to a bridle trail, and again, further down, to a deserted logging road. From any west-facing window in the house, they could look down onto the pointed tops of evergreens, dark and splendid against blue sky or grey.

More blue than gray, really. Mrs. Caldecote had a knack with the weather. She spoke to the sky, and the sky answered favorably. It might be inherited from her alleged ancestors, the Fair Folk. It might be because she was a McBride, and when a McBride said a thing, people and the weather listened. It might be the period of blessed weather simply coincided with the Caldecotes' life on the side of the mountain, and that Mrs. Caldecote just liked to talk to things. But nobody could deny the beauty of the sky during those years.

They built the house large, to accommodate the space requirements of their children (though, at the time, there were only Sophie, Maud, Cole, and Aida Kay—Dandy and Gabriel were to come later). Only Sophie and Maud were old enough to remember the time before they lived on the mountain, and even those memories were fragmented. Maud could call up the satin gleam of the sun on a greening church bell, or the flavor of an egg salad sandwich shared with a neighbor boy, or the sound of her tricycle wheels on sidewalk. Sophie could remember the playground at her preschool, and that boy Rodney who licked all the salt from his crackers, and the small fish she caught for Kitty and brought home in a strawberry flat.

The Caldecotes left the trees alone, since few grew on that sharp mountain bone that held the house's foundation. Mr. Caldecote cut some trees above the house to make space for his garden and the eventuality of horses. Sophie and Maud played while he split the logs, and helped to stack the wood that, when aged, would stoke fires in the fireplace.

In the center of the future pasture rose three venerable stumps, old-growth cedar logged long ago by the same men who had cleared and abandoned the logging road. One was too tall for climbing. It was a good place for birds to nest. One was shorter, and served as a nursery stump for huckleberries. The third, and broadest, was crowned by a big granodiorite erratic, kissed here and there with lichen, crevices already wearing away to sparkling sand. This became one of the children's favorite spots, a place where Sophie practiced jumping, first from the stump, then from the boulder.

Maud liked the boulder, but she, unlike Sophie, was too afraid to jump from it. Even when her mother stood below, arms outstretched with a promise to catch her, Maud hesitated and backed away, burning with fear and shame. The best she could manage was to sit on the stump and half-slide into her mother's arms. Even then, she was crying.

"It's all right, honey. Don't worry. You're at the beginning of the beginning."

Maud knew what that meant. Every new thing had a beginning of a beginning. It happened when Mama taught her to play Old Maid and Go Fish. It happened when Papa taught her to blow bubbles with bubble gum. But it seemed like every one of Maud's beginnings of the beginning had to include crying.

Mr. and Mrs. Caldecote took walks with the children. Mr. Caldecote carried Cole when his two-year-old's legs grew too tired, and Mrs. Caldecote carried baby Aida Kay. They taught Sophie and Maud the names of the trees in the woods: Douglas fir, western hemlock, western red cedar, slide alder, big leaf maple (not sugar maple, to the dismay of the children), and vine maple (which grew in mossy tangles that looked like monstrous spiders). They taught them to know salal and Oregon grape, red huckleberry and blackberry and salmonberry; how to beware stinging nettle and treacherous devil's club; and how to respect (and never pick) trillium.

All around were small animals the children could hold in their hands—garter snakes, lizards, toads, sometimes a sticky and beautiful brown tree frog. There were other animals Sophie and Maud dreamed of seeing, and sometimes attempted luring out—rabbits, porcupines, raccoons, and skunks (which the children thought adorable, and believed only smelled when encountered dead on the highway).

Sometimes, in a sunny clearing, a deer would stop and watch with graceful immobility the more awkward frozen stances of the children, who longed until their hearts nearly broke to creep up and pet that soft muzzle. And once, Mr. Caldecote glanced up from his morning coffee to witness a cougar sharpening her claws on a nearby tree.

When it was too rainy to play outside, there were inside things to fascinate the children. Mama had kept from her childhood a model horse collection. The horses were cast in bronze, with tiny ball-chain reins. She also owned a china doll in a shattered, ruffled yellow silk dress, that she was given for being an attending princess in the Salmon Queen pageant. She had ridden on the float with the Queen, and waved, and had worn a little crown of her own.

She kept from her high school days a pair of high-heeled shoes with clear plastic straps and Lucite heels. The heels had a pattern of flowers on them, and the petals of the flowers were rhinestones.

"What are rhymestones?" Maud asked.

"They're artificial diamonds." Mama said.

Sophie and Maud, and later Aida Kay and Dandy, desperately wanted to wear these high-heeled slippers for games of Cinderella (which they played when they were set to work scrubbing the kitchen floor—Mrs. Caldecote hanging out, just out of sight, to listen to them). They dreamed of being able to wear them when they were old enough to date. Of course, the girls all grew up taller than their mother, and by the time they were dating age, their feet were too big to fit into the glass slippers.

"I guess we're just a family of ugly step-sisters," Sophie said with a sigh.

Mama had other things. There were two jewelry boxes. One was from Japan, black lacquer with delicate painting of willows and bridges and streams. When you opened the lid, it played "Stardust." Maud was well into her thirties before she realized "Stardust" had words. She had always imagined it to be unique to Mama's music box. The other jewelry box was pale blue leather, with a catch that closed with a satisfying snap.

Mama's wedding dress was safely packed away in a big, gold-foil box, which nobody was allowed to open, not even to peek. But her white tulle prom dress, spangled with rhinestones, hung in the back of her closet and was sometimes taken out to be carefully admired.

In one drawer, Mama kept a book with a lock and the words "My Diary" stamped on front in gold that was wearing away. Maud used to look for the key but never found it.

As it happened, Mama's diary was full of the misery of her growing up, the misery and conflict in the home that she couldn't wait to leave. Mama couldn't bring herself to throw away the diary, so she threw away the key, instead.

Papa had interesting things, too. The best was a bronze piggy bank in the shape of a little book, with the three little pigs and the big bad wolf on it. There was money inside of the piggy bank; it rattled when you shook it.

It never occurred to Maud, when she was a child, that her parents had ever been children, with children's things; that they could be as fond of certain things as she was of Popcorn the stuffed dog; that they might want to preserve from their children's careless hands the things that had survived their own childhood carelessness.

For Christmas, Papa's lively younger sisters sent a big box of dresses, shoes, and hats—things they had once worn until worn out or out of fashion. There was a pair of red satin high heels that the girls called the Ruby Slippers. There was a shiny green satin dress that swallowed Cole and turned him into Colleen. The little boy, with his broad nose and his white-blond butch haircut, sashayed like a princess, which was especially poignant when he raised the skirt to reveal his cowboy boots and rolled-cuff Levis.

The house on the mountain was a good place to be a child. Gradually there appeared other houses on the mountain, though not many, and most of them held other children. When Maud was eight, her two nearest neighbors were Randy Bundy and Julie Chance.

Randy Bundy, at twelve, was the oldest kid on the mountain. Mama said he was wild. He rode a mean-spirited buckskin gelding named Outlaw, and he told stories. His most infamous was of witnessing a plane crash at the top of the mountain. He said the pilot's severed arm hung by a single blood vessel. That was how Maud learned about blood vessels, and how she learned about slick little liars, which was what Papa called Randy Bundy.

Julie Chance, at eleven, was a year older than Sophie and was both knowledgeable and fearless. She rode her palomino, Blondie, the two miles down to town all by herself. She knew how to buy milk and eggs for her mother and bring them back in a saddle bag. She knew everything about their neighbors on the mountain—the names of their children, their dogs, their horses. She knew the best places to pick blackberries. She showed them how to eat wood sorrel, which tasted just like lemon.

She taught them how to discover the first initial of their future husband by reciting the alphabet while twisting an apple stem. Maud was in love with a boy named Arnie, but of course the apple stem never broke on "A." Instead, it always broke on "L." The only "L" she knew was Lionel Pipping, who was mean. She frequently cried after twisting apple stems.

Most importantly, Julie Chance knew the way to the Mansion.

For children, the way to the Mansion was learned through initiation. You knew you had crossed an important line when you were deemed old enough to hike to the Mansion. The way was long, full of switchbacks and very few level stretches for resting the legs. A trail had been cleared pretty well, but there were still the roots of trees to watch out for, and big rocks, and the shiny black and gold centipedes that seemed to inspire universal revulsion.

It mattered who took you up there. Randy Bundy offered, but Mama said no. Sophie and Maud ended up going with Julie. Mrs. Chance fitted up the three kids with a canteen each of lemonade, and gave Julie the backpack that held lunch. Maud asked, in a hinting sort of way, if Blondie might want to go to the Mansion too, but Mrs. Chance said no, parts of the trail were too narrow for a horse, but maybe the kids could go riding in the pasture the next day.

They followed the upper road until they got to the top of the hill, and Julie turned up a steep trail.

"Randy Bundy says this trail was made by a prison chain gang," Sophie said. "He said one of the prisoners escaped and is still hiding on the mountain."

"I can't stand Randy Bundy," Julie said. "He makes up stupid stories that never even happened, just so you pay attention to him. Believe me, lots of things happen on this mountain that he doesn't know about. Lots of things that would make him pee his pants if he knew."

"Like what?" Sophie asked.

"Oh, things. Did you know that Mrs. Lawrence always carries a pistol when she goes riding? I haven't see it, but she showed it to Mama once and said Mama ought to get one, too. It's not for bears. It's not for cougars."

"What's it for?"

Julie said, "The crazy hermits. There's an ugly old man and an ugly old woman, and they have three ugly old dogs. If you get too near their property they sic their dogs on you. And if their dogs can't get you, they come get you themselves."

That was enough for Maud. A plane crash and a dangling severed arm? All right. She'd had time to get used to the idea that Randy might have made that up. But crazy hermits with ugly dogs? Julie Chance was honest as the day was long. If she said there were crazy hermits, there were crazy hermits. Maud didn't even know what a hermit was. She didn't care.

She cried. Sophie got mad. Julie got impatient. The two older girls had no time for an eight-year-old crybaby when there was such an important hike on.

"Just go home," Sophie said.

So she did. Ashamed of her own cowardice, she ran back down to home and Mama and safety. She was disappointed, too, and she felt a sick, anxious hunger for Sophie to come back and tell her all about the Mansion (and prove that the crazy hermits and their dogs hadn't got her).

"It's not really a mansion," Mama said soothingly. "It's just an old stone vacation house that's been boarded up for years. Papa and I will take you up someday, all right?"

"What about the crazy hermits and the ugly dogs?"

"Oh, I think I know who Julie was talking about. There's an elderly couple who have a cabin back in the woods, far west of here. I don't think you're in any danger of running into them or their dogs, but if you did, I don't think they'd do you any harm. Some people just like to be left alone."

"But Mrs. Lawrence has a gun!"

"Mrs. Lawrence is a cautious woman. That gun is probably as much for cougars as it is for anything else. Parts of this mountain are still wild. Don't worry so, Maud."

Sophie returned well before suppertime, thoroughly disillusioned about the Mansion. "Our house is more of a mansion than that little old thing," she said. She brandished the library's copy of *The Four-Story Mistake* and said, "It's nothing like the mansion in this. But the Anvil is kind of neat. You can see for miles and miles and miles."

And Maud felt disappointed all over again.

That summer, Danielle Jordan Caldecote was born. Nicknamed Dandy, the baby was like a living doll to all the girls in the neighborhood. Everybody took turns toting Dandy around, or feeding her, or playing with her. Maud learned to change her diapers, a distasteful task. It was more fun to fold the clean diapers, fluffy and warm from the clothes dryer.

That summer, also, Mr. and Mrs. Chang built their house the next lot over from the Caldecotes'. Mrs. Chang was very feminine and proper, but her breath smelled like rubbing alcohol. Her twins, Candy and Cindy, were a year older than Dandy and too big to tote around, to the dismay of motherly Aida Kay. Even as toddlers they seemed to spend more time at the Caldecote house than they did at their own. As they grew, Mrs. Caldecote sewed them matching playsuits to change into because they were, to their mother's bafflement and disgust, rough and tumble girls and would spoil the dainty dresses, the lace trimmed socks. And so Dandy, Candy, and Cindy grew up almost as sisters together.

That fall the Caldecotes got a piano. It was an upright piano with a bench. Maud would have preferred the kind of stool that twirled. The wood of the front panel had a mirrored grain that looked like nothing so much as a squat toad. Maud immediately called this "Conductor Frog."

There had always been music in the Caldecote house. Papa had a steel-string acoustic guitar, a Harmony Monterey. Sometimes he played Spanish music on it, his fingers rapidly fanning against the strings. Sometimes he played songs with words that he would sing. There were fun songs like "The Fox Went Down." There were sad songs like "500 Miles." And then there was "Grandma's in the Cellar," which made Mama protest, "John Jordan Caldecote, don't you sing that awful song!"

When Papa wasn't playing, the radio was on, or the stereo, and the children grew up on classical music, folk music, and show tunes. Mama, too, was always singing as she worked. She woke them in the morning with "Good Morning to You," and she put them to bed at night with lullabies.

Now Sophie and Maud began piano lessons in a room hung with different musical instruments and a copy of Picasso's "Three Musicians," the latter of which confused Maud. Sophie took to the piano as if she'd been born to it and far outstripped Maud, who was more interested in using the loud pedal and transposing her assignments to minor keys than she was in actually practicing. But what she preferred over that was to sing—loudly, dramatically, without a trace of self-consciousness. Her voice was husky but melodic. Happily, the piano teacher also taught voice, and so Maud switched from playing scales to singing them.

Maud applied herself to voice lessons, which was a good thing, since she applied herself to very little at school. During open house, Maud's teacher, Mrs. Meachum, pulled the Caldecotes aside.

"This will likely come as no surprise to you," she said, "but Maud is a challenge to all my years of teaching. Math reduces her to tears. The longer and more patiently I try to walk her through a problem, the harder she cries. I don't know how many times I've had to send her to the nurse's office to lie down.

"History goes right over her head. The only thing that interested her was the story of Roanoke Island, and then she pestered me with questions as if her life depended on it. She's all right in geography, since she likes the sound of foreign names and she loves the maps and the globe. She enjoys art but not in any serious way. And Mr. Caldecote, I hope I will not shock you to say the poor child couldn't write her way out of a paper bag."

For Mr. Caldecote edited and published the town's newspaper.

"It strains credibility," Mrs. Meachum said, "that she could be Sophie's sister…or your daughter, Mr. Caldecote."

"I promise you, she is," said Mrs. Caldecote, a little tartly.

Mrs. Meachum cleared her throat and continued hastily, "The only time Maud seems to be happy and engaged is during music class. But let's just say she won't be singing for her supper with that rough voice of hers…" She trailed off when Mrs. Caldecote gave her a McBride look.

"Maud will find her way," Mr. Caldecote said. "Maybe not this year. Maybe not next year. But she will find her way."

Maud herself was not so sure. It was hard to be two years younger than Sophie and constantly compared to her. Sophie was blonde, whereas Maud was dark. Sophie was of average height, whereas Maud had always been the tallest in her class. Sophie was good at school and good at piano. Maud wasn't good at much besides singing and pretending. Sophie excelled at sports. Maud was far too awkward and was always chosen last for teams. Sophie wasn't popular, but she was popular enough. Maud had acquaintances but no real friends. Not able to travel her older sister's path, Maud found her way overgrown as if with devil's club.

When Maud was twelve, she finally hiked to the Mansion. It was on a bad day that found her sitting on the dusty ground beneath a cedar tree. Rain pattered everywhere, but she stayed dry and hidden under the boughs that swept the ground. The ditch water gurgled and rushed. Mab and Nut, the Caldecote's mares, grazed nearby, their hooves thumping gently as they walked. Down below, the house was warm and light and noisy, Cole and her sisters shouting to each other, baby Gabriel crying. They'd been playing Monopoly, and Maud had left in a huff because of some younger-brother thing Cole had said to her. They could call her in, call her back, if they wanted her; but they never did. They let her do as she pleased.

"Let her go. She'll come back." But what if she *didn't* come back? What if she *never* came back? They'd be sorry then. They'd never know what had happened to her. Maybe she'd get to be famous. She'd be beautiful, of course, and rich. She'd even change her name.

The ache inside her was nearly intolerable. Why didn't they call her back? Why didn't they *ever* call her back? She could be dying out here, crushed by a fallen tree branch. She'd die because nobody came to check on her. Too late. They'd find her dead and cold. *Maud...we always knew she'd never amount to much. At least we don't have to put up with her any more. Life will be fun without Maud.*

And she wondered if maybe she were already dead. *Part of me is dead, and part of me isn't.* She imagined her own funeral, and saw the pain and the grief of her mother and father, and wondered if maybe she shouldn't let a tree branch fall on her and crush her, after all.

She was crying in pity for her dead self when she decided to strike out for the trail. Fine. She'd just hike to the

Mansion and not let anybody know. Mama and Papa and Sophie said it wasn't really a mansion, just a little stone vacation house that nobody had ever lived in, but maybe it would be a real mansion just for Maud. Maybe she would find a way to get inside—a secret passageway that nobody else had discovered. She could live there all alone—haul up groceries, draw water from a creek, and gather firewood for her fireplace. It would snow and nobody would be able to get up the trail, and she'd be cozy on top of the mountain in her Mansion. No diapers to change, no screaming brothers and sisters, no school, nothing but peace and quiet.

The way was steep and rocky. She felt every root and rock through the thin soles of her tennis shoes. Despite the cold and rain, she grew hot and sweaty in her light coat, so she took it off and tied it around her waist. Her mouth was dry; she wished for water or a piece of gum.

About a mile up the trail, a young doe who wasn't afraid of her stopped to pee. She peed just like a female dog. Maud thought of the fawn in *Through the Looking Glass* and the forest where nothing had a name.

"If this were that forest, I know one thing for sure. I wouldn't be a Caldecote. I'd leave my troubles behind."

Maud sometimes tried to imagine how this would work. Would you go out into the country and throw your troubles out of your car, the way some terrible people did with their dogs and cats? She'd heard stories of other dogs and cats who made amazing cross-country journeys. Would your troubles be able to find you, the way those gallant dogs and cats had found their own careless families?

Maud was growing weary. She wished she had counted the switchbacks. This must have been the thirtieth. She rested facing down the trail, her hands on her knees. The sting of Cole's words and her family's indifference were beginning to fade. Home sounded comfortable. But she had committed to running away, at least to see the Mansion, and so she continued.

As it was, she had only one more switchback before the trail leveled off, and she stood on the top of the mountain. There lay the giant erratic called the Anvil. She hurried to it and clambered up it. Standing tall, she regretted the rain and the low-lying clouds that obscured the view. She called out "Hello! Hello! I am Maud of Sky, and I am going to conquer the world!"

She remembered one of Randy Bundy's wild stories, that he had almost been struck by lightning while standing on the Anvil. The scorched black spot, she reckoned, was more likely from a campfire than a lightning strike. Randy Bundy, now sixteen, had moved away with his family, but his stories remained.

She slid off the Anvil and went in search of the Mansion. It wasn't far, tucked within a protective ring of trees that had been seedlings when the house was built. It was a single-story stone cottage, 1920s-style storybook rustic. The windows and doors were boarded with heavy plywood of recent vintage. A partially frayed blue tarp covered the roof. The only sign of vandalism was a series of initials scraped into the moss that covered the stones of the north-facing wall. Maud walked around and around the house, trampling wet, winter-killed bracken, looking for the slightest chink in the plywood. She longed to see what the inside of the Mansion looked like. Was it fully furnished? Were there dishes in the cupboard and logs in the fireplace? Were there books and a piano and a trunk of beaded 1920s evening gowns?

Maud was soaked with sweat and rain, no longer warm with exertion, and her teeth chattered. She put on her jacket, which hardly seemed up to the task of warming her. She became aware that it was not as light as it had been.

The thought of descending the rooty, rocky trail in the dark made her hurry away.

She went down the trail as quickly as she could. Sometimes she skidded on small, loose rocks or fir cones. Sometimes she slipped on a patch of mud. She sang loudly to herself as she hiked down, trying not to think of winter-lean cougars. By the time she finally came to the trailhead, she could barely see the pale blobs of her feet in her sneakers. There was the road, and there, her driveway. And soon she was in her own warm kitchen, where another game of Monopoly was being played without her.

"Where have you been?" Mama asked. "I thought you were in your room."

"Oh, I just went up to the Mansion," Maud said.

"By yourself?"

"Uh-huh."

"Did the crazy hermits get you?" Sophie said unkindly.

"Shut up."

"Go change out of your wet things," Mama said. "You're about to shiver to pieces."

Maud went down to her room and changed. She sat on her unmade bed, wrapped in a blanket, and thought about the Mansion, and of an untouched world within, protected by boards and tarp. She felt, though she couldn't say how, that it waited for her, and that one day she would, in perfect solitude, discover its treasures.

Maud, always the tallest child in her class, was six feet tall by the time she turned thirteen. With puberty, her public shyness mutated into an excruciating self-consciousness that nothing could assuage. She didn't know what to do with her body, so she slouched, wrapped at all times in her long winter coat. She was an awkward girl, terrible at sports, much to the chagrin of the girls' basketball coach, who could have used Maud's height on the team.

Not a brain like Sophie, not social like Cole, Maud clung to the few other shy girls in school and tried to avoid detection. The borage amulet that Mama made to help Maud be brave didn't seem to do her a bit of good, but she wore it anyway, underneath her tops, and hoped that one day it would work.

In her first year of high school, Lionel Pipping, long her nemesis, now a popular jock, struck on a new way to torment her. In the cafeteria, in the one class they shared, or in the hallway, he had taken to calling out to her, "Maud, I *love* you," and then laughing with his friends. This mockery had made her turn red and miserable with shame. Of course, she knew what it meant—that she was considered a dog, and that being a dog was the worst thing a girl could be. She dreaded her class with him, dreaded meeting him in the hallway, and spent more than one evening at home crying over the humiliation.

"Just tell him he's a disgusting puddle of puke," Sophie said. But Maud could tell that Sophie was embarrassed, not for her, but of her.

Sophie was the self-appointed arbiter of appropriate behavior. Hers was a losing battle. Nobody acted properly, except maybe her father, though he was really too shy and should assert himself more at the town's 4th of July picnic. Cole didn't take anything seriously, and he called her friends unflattering nicknames. Aida Kay's glasses and haircut weren't fashionable enough, and she sometimes sassed her teachers. Dandy played with Candy and Cindy and let them boss her around. Gabriel was all right, except his hair was too long, too gold, too curly. Maud didn't care enough about serious things, brought home Cs, and was too shy and awkward.

And Mama, well, Mama was hopeless. She didn't understand that, as a McBride, she had a position in the town. She ought to get her hair cut more often, and wear makeup, and throw away her cowboy boots and her sweater that she'd worn in every driver's license picture for the past six thousand years.

Sophie had the misfortune of being with Mama the day Mama had her epiphany at the butcher's shop. "Looking at all these pieces of dead creature...I just can't do it, any more than I could buy dog meat or cat meat or horse meat."

Of course, she was a McBride, so she could do as she pleased. But the amount of meat her children ate was going to make a not inconsiderable loss in the butcher's income. When she came in the next day, her face resolute and the fire of McBride cussedness in her eyes, he wondered what she was going to spring on him.

"Bean curd!" she said, without greeting or preamble. "You need to stock bean curd. Tofu, it's called. Also tempeh, a textured product of the soybean. Finally, seitan, which is a meat substitute made of wheat gluten. Give me some paper and a pencil, and I'll write it all out for you."

"You can't feel a whole lot of affection for a salmon, can you?" the butcher said hopefully.

"How do you know?"

"Well, a shrimp, then. Or a clam. In matters of personality, they can't be said to possess much."

"Too expensive," Mama said.

Well, what could he do? She just had it in her blood. Maybe it was a curiosity that it hadn't come out this way before. He felt bad for John, who was a Texas carnivore through and through.

They heard later that the minister of a different church preached a sermon against it a few Sundays later. "Is it a coincidence that this mock meat is called Satan?" he demanded of his congregation. He'd referred to Mama not-so-obliquely as a cafeteria Christian and a known kitchen witch with a house full of heathen fetishes.

Sophie, whose best friend went to that church, was mortified.

Her family's defects were an acute source of humiliation for Sophie. She wanted to shake off Sky like it was a bug crawling on her shoulder. She dreamed of a day she'd go someplace where nobody knew them, and where nobody told her things Cole had said, or Maud had worn, or the lip Aida Kay had given this teacher, or how Dandy had been crying at recess.

But nothing torched Sophie's propriety-loving soul quite so thoroughly as when Maud came home from choir camp with a pack of menthol cigarettes.

When Maud got back from choir camp the Spring Break before she turned 16, the first time she had been away from home for any length of time, she wasn't the same girl she'd been before she left. Mrs. Caldecote noticed it first—a new, easy grace of motion in her lanky limbs, the way she held her chin just a bit higher, the subtle movements of her head that would send her spire of dark hair swishing over one shoulder, then the other. There was something different in the way her clothes hung on her...same clothes, different effect. When she stepped off the old school bus, the last one to get off, taking her time, her mother noticed at once.

There is a code of clothing and adornment so subtle, so varying from one generation to the next, that it can't be perceived by anybody outside of that particular generation. Maud couldn't look at her mother's old yearbooks, for example, and pick out the "bad" girls from the "good," though to

Mrs. Caldecote it was immediate and obvious, in the part of the hair, in the choice of blouse, even in the size, measured in millimeters, of the pearl earrings. Mrs. Caldecote assumed the same would be true for Maud and her generation... subtle differences that would show clearly one's standing, and the standing of one's parents...but she couldn't see it. Her own code was outmoded and useless. Even so, she had faith that the rolled sleeves of Maud's striped T-shirt meant something other than "bad" girl, as did the ponytail on top of her head instead of at the nape, and the new confidence in her walk.

A phrase came to her mind that she would never have associated with Maud, not in a million years. And that phrase was "savoir faire." There in the high school parking lot, Mrs. Caldecote knew that her second daughter had achieved something even her accomplished oldest hadn't. She saw it with admiration and pride, not unmingled with some heartache and even a pang of fear. Others would admire her daughter and covet her.

It wasn't until she was home, and in the presence of the whole family, that Maud very deliberately opened her purse, took out a cigarette from a full pack, and lit it. The girls gasped. Cole wrinkled his face into a look of disgust. Mama and Papa glanced at each other. Mama raised an eyebrow; Papa sighed.

Sophie was livid. "Aren't you going to make her stop?" she demanded, following Mama around the house in an electrical storm of outrage after Maud blew smoke on her and told her to mind her own damn beeswax. "You are her mother, after all."

"Your Papa and I have decided to wait and see what happens," Mama said. "At least she's doing it out in the open."

"You mean it's all right with you?" Sophie looked as if she were about to strangle on her own moral outrage.

"I did not say that, Sophia."

"But you're just going to let her smoke and swear?"

"For now. We've told her she may not smoke at school or in any other public place."

"Cigarettes are addictive, you know. She's going to get lung cancer and die. If she doesn't burn the house down first, that is, and kill all of us."

"Sophie, let it go," Mama said. "Maud, don't blow smoke on your sister anymore."

Fortunately, Sophie was working part-time at the nursing home that spring, so Maud didn't see much of her.

The source of the cigarettes, and the inspiration for Maud's new poise, was an 18-year-old girl named Bonnie who came to choir camp from the city. Bonnie was bold and daring, stood six foot one in her stocking feet, wore high-heeled boots, and gave not a single damn about anything. From the first day, she'd taken shy Maud under her wing. She wore her ponytail at the top of her head to make herself even taller and encouraged Maud to adopt the style. When Maud told her about Lionel Pipping and his *I love you*s, she said, "Just say 'I love you' back in the same snotty voice and he'll shut up." Maud couldn't quite believe that was true. Besides, she was a romantic. The first time she said "I love you" to a boy, she wanted to actually mean it.

Bonnie could talk to anybody with ease, including teachers, including boys. She flirted with everyone, and even the short boys grew infatuated with her. She swore and smoked and made both look sophisticated.

For weeks, the Caldecotes were subject to what Bonnie said, what Bonnie did, how Bonnie wanted Maud to come visit her in the city. Maud and Bonnie wrote letters to each other. Increasingly, Bonnie's letters were full of boys and how she was attracting them at a prodigious rate.

It never occurred to Maud to try attracting a boy. Despite her adoration of Bonnie, she thought most flirting was actually sort of disgusting. It clashed with her ideas of dignity and heroinehood. Dippy girls flirted. Minor characters flirted. So the notion of an apprenticeship in love simply never would have occurred to her. That it did occur to Bonnie both annoyed her and surprised her with a conviction that maybe Bonnie wasn't so perfect, after all. It was the McBride coming out in her. She became disappointed in a friend for being merely human.

But Bonnie's other lessons held. Maud embraced her height. She took to wearing cowboy boots with two-inch heels and wore her ponytail on top of her head. Most importantly, the first time Lionel Pipping called out "Maud, I *love* you" to her in the cafeteria, she'd had it. She went from fearful to furious in that moment, just as if she'd been released from physical restraints. She strode over to him, her head held high.

"What did you just say?" she demanded.

"I *love* you, Maud," he said with a smirk.

"Prove it," she said. "Kiss me."

"What?" He turned to look at his friends, who laughed and whistled.

She planted both hands on his chest and shoved him back. "Come on. Kiss me. I dare you." She gave him another shove.

He looked at her with new eyes. "Are you kidding me?"

"Yes, I am. Because I'd rather kiss a slug than kiss you."

"But—"

"You." She pointed her finger at him imperiously. "Go out right now and pick up the biggest, juiciest slug you can find and bring it to me. What are you waiting for? I told you to bring me a slug."

"But I've got class."

"I don't care. Be late for class. But bring me that slug."

Her next class was Intro to French. She was conjugating verbs when Lionel Pipping came in, nodding in apology to Madame Whitman. On his PeeChee, which he held out flat in front of him, was a sizable banana slug.

Maud stood and took the slug in her hand. She let it settle itself as if handling slugs were the most natural thing in the world.

"You're a disgusting creature," she told it, "but compared to Lionel Pipping you're a pure beauty."

She bent and kissed the slug. The class, including Madame Whitman, gasped and groaned. Maud put the slug back on Lionel's PeeChee.

"Now take this fair creature back outside, and don't you *dare* say one word to me *ever again.*"

That night, Maud came down with the mother of all colds. She was home sick for an entire week. But when she came back to school, Lionel Pipping and the other bullies gave her a wide berth. Whenever she saw him, she made a kissy face at him.

Maud's friends started calling her Maud, Kisser of Slugs, with humorous admiration.

"I never thought I'd feel sorry for a Pipping," Sophie told her.

When word got back to Mama, she wondered what else had changed in Maud. She warned Maud to be careful with imprecations. "I think you must have a strong streak of McBride in you," she said. And despite her unhappy relations with her birth family, she looked proud when she said it.

By June, Bonnie's letters trickled off to nothing. Maud was both disappointed and relieved. It wasn't long before she found a new passion, courtesy of the county library.

On a whim, she checked out a historical novel called *Grafinia* and found herself lost in a world of Russian countesses, handsome highwaymen, husbands killed in the Crimean War who came back to life, romance, cattle ranching, the gold rush, vigilante groups, and the losing and gaining of fortunes.

With typical older-sister bossiness, she insisted that Aida Kay read it as soon as she'd finished. She needed somebody sympathetic to discuss it with, and Sophie was out of the question, being too interested in important books like *The Gulag Archipelago* to mess around with mere romance fiction. Aida Kay was sucked into the story as well, and from that moment on, they could hardly talk about anything but the novel and the characters.

If the author was a bit careless with her facts and her history, Maud and Aida Kay didn't notice. They had always loved stories set in the olden days, and they had always loved stories of beautiful girls and dashing bandits, and that was really all that mattered to them. Maud took to using Russian words, which she mispronounced, causing her mother and father to smile at each other when she wasn't looking.

"Did Natasha smoke cigarettes?" Aida Kay asked once, after Maud had lit one.

"Of course not. They weren't invented yet." Maud thought a bit. "But I'll bet she would have if they were."

Grafinia would have occupied them for the rest of the summer had not, one week later, come the passion to end all passions.

Maud's favorite place in town was the Blue Mouse Theatre. She adored this temple to make-believe, a little jewel box of a theater quite unexpectedly opulent for a town the size of Sky. Mr. Dougal Avery, the owner, had bad luck with the films he received. The current Hollywood blockbusters never made it to the Blue Mouse. Rather, anime, Godzilla,

Hong Kong action movies, SciFi and horror, old musicals—
the fantasies of the wider world, both art house and psycho-
tronic—passed through the little theater. Not a few children
learned to read first by reading subtitles.

Ever hopeful at finally getting a print of *Marmots in
the Family*, Mr. Avery received an astonishing eight cans of
film off the noon train. And so it came to pass that *Kuch
Kuch Hota Hai* introduced the people of Sky to the world of
Bollywood.

Maud was there for the first showing. At the intermis-
sion, as conversation gradually started up, she found her
own language jarring and alien. She had grown used to the
flow of English-sprinkled Hindi. She was startled by her
own whiteness when she looked at herself in the restroom
mirror. Everything had changed. Her eyes had changed, and
her ears, too. What she had grown up seeing and hearing
had become foreign, and sad, and boring.

By the time the final credits rolled, Maud was congest-
ed with crying, and her heart beat like a drum. She wasn't
watching where she was going when she came out of the
theater into the soft June rain, and she walked right into a
man so tall she really ought to have seen him.

"Whoa! Watch where you're going, Lightning," said his
companion.

"Sorry, miss," the man said.

"Sorry," said Maud. She went on her way a bit more
carefully, suddenly critical of her surroundings. The grays
and muted greens of the hills, the darker evergreens stark
as swords, shocked her eyes. Hers seemed suddenly a world
of spikes and spears. She longed for a different world of
lush and sudden rainfalls, of candy-colored sarees, of dancing and singing, loving and weeping. How wrong her jeans
and T-shirt felt to her. How huge and clumping her cowboy

boots. Bells on her ankles, bangles on her arms—that's what she needed.

She'd seen American musicals before, of course, and she had long known that music made people fall in love. The serenade underneath the window, the song like an apology, the sung confession of love—they were nothing new to Maud. But there was something about the combination of college fantasy, the love triangle of Rahul, Tina, and Anjali (and after the interval, Rahul, Anjali, and Aman), and the exotic locale that utterly arrested her.

And Maud wasn't alone. Other girls came out of the theater wide-eyed, stunned, elated. The boys didn't want anything to do with it, naturally, besides to make fun of all the bursting into song and dance. But it was the most glamorous thing the town girls had ever seen, and all of a sudden, India was all the rage. The drug store sold out of black eyeliner. Girls raided their mothers' jewelry boxes for bracelets, for jewelry to hang on their foreheads. Women wondered what happened to their flat sheets, and didn't know that they draped like sarees around their daughters, who practiced dancing in front of mirrors when nobody else was looking.

Some of the girls saw the movie three or four times. These regulars cheered during the credits, and chanted "No short skirts in college!" and "Miss Briganza…uh-huh!" with the characters.

Maud saw it every day. She spent every penny of her babysitting money on theater tickets. She couldn't keep away. It fed a hunger in her that she had never before realized existed. And it validated her, for the actress who played Tina had a husky voice just like Maud's. On the strength of it, Maud identified with the sophisticated but doomed Tina far more than with tomboy heroine Anjali.

Aida Kay often accompanied her, nearly as crazy about the movie as she was. Once, her parents came with them to see what all the fuss was about. She was embarrassed to have them there. It seemed almost indecent to go into that dream world with them nearby.

When after two weeks the film left, Maud cried for an hour. She couldn't believe it was gone out of her life.

So she decided to recreate what she loved.

By that time in their lives, both Maud and Aida Kay were really too old to play pretend anymore and still maintain their dignity. So they turned to writing plays (until they tired of that) and then acting what they'd written. That way, they could still play dress-up, and be other people in other places, except to a purpose, which was to become famous.

Maud decided to spend the rest of the summer at the top of the mountain, writing a Bollywood-style musical version of *Grafinia*. It seemed like a perfect plan to her. She and Aida Kay would act out the parts, Maud taking the role of the dashing Countess Natasha, Aida Kay the more subdued and traditionally feminine role of Charlotte. Dandy, who was seven, begged to come with them, and since they both loved an audience, they agreed.

"Mind your manners while you're up there," Mama said. "The Mansion has got a new owner, and he's posted 'no trespassing' signs all around his property."

Maud heard this with a derisive snort. Since coming back from choir camp, she baited and mocked fate, and Mama worried incessantly. There were only so many protections she could devise for her child, especially if she refused to wear them. The herbal amulets would be found somewhere beneath the bed, if not, as on one particularly memorable occasion, wrapped around a headless Barbie Doll with the note: "IT DIDN'T WORK" stuck through her soft leg with a sewing pin.

When Maud saw the new NO TRESPASSING signs posted at the Anvil, her defiance was second only to her indignation.

"He may own the Mansion," she said. "I'm not saying he doesn't. But how can he own the Anvil? That's like saying he owns the Statue of Liberty."

She climbed atop the Anvil, took off her cowboy boots and socks, lay down, and flexed her toes. Clouds were moving in quickly, but the granodiorite was still warm on her back. Aida Kay and Dandy wouldn't follow her. They waited nervously beside the NO TRESPASSING sign, fully expecting the new owner to show up (possibly with a shotgun).

Maud had brought up her last cigarette from the pack Bonnie had given her at choir camp. She smoked it now, flicking her ash onto the spot where Randy Bundy had said lightning had almost struck him.

"Lightning, my eye," she said. She shouted down to her sister, "How about this, Aida Kay? We'll have a scene where Joshua and Natasha get caught in the rain and dance together in a gazebo like Rahul and Anjali."

It looked like rain was imminent. Directly overhead lay a dark gray cloud so low that Maud thought she might almost touch it if she stood on tiptoes. She stubbed out her cigarette on the lightning-struck spot and stood. "Maybe I can dance the lightning down." She waltzed, or imagined she did, her arms held out to an invisible partner, humming the theme song to *Kuch Kuch Hota Hai*. As if on cue, it began to rain. Aida Kay and Dandy ran for the cover of a cedar tree.

"Hey, lightning!" Maud called to the sky. "Randy Bundy's afraid of you, but I'm not! Come and dance with me if you dare!"

Suddenly, Aida Kay and Dandy began to shout for her over the building wind.

"Maud! Maud! Get down!"

"What?"

"Come *on*!"

Then she saw him—the same tall man she'd bumped into leaving the Blue Mouse Theatre. The same tall man who had called her "miss."

"Hey!" he shouted. "What the hell are you doing on my land?"

She scooped up her boots and socks and jumped off the Anvil.

"Run! Run! Run!"

They made it to the trailhead and pelted down the trail, drenched, shivering, Dandy crying.

Maud, barefoot, said, "Damn! I dropped one of my boots."

"Don't go back for it," Aida Kay begged. "Just come on. Please!"

"Hey, Dandy, it's okay. Don't cry. He's not following us." Maud grabbed her youngest sister in a hug. "You settle down now, okay? Huh? Okay, Dandy?"

"Did he have a gun?" Dandy quavered.

"No, he most certainly did not have a gun." Then Maud laughed. "Wow! That was something, wasn't it? Mister Big Scary Guy yelling at us to get off his land. *His* land. As if anybody could own the Anvil. He might as well say he owns the Taj Mahal."

"Are we going to tell Mama and Papa?" Aida Kay asked.

"Only if they ask," Maud said, and winked.

But the next day, the man drove into their driveway in a pickup truck and got out with Maud's boot in his hand. "Mrs. Caldecote, I'm David Levain. I believe this belongs to one of your kids."

"That's yours, isn't it, Maud?" Mama asked.

Maud went to take it. "Thanks," she said. But he wouldn't let the boot go.

"Mrs. Caldecote, I need to talk to your kid about trespassing on my land."

Maud was not almost sixteen anymore, not a woman of the world at all, but six, and in big, big trouble.

"Maud, what did I tell you yesterday?" Mama scolded. "You've got better manners and better sense than to make a man warn you off his land. Or you ought to."

"Do you want to tell your mother what you were doing on that big rock up there, or do you want me to tell her?"

"I was dancing," Maud said, feeling foolish.

"No. Before that."

"Oh, that?" Maud waved her hand. "They know I smoke."

"You left your cigarette butt up there. I would have brought it down to you, but I expect you to clean it up yourself. Do you know what the penalty for trespassing is in this county?"

"No," Maud said, her voice barely audible.

"Thirty days in jail and a $500 fine."

"Mr. Levain, I'm sure Maud meant no harm."

"Mrs. Caldecote, I'm serious about keeping trespassers and vandals off my property. I'm not going to be here all the time, and I need to know my property will be safe in my absence. If I let this go, I'm going to be sending a message to every juvenile delinquent—"

"Excuse me?" Maud said.

"—in Sky that my property is fair game. I'm not going to let that happen."

"My daughter is many things, Mr. Levain, but a juvenile delinquent she is not."

"I figured that was the case," he said. "That's why I'm not inclined to prosecute. If you and your husband are agreeable, I propose that she come up to my property for thirty days and work for me. I've got a lot of cleaning to do on the house alone."

"No," Maud said, emboldened at last. "No, no, no. I'm going to eat ice cream all summer long, I'm going to lie in the grass and write a musical, I'm not working for him for thirty days, no way."

"I guess you leave me no choice but to prosecute," he said.

"Mr. Levain, you have to understand that the children here are used to hiking up to the Anvil."

"And you have to understand that they'll need to get un-used to it. I'm not going to tolerate trespassers, and that's that."

"Well, Maud, I think there's nothing for it," Mama said. Maud could tell she was angry, both at Mr. Levain and at Maud for causing trouble in the first place. "Mr. Levain, I'll talk to my husband and see what he thinks. Is there a number where I can reach you?"

"I'm staying at the Sky Hotel for now." He handed Maud's boot to her. "Let me know what you decide."

"Well, this is a revolting development," Mama said after he had driven off. "Maud, what were you thinking? What if he'd taken a shot at you?"

"He didn't have a gun," Maud said sullenly.

"You didn't know that when you trespassed."

"Mama, do I *have* to work for him?"

"We'll see what Papa says when he gets home, but I suspect you do."

Maud slapped her hands to her head with a cry of anguish.

"Maud, you need to learn to think before you act."

Maud didn't have the heart to say that she had.

Papa was angry. He'd met Mr. Levain in town and been apprised of the situation. He had taught his children to always obey NO TRESPASSING signs, and he couldn't believe that Maud was so knuckle-headed as to ignore one and encourage her little sisters to do the same.

"He might have shot you," he said.

"Why does everybody think he had a gun?" Maud said through her tears. "He didn't have a damn gun. And anyway, I was on the Anvil. How can anybody own the Anvil? He might as well say he owns the Eiffel Tower."

"He owns thirty acres of that mountain top, and that includes the Anvil. It doesn't matter what anybody used to do, Maud. It's his property now, and he's got the right to keep people off it.

"Now I'm going to ask you a question, and I want you to think very carefully before you answer. Since you've been back from choir camp you've been smoking and swearing and acting out. Your Mama and I haven't said anything because we want you children to find your own way of being in the world. But I'll ask you now—what foundation are you laying for your future?"

"What do you mean?" Maud asked, and blew her nose.

"Everything that you do today lays the foundation for who you will be tomorrow."

"I don't know," she said. "I haven't thought about it."

"You're nearly sixteen years old. I think it's time you started."

Maud sighed. "Okay. I will. But do I have to *work* for him, Papa?"

"Yes. You have to work for him. Thirty days, starting tomorrow. He'll pick you up after breakfast."

"Pick me *up*?"

"He'll drive you up there so you don't have to waste time hiking."

"There's a *road* up there?"

"Yes, Maud. That's how the workers service the radio tower."

"Oh." And Maud felt resentment that she'd never known about the road before. It was as if they'd deliberately withheld the information. She could have been riding Nut or Mab up to the Anvil all this time, and now she couldn't any more. Life was being deeply unfair to her.

"Jordan, will she be safe?" Mama asked. "We know nothing at all about him."

"We know he's got a stick up his butt," Maud grumbled. Mama swatted her.

"Here's what he told me. He inherited the property from old Mr. Levain, his grandfather, and he intends to live up there off and on. He's a carpenter by trade and does a lot of traveling. He went to college with Howard Waters. Howard vouched for him."

"That's all well and good," Mama said, "but Maud is going to be alone up there with him."

"I told him that he might not have a shotgun but that I do," Papa said. "He seemed to think it unnecessary that I was warning him about a kid."

"Just so long as he doesn't *forget* she's a kid," Mama said.

By this time of life, Maud had gotten over the idea that the Mansion was anything other than what people said it was—a simple mountain cottage too rustic for old Mr. Levain's wife and so never lived in. Knowing she would have to work there for thirty days instead of working on her musical stripped it of whatever allure remained. It was Mr. Levain's house now, and it would never be hers.

He picked her up at 9:00 the next morning. As they drove up the strange, rough road, he told her what he expected.

"You'll be working clearing all the weeds away from the side of the house," he said. "Everything within a yard of the walls. I've got a pair of work gloves you can use. You'll load everything into the wheelbarrow and take it to my compost heap. At noon I'll drive you back down to your house and you'll be done for the day. I expect you to work every day but Sunday. Do you understand?"

"Yes," she said sullenly.

"Yes what?"

"Yes, sir," she said.

It irritated her to have to call him "sir." Was he even thirty years old? She looked him over and conceded to herself that he was a bit handsome. If he were an actor or a singer she might be inclined to get a crush on him. But a slave-driving carpenter? No. Never.

"You know what?" he said suddenly. "Never mind calling me 'sir.' Everybody just calls me Lightning."

"Why would they do that?" Maud asked scornfully. "Did you electrocute somebody?"

"Sir it is," he said. They were at the Mansion. He put the truck into park. "You know, you might have saved yourself all this trouble if you'd just bothered to apologize in the first place."

Maud got out and surveyed the weeds growing up around the house. This was going to take forever.

"Why would I apologize?" she demanded.

"For trespassing," he said, aggravated. "That's why you're here, remember?"

"I wasn't trespassing because you can't own the Anvil," she said in a blurt. "It just isn't right."

"Why is that, Maud Caldecote?"

"Because it belongs to everybody. It's where you go when..."

"When what?"

Maud shook her head. "You might as well say you own a mountain or a river or the United States of America. Nobody owns those things. They belong to everybody."

"Sorry, but the Anvil is on my property, which makes it mine. I posted NO TRESPASSING signs, which you ignored. Now stop arguing with me about it and get to work."

And that was that. Because of her stubbornness, her fate was sealed—sealed away, like a walled-in Gothic heroine awaiting rescue. Why couldn't it be sealed in an envelope, awaiting the glamorous announcer to open it and stun the world amid huge applause? She thought about her musical and ripped at the weeds with ferocity. And what was Mr. "everybody calls me Lightning" doing?

As she ripped at the weeds, she sang, to the tune of "Scotland the Brave," "Lightning's a pile of goo, Lightning's a stinker too, Lightning's a rotten rat, Lightning's a skunk."

"I can hear you," he yelled from around the corner of the house.

Good, she thought. But she sang more softly after that.

Lightning took the plywood off the windows and doors and spent hours trying to get the windows open. Maud was curious about the inside of the house, but Lightning wouldn't allow her in. He said the floors were dirty enough without her tracking in more. Once the windows were opened she looked inside, but the house was empty and gloomy and stripped of allure.

She spent the first five days clearing away the weeds. The stench of Herb Robert clung to her despite her work gloves, made her itch and raised welts on her arms where she scratched them. She always hated Herb Robert from that summer forward and could see no beauty in it. She cleared away dandelion and other wild asters, and bracken. Lightning's compost pile grew.

"Good for my garden next summer," he said, and she thought he seemed too young to have a garden. Gardens were what fathers did.

She went home sore every noon from stooping, bending, standing, and was too tired to do anything but lie around. Fortunately, she wasn't too tired to eat ice cream or to read novels.

Next he set her to scrubbing the stone walls. She took off her boots and socks to preserve them. The soapy water quickly turned dirty. She knew she was going to wear out the scrub brush long before she'd got so much as a square yard of the wall cleaned. It was an impossible task. He had to know it was impossible. He'd been speaking to Venus, or to the king in Rumpelstiltskin. She'd be here forever. She'd be forty years old and still scrubbing these damn stone walls. Her fingers would look like prunes. She'd stink like Herb Robert, and her back would be crooked. This was the future he had in mind for her, and all for a little trespassing. It was unfair. Every little dirty soap bubble of it.

The soapy mud between her toes was about to drive her crazy. She wanted to soak her feet. She wanted to wash the dust and the sweat from her face. She thought of the creek that ran beneath the red bridge to Sky and sighed. How nice and cool it would be there, hanging over the creek, lying back on a moss-covered log. She could hear it in her imagination, that cool endless slither of water over stones, over wood, over sand.

A smooth, clear animal, the creek was. She thought about living in a houseboat down where the creek became broad and deep. She could moor it to a Douglas fir, and that way she'd always feel the water running beneath her house but never drift away. She imagined what her houseboat would look like. Very small. She liked small places. *I'll have a rabbit*, she thought. *It will be tame like a cat, and sleep on a pillow next to mine.*

"Maud Caldecote!"

She shook herself from her daydream. "What?"

"It's time to go home. Where were you just now?"

She made a face. "Not here, that's for damn sure."

Mama kept an herb garden that was a feast of scents and colors—hyssop flowering a deep violet blue, thyme flowers a paler purple, Empress of India nasturtiums' blue-green leaves as big as saucers for tea cups, flowers deep scarlet. Come school exam times, Mama didn't have to bake because people came for sprigs of her incomparable rosemary for their children. She wouldn't take any money for her herbs but would accept a loaf of bread, a cake, a plate of cookies. The kids loved exam time for the extra treats.

Aside from the prosperous rosemary, Maud was most fond of the thriving orange calendula, its leaves sticky with oil, its fragrance faintly sulfurous but not unpleasant.

Mama kept a big hex jar of olive oil and calendula petals on the kitchen windowsill. When Maud shook the jar, the petals swirled in the golden oil like a cloud of oblong gold flakes. Mama preserved the petals in oil for their healing properties—treating chapped lips in the wintertime, bug bites and sunburn in the summertime, scrapes and scratches anytime. Maud associated the scent with her mother's comforting touch.

During those thirty days, Maud made liberal use of the calendula infusion on her scrapes, cuts, and bruises. She was indignant when Mama poured some off into a smaller bottle and gave it to Lightning.

"He's the enemy!" she said.

"He's a neighbor," Mama replied.

"A bad neighbor."

"All the more reason to be a good one." Mama sighed and stroked a strand of hair away from Maud's forehead. "He's from the city and hasn't gotten used to our ways yet. Give him time and try to be kind. Life hasn't been particularly gentle with him."

"What do you mean?"

"Think about the McBrides," Mama said, "and then think about me, and how I didn't fit into my own family. Lightning has experienced the same with his family."

"How do you know?"

"Oh, we've chatted a bit."

"Chatting with the enemy," Maud said.

Mama was divorced from her family, and they from her. The McBrides left Sky, the only place she had ever been happy (and no thanks to them), when she started high school. She met John Jordan Caldecote in college, married him after a year of teaching high school math, and persuaded him that Sky was the best place to raise a family. She didn't see her parents, nor did she want her children to know them. The only family member she loved and kept in touch with was her Aunt Helena McBride.

Aunt Helena came to visit from the city from time to time, and always treated her great-nieces and great-nephews, when she did, with trips to the dollar store and the Diamond Drive-In. She was a wealthy single woman who sent extravagant gifts for Christmases and birthdays, and she had promised to help with the children's college expenses, since Papa, the publisher of a small-town newspaper, didn't have an overabundance of cash for that purpose.

When Lightning dropped Maud off one afternoon, she found the house busier than usual. Aunt Helena had called and invited herself for a visit and would be arriving the next day on the train.

"Maud, I know you're sore from working, but I really need your help. I'd like to put Helena in your room, and I need you to clean it."

Maud groaned. The floor of her room was booby-trapped with notebooks, paperbacks, records, drawings, heads she'd made out of modeling clay, piles of dirty clothes. She tackled the mess until supper and asked Mama if she could skip working for Lightning the next day.

"No," Mama said. "Just do what you can tonight."

Maud did what she could. Mama was satisfied that her room was now suitable for Aunt Helena. Maud would sleep in Sophie's room, which might be fun, since Sophie talked in her sleep. It was the only time to have a conversation with her that wasn't in some way acrimonious.

Maud wasn't in the mood to be a good neighbor or a good worker the next day. She scrubbed the stones listlessly, thinking about how all the other kids would be getting dressed up to meet Aunt Helena at the train depot. Aunt Helena always took everybody out to lunch when she arrived, usually at the elegant Sky Cafe. Maud would be missing that treat, and it made her mad. She sang her Lightning song at the top of her voice, repeatedly. And perhaps Lightning was learning to be a good neighbor because he laughed where she couldn't see or hear him, and shook his head, and muttered "Crazy kid" under his breath.

The house was empty when she got back at noon. She quickly showered and changed into a dress. When she heard the van in the driveway, she ran out to meet it. Aunt Helena hopped out and grabbed Maud in a fierce hug.

"Is this my little Maudie? Look at you! You're so tall and gorgeous!"

Aunt Helena was glamorous, well-dressed in neatly creased black slacks and a summer-weight black cashmere sweater, a string of pearls at her throat and gemstone rings on every finger but her thumbs and pinkies. Her hair was bobbed to her shoulders, snowy white and fragrant of L'Heure Bleue, "my signature scent," she said. She wore no makeup but for a bit of mascara and dark red lipstick. The skin of her face and hands was soft and moist with perfumed creams. A hug and a kiss from Aunt Helena, and you came away smelling amazing.

Everybody went into the living room. Maud, in her excitement (and in the mood to show off), lit a cigarette from a new pack.

Aunt Helena sighed and shook her head. "Maud, I never thought I'd see you a slave to anything."

Maud felt bad for disappointing her but said airily, "The only slave I am is to that heathen on the top of the mountain."

"Your mother and father told me a little bit about that. Why don't you fill me in?"

Maud went off on a litany of complaints about Lightning and the work he was putting her to.

"Well, at least we'll have afternoons and evenings together," said Aunt Helena.

Aunt Helena had been there for a week when one evening, as she and Maud were helping Mama to make dinner, she said, "How would you like to come stay with me for a month?"

Maud put down the potato she was peeling. "In the city?"

"Yes, in the city."

"I'd love it!" Maud cried. "Oh, Mama, may I?"

Mama smiled. "We'll see."

"I do have one stipulation. If you want to come, you'll have to quit smoking first."

Maud ran to find her purse and dug out her pack of cigarettes. She took it back up to the kitchen and ostentatiously broke each one in half before throwing them out.

Aunt Helena smiled. "No buying more allowed."

"I won't buy any more!"

"Do you promise?"

"I promise, I promise!"

"Good. Now let me tell you about the party."

"Party?"

"There's a family I know named MacDonald. Their son Paolo is turning eighteen in a few weeks. His parents are going to throw a big party for him. Do you think you'd like to come with me?"

"Mama, may I go? Please, please, please?"

"We'll see."

"May I wear your prom dress?"

"We'll see."

What Maud didn't know was that Mama had asked Aunt Helena to ask her to visit. She wanted Maud to see something other than the world of Sky. And though she lived her life as a deliberate rejection of McBrideism, she could sense the McBride coming out in Maud in certain ways. She would much rather Aunt Helena serve as a model for Maud than have Maud thrash out her McBride tendencies without a guide.

"Why me?" Maud asked, almost afraid of jinxing herself. "Why didn't you ask Sophie?"

"Sophie is too busy working and earning money for college," Mama said. "You know that going to college means more to her than anything else."

"Sophie will stay with me a few weeks before she moves into the dorm," Aunt Helena said. "We'll have a good visit then."

"But the party?"

"I think you're far more likely than Sophie to enjoy the party."

Maud was relieved. Despite their frequent bouts of head-butting, she loved her older sister and wouldn't want to deprive her of a pleasure that, as oldest, was rightfully hers.

"Does that mean I really get to go?"

Mama smiled again. "We'll see."

If the prospect of the party made Maud feel like Cinderella going to the ball, then Lightning handily fulfilled the role of Wicked Stepmother. Maud scraped and scrubbed moss off the north wall as far as she could reach. Lightning, on a ladder, scrubbed higher.

"So your mom says you might have a trip to the city coming up," he said. He often tried to start conversations. She usually answered with a sullen syllable or two. Today she surprised him.

"There's going to be a big party. I've never been to a grown-up party before. I wonder if there will be caviar and champagne."

"Do you like caviar and champagne?"

"I don't know. Don't you?"

"Not much. So now you're going to add drinking to smoking?"

"Oh, I quit smoking," she said. She didn't mention that that was one of the conditions of her going to the city.

"Good for you. Those things make you stink to high heaven."

"Gee, thanks."

"So there's going to be a big party."

"Yes, and I might get to wear my mother's old prom dress."

"I hate to say it but your mother is not exactly tall."

"It may be a bit shorter on me…"

"A bit."

"It's so gorgeous, I don't care if it comes up to my knees. It's all layers of tulle with little tiny rhinestones scattered over it. We used to cry when we were kids because she wouldn't let us wear it for dress-up. When I was young, I thought she was just being selfish."

"And now that you're an adult, you understand that your parents are human beings, just like you," Lightning said, grinning at her assumed age. She just stared up at him, thunderstruck by the notion of her parents being human beings.

"Your mother is a beautiful woman," he said. "She might want to wear that prom dress again someday."

Maud continued to stare at him, utterly aghast.

That afternoon, when she went home, she scrutinized her mother, amazed that a man as young as Lightning would find a 40-year-old woman beautiful. She allowed as how her mother had beautiful eyes; and Maud had always envied her broad cheekbones. And maybe there was something elegant about Mama, despite the cowboy boots and the hand-knitted sweaters that were a deliberate reaction to McBrideism.

"What are you staring at?" Mama asked, baffled by her daughter's scrutiny.

"Mmm-mm, nothing."

Maud went into the bathroom, looked into the mirror, looking for her mother in her face, looking for beauty there. And for the first time, she wondered what Lightning saw when he looked at her with his blue, blue eyes.

Maud tried on the prom dress. Though she was much taller than her mother, and much smaller in the bust, the dress would fit well with only a little alteration.

"You're supposed to wear it with a hoop," Mama said. "But without, the hem just skims your ankles. I think this will work, baby."

Aunt Helena, however, was not enthused. "Maudie, it's a beautiful gown, but it's a good twenty years out of date. Wouldn't you like something new and fashionable? My treat."

Maud shook her head. She turned and swirled, looking at herself in Mama's full-length mirror. "I have always wanted to wear this dress, and now I finally have the chance."

"We'll need to buy you some shoes," Mama said. "Let's go down to Mrs. Diamond's shop and see what she has."

"She never has shoes big enough for me," Maud complained. "Nobody does."

"Well, you can't wear cowboy boots with this," Mama said. "Maybe Mrs. Diamond can order some shoes in your size."

Maud reluctantly took off the prom gown and put her jeans and T-shirt back on. She'd felt beautiful in the gown. Now she just felt ordinary again.

Aunt Helena asked Mama for certain herbs. "I can get them in the city, but yours are always more powerful." They went into the shed that served as Mama's stillroom and selected from among the bottled tinctures and dried herbs.

"We've got to persuade her not to wear that dress," Helena said. "The MacDonalds are fashionable people, and so are all their friends. Maudie would stick out like a sore thumb in that thing."

"It's what she wants, Helena," Mama said. She hated how defensive she felt. This was Helena, after all, who had been a friend and an ally during a time when Mama had desperately needed both. If Helena was a McBride, though, so was Mama. Pride was one of the greatest of the McBride's sins.

"They'll laugh at her," Helena said.

"If that's the case, they're not worth knowing, and she can skip the party."

"I just don't want her to get hurt."

"I understand that. But you don't understand the extent of Maud's stubbornness. She's made up her mind. You can try in the city. You can take her shopping. But I am telling you, when she goes, that dress is going with her."

"I'm going to turn sixteen while I'm in the city. It'll be weird not having my birthday at home."

"Will your aunt throw you a Sweet Sixteen party?" Lightning asked.

"We don't do that in my family," Maud said, with an air of superiority. "It's tacky."

"Sorry I said anything."

"I mean, come on. 'Sweet sixteen and never been kissed?' How gross is that?"

"Very, evidently. When are you heading to the city with your aunt?"

"Not until next week, so you'll get your stinking thirty days."

"Nah. Let's wrap it up. I guess you've worked pretty hard. Let's call it even."

Maud dropped her scrub brush. "Really?"

"Yeah, absolutely. You've done well."

"Woo-hoo! I'm free! I'm free!"

She wasted no time on good-byes but declared that she was going to celebrate by hiking down the old trail. When she got to the Anvil, she looked behind her. As she suspected, Lightning was nowhere in sight. She climbed up to the top and stood tall and straight. The day was sunny, the air almost perfectly clear. She could see for miles and miles. She imagined where the city might lie, and imagined what it might look like. She imagined her future as full of delight.

"I am Maud of Sky," she shouted, "and I am going to conquer the world!"

The week before her sixteenth birthday, Maud went to the city. It was the first time she'd been in the city since she was a small child. Helena took her downtown to visit the big department stores and shop for her school clothes for the upcoming year. Maud was too tall for most ready-to-wear but she was learning workarounds—Men's Levi's 501s to be taken to Helena's tailor to be taken in at the waist, skirts worn with black tights to mitigate their shortness, sleeves that could be pushed or rolled up to the elbows and look intentional.

They visited museums and went to the Japanese garden to feed the koi. They ate out every night, and Maud was introduced to Indian restaurants, Thai restaurants, Italian restaurants. The food was what Maud remembered most about the visit.

She also remembered a funny little house in Helena's neighborhood. It was wedge-shaped, like a piece of cake, on a wedge-shaped lot. The outside of the house was apricot buttercream stucco trimmed in raspberry-sauce red.

"Oh, that?" Helena said, when Maud asked about the little house. "That's A. C.'s house."

"Who's A. C.?"

"A. C. stands for Admirable Cat. Everybody in the neighborhood knows A. C. She belonged to Professor Day, who taught music at the University. Every evening, Professor Day and A. C. would go walking down to the bascule bridge over the canal to watch the sailboats go by. He died a few years ago. A hit and run, I believe it was. A terrible thing. His daughter still lives in the house, and she takes A. C. for her evening walks now. Maybe we'll see them while you're here."

Several evenings, Helena and Maud took walks down to the canal bridge to watch the boats. One night a Chinese junk with red sails floated past them. But they never saw A. C.

One morning after breakfast, Helena said, "Maud, come see my consulting room."

Helena unlocked a door that Maud had never seen opened before. Here was a room of curiosities. The walls were painted oxblood red. There was a Persian carpet on the floor, heavy damask drapes in the widows. Here were objects on an antique table—a crystal ball on a bronze base so tarnished it looked like black ceramic, a pack of flexible tarot cards, edges furred with use, wrapped in a vintage silk Hermes scarf, jars of frankincense and copal resin, and a blackened bronze censer, a Baltic amber rosary. Beeswax votive candles burned, with the scent of hot honey, in upended antique Whitall Tatum Co No 1 green glass insulators, which kept the eclectic elegance of the room in tongue-in-cheek check.

"This is a statue of St. Brigid. She's very important to this family. The name McBride means 'son of the servant of Brigid.'"

"We don't have saints in our church," said Maud.

"That's because you go to your father's church. Now this is a statue of Cernunnos."

"Who's Cernunnos?" Maud was shocked and not a little titillated by the statue's pronounced genitalia.

"He's the ancient Celtic horned god." Helena said. She waved her hands. "As you may have guessed, he's a god of fertility. To be honest with you, most of this is just window dressing. People expect to see these things."

"Wait a minute…are you *actually* a witch?" Maud asked, excited by the possibility that the old family joke could be a reality.

"Honey, I'm a McBride," Helena said, as if that explained everything. "And so, I believe, are you."

"But what does that even mean?"

Helena smiled. "I'll tell you what. Let's try an experiment. Sit down and look into that crystal ball. Just relax and breathe regularly, and tell me what you see."

Maud didn't see anything but the room, small, upside-down and curved. Had she seen anything else, she would have been frankly astonished.

"Anything?" Helena said.

Maud shook her head.

"That's fine," Helena said. "Let's try something else." From a drawer she produced an oblong, fist-sized chunk of clear quartz crystal, irregular with multiple conchoidal fractures. "How about this? This is yours, I think. It looks right in your hand. How does it feel?"

"Cool," Maud said. It was heavy and literally cool to the touch.

"Now place it in front of the candle, long side up. It's a bit of a delicate balance. There you go. Now gaze at it and just imagine. Imagine what you could see in the crystal, *if* you could see something. Take your time. Don't worry. Just daydream."

Maud let her mind wander, which was the easiest thing in the world for her. The gleam of the candle behind the crystal multiplied in the fractures. Her gaze softened and

115

lost focus. She was in the room and out of it. She was wearing her mother's prom dress.

There was a rose on the front of her dress, opening like a stain. No, not a rose. It was a pomegranate, broken open and spilling seeds, seeds spilling down to the polished wood floor, spilling and sprouting, sprouting and climbing, a briar twisting around and around her, as if she were a doll wrapped in thorns. The thorns didn't quite touch her. She held her arms stiffly to her body, every muscle tensed and shrinking away from the thorn points. *Don't move. Breathe shallowly. Don't cry. Whatever you do. Do. Not. Cry. Be strong. Be an-*gry. *Gather in one big breath and it's going to hurt like hell but you have got to* shout!

"Did you break the thorns?" Helena asked.

Maud was surprised to realize that she'd been speaking out loud. She blinked rapidly and rubbed her chest, which was warm, which itched as though scratched by a thorn. She expected her fingers to come away red and wet.

"I don't know," she said. She felt like crying, and she didn't know why. She gave in to the desire. Helena hugged her tightly.

"It's all right, Maudie. It's all right. You're stressed out about this party, aren't you?"

"I guess so," she said. "I want to go. I really, really do. But I've never been to a grown-up party before. What if I do the wrong thing? What if I say something stupid?"

"Then you'll be exactly like everybody else in that room at one time or another. I promise you that. Come on. That's enough for today. Cry yourself out. It's good for you. And I'll make you a cup of your mother's excellent chamomile tea. Oh, Maudie, I knew it! I knew you were a McBride!"

But her triumph was tempered by concern over Maud's vision. Those were specific and potent symbols—the rose, the pomegranate, the briar. Maybe it was just nerves coming out—a brief spiritual ailment, similar to somebody used to plain fare getting sick after too much rich food.

Once Maud had blown her nose and washed her face, once she'd drunk her tea, she seemed fine. She played with Helena's cat Caliban and talked about the Caldecotes' cats— Smicky, the easygoing gray longhair who napped in the oven if anybody left the oven door opened, Kitty, the mean calico who would nonetheless come to comfort you if you were crying.

Over the next several days Helena tried Maud on the tarot cards and on the crystal ball again, but only the chunk of quartz, which Maud referred to as the daydream rock, produced results. Maud was like the daydream rock itself, a raw, rough mineral in its natural state. Maud loved to feel its surfaces, some nearly as sharp as glass, some smooth, some rippled. It became a sort of fidget stone for her when she wasn't using it to gaze. She couldn't believe that Helena had given her something so beautiful, and that she got to keep it, that she'd be able to take it home with her. She was awed that the earth had produced something so imperfectly perfect. She couldn't have been more pleased if Helena had given her one of the gemstone rings that adorned her fingers.

One day Helena took Maud downtown to a dark little shop beneath the vast public market. The shop smelled of herbs and incense and tea, and was crowded with curious objects that might have been at home in Helena's consulting room. The clerk knew Helena well and studied Maud curiously.

"Is she a McBride?" he asked.

"That she is," Helena said proudly. "We've come to buy her her own wicked pack of cards. I think we'll start her with the Rider-Waite."

"Excellent choice," said the clerk. He produced an unopened deck of tarot cards. Helena let Maud choose an elaborately embroidered silk bag to keep them in. After Helena paid, she handed the deck and bag to Maud.

"They say a deck of tarot cards should always be a gift. Happy early birthday, Maud. May you use them in good health, and may they serve you long and well."

They went to the Greek restaurant next to the little shop. Over lunch, Helena tried to explain her relationship to the MacDonald family. "To be a McBride is to have unusual abilities. Because of these abilities, I act as a spiritual advisor, almost a kind of fairy godmother, to the MacDonalds. I counsel the family, bless it, and help it to prosper. I have advised Magnus MacDonald for many years now, many, many years. His son is a skeptic who chose a different path, the way your mother chose a different path. Paolo doesn't get along with his family, so I thought you might be able to help him. Perhaps in future you might have a relationship with him similar to the one I have with Magnus. And so it would be good for you to bless him at the party."

"I don't even know where I'd begin," Maud said. "'God is great, God is good, let us thank Him for this dude?'"

"You could say something as simple as 'may your life be happy, healthy, and prosperous,'" Helena said. "Daydream on it and see what comes to your mind. Before we go home, we need to go shopping for a blank notebook and a good pen for you. It's best to get into the habit of writing down your daydreams and observations, not to mention your tarot readings. You'll want to have a record of such things as you go along."

Helena advised Maud to sleep with the tarot pack under her pillow for seven days before using it or even opening it.

Maud slipped the deck into the silk bag and tucked it under her pillow.

As for her vision, it never repeated itself. Now when Maud gazed at the daydream rock, she saw ordinary things, things she'd daydream about in any case. Her curiosity about Paolo MacDonald fueled most of her daydreaming sessions. She wondered what he was like, if he were the type of person who could make her laugh, or if he were serious, or snobbish. What would they talk about when they met at the party? Would he ask her to dance?

One afternoon, before eating an apple, Maud twisted the stem while reciting the alphabet. She wondered if she would finally make it past "L," perhaps this time land on "P" for Paolo. But no, the stem broke on "L," just as it always had.

"I didn't know girls still did that," Helena said, smiling. "Who do you know whose name begins with an 'L'?"

"Nobody, since that jerk Lionel Pipping moved away."

"What about Lightning?"

"Oh, gross!" Maud exclaimed. "That slave-driving heathen is at least thirty years old. I'd sooner find out where Lionel moved and marry *him*."

"You're not even sixteen yet. You've got a long time to go before even thinking about marriage."

"Oh, I know. I doubt I'll even get married. I've changed too many diapers to ever want kids of my own."

"That may change, too."

"I'd rather be like you, anyway."

Helena smiled. "We'll see. Have you moved past 'let us thank Him for this dude?'"

Maud grinned. "But I really like the ring of that."

On the afternoon of the party, Aunt Helena took Maud to a makeup counter at the fanciest of the downtown department stores. The makeover would be Maud's birthday present. The makeup artist sat Maud down on a stool and applied foundation and powder while Aunt Helena described Maud's outfit.

"Nice," the makeup artist said. "I love vintage fashion! Why don't we go full retro with her makeup? Winged eyeliner and a blood-red lip? Do you like that idea?"

Maud definitely did.

"That's not quite the period," Aunt Helena said cautiously. "I was thinking more along the lines of Grace Kelly in *Rear Window*."

"Oh, please?" Maud said. "I really want cat-eye eyeliner!"

"Well, Maudie, it's your face."

Maud loved the results. The eyeliner emphasized the natural upward tilt of her eyelids, and the red lipstick made her look (she thought) older and more sophisticated and actually rather sexy. She was almost sorry she'd given up smoking. A lit cigarette would have been the perfect accessory for her vampy mouth.

Aunt Helena bought her all the makeup that had gone into her look, plus her very own bottle of L'Heure Bleue. Maud was ecstatic, and hoped that Mama wouldn't confiscate it the instant she got back to Sky. Mama didn't believe in wearing makeup (except lip gloss) before age eighteen.

Back at Aunt Helena's house, they dressed for the party. Maud sang as she dressed. When she was done, she could hardly believe her reflection in the full-length mirror. When she came out, Aunt Helena said, "Oh, Maudie. You look so grown up."

From her garden Helena plucked the blossom from a Madonna lily, and went in and pinned it to Maud's hair, behind her left ear. "Now you're absolutely perfect," she said.

They took a cab downtown to the University Club, a majestic old white building with a frieze of white and blue terracotta depicting bespectacled, book-reading walruses. The party was being held in a rotunda capped by a stained-glass dome of blooming wisteria and a magnificent chandelier. A pianist played popular tunes on a grand piano. Waiters circulated with trays of hors d'oeuvres and flutes of champagne. There was a wet bar and a buffet table, the latter dominated by a gigantic tiered birthday cake. And the guests of all ages, from a two-year-old in a tuxedo to a very old woman in a beaded gown, were all dressed elegantly.

Helena looked around. "Paolo is nowhere in sight. I wonder if he's hiding in the bathroom."

"Why would he do that?" Maud said. "This is *wonderful!*"

"I think you and Paolo have different ideas of 'wonderful.'"

Francesca MacDonald, Paolo's mother, glided up to Helena. She was a petite lady in her early 40s with a neat chignon of tastefully blonde hair. Her mermaid gown glittered with beads, her throat with diamonds. "Good evening, Helena."

"Good evening, Francesca."

"And who is this?"

"This is my great-niece, Maud Caldecote."

"How do you do, Maud? So nice of you to join us. Helena, you naughty thing. Did you tell Maud this was a fancy-dress party? I'm afraid she's the only guest in costume."

Maud looked to her aunt for guidance and understanding. Helena's expression was pinched.

"Maud is fond of vintage fashion. It's considered chic these days."

"Oh, is it? I hadn't heard. Pity about the shoes. But I suppose a girl as big as you are has a difficult time finding decent shoes that fit, isn't that right, Maud?"

"Uh…yes…." Maud said. She wondered what was wrong with her white satin flats. The shoe store clerk had told her that if she wanted to, she could dye them a different color, which she thought was neat.

"Maud is *tall*. She's not *big*."

"Hmm…semantics. You must admit, she's huge, certainly compared to somebody like me."

Maud was struck speechless. Never before in her life had an adult been so deliberately and gleefully rude to her.

"At least she's not fat. I simply cannot tolerate an obese person. Thankfully, all *our* friends are thin. It's a pity about Magnus's set. Do enjoy the party, Maud."

Magnus MacDonald beckoned to Aunt Helena, and she excused herself. "I'll be right back, Maud."

Francesca MacDonald wandered off with a vague murmur. When a waiter offered Maud a flute of champagne, she took it. Aunt Helena had given her prior permission, with the stipulation that if she didn't like it she'd admit it and find something non-alcoholic to drink. She wondered if she looked older in her gown and makeup. But no, other kids her age were drinking, too. They must be Paolo's friends, from school or whatever organizations he belonged to. Maud took a cautious sip and smiled. It was love at first taste. The champagne fizzed like pop but otherwise was nothing like it. It made her think of sunshine on the Mountain, when the glaciers glinted. She hummed to herself and sipped and felt happy, even alone in the crowd.

But she wasn't alone for long. A young man sauntered up to her, hands in his trouser pockets. He was dressed in a tuxedo with a carelessly tied bow tie and his dark hair looked uncombed and overdue for a trim. He was a few inches shorter than Maud, and not what Maud would call good-looking, but he had a nice smile, and his eyes were dark and intelligent.

"Nice kiss-off you're giving this crowd of losers," he said.

Maud was startled. "I beg your pardon?"

"The outfit. If you'd come in here in nothing but a T-shirt that says 'Go to Hell' you couldn't have spoken any louder or clearer."

"But I wasn't trying to tell anybody to go to hell," Maud said, confused. "What's wrong with my outfit?"

"Are you serious? You are! That makes it even better. I'm Paolo MacDonald, by the way" he said.

"I'm Maud Caldecote."

"Welcome to my party, Maud Caldecote."

"Thank you. Happy birthday," she said, and then added shyly, "It's my birthday today, too."

"No way! Happy birthday. How old?"

"Sixteen."

"'Maud is not seventeen. But she is tall and stately.'"

"Tennyson. I know that one like the back of my hand. Thank you a million times for not saying 'sweet sixteen and never been kissed,' because that is just so gross."

"I never would. But just so you know, I'm eighteen, and I've never been kissed. Not that I'm hinting or anything. No pressure."

"I won't kiss you if you won't kiss me."

"You've got yourself a deal."

"How did somebody with a last name like MacDonald end up with a first name like Paolo?"

"Italian-American mother," he said. "I'll tell you what. Let's pretend that this is *your* party and I'm your guest. I mean, it really isn't for me. It's for Mother and Father. They didn't bother to ask what I wanted."

"What do you want?"

"Out of here. What do you want?"

"A new pair of cowboy boots and another glass of champagne."

"Your wants are simple, Maud Caldecote. I envy you. I've been watching you since I snuck back in. Why aren't you out on the dance floor?"

"Oh, I don't know anybody here. Besides, I don't know how to dance."

"You don't know how to *dance*?"

"I don't know how to dance."

"I can teach you. I mean, if you don't mind that I'm shorter than you."

"Why would I mind that?"

"Are you sure? I'll bet I could borrow a pair of my father's elevator shoes."

"What, do you push a button to make them go up or down?"

"Maud Caldecote, you are either remarkably naive or remarkably sarcastic. I don't know which I would prefer."

"It's just such a funny phrase. Elevator shoes."

"Well, they can't exactly call them high heels. That would be too girly."

"If it makes you feel any better, your mother just told me I was huge."

"My mother is an idiot," Paolo said, glaring at his offending parent.

Emboldened, and still stinging from the disparaging comments about her height, Maud said, "She's nothing but a pampered little pipsqueak."

Paolo laughed, astonished. "I am so stealing that. How much champagne have you had? Or do you always talk like a wisecracking broad?"

"I think I'm a little bit tipsy."

"Then tell me the truth. Do you have a crush on me? Be honest. This is for research purposes only."

"For research purposes only?"

"Swear to God."

"Okay. Well, I think I've got a little crush on you."

"Just a little one?"

"I only met you like thirteen seconds ago."

"True, true. I haven't had time to make you fall desperately in love with me yet. Give it a few hours."

Maud had never flirted before. It was as intoxicating as the champagne. She felt flushed and giddy with happiness. She was doing well. She was making him laugh. And he was making her laugh.

"Does everybody fall desperately in love with you?"

"Only the people who matter," he said.

"Paolo, darling, you have other guests." His mother tsked, took hold of his bow tie, untied it, and redid it properly.

Paolo fidgeted like a small boy. "I know that, Mother. I'm avoiding them."

"I'm sure Mag will excuse you."

"Maud. Her name is Maud."

"All right. Maud. I'm sure Maud will excuse you. Won't you, Maud?"

"What if I don't want to be excused?" Paolo said.

"Don't be boring, darling."

"But I'm so good at it, Mother."

"Paolo, don't make me get your father."

"Sorry, Maud. I guess the dance lesson will have to wait. See you around."

Maud was alone again. Being a stranger at a party is one of the most uncomfortable of human feelings, especially when one's champagne flute is empty and one is noticing people giving one disdainful glances. She could go stand with Aunt Helena, who was in conversation with a couple of imposing-looking people. She decided instead to find a nice, out-of-the-way seat where she could watch the party. And by party, she meant Paolo.

Paolo made the rounds with his mother, saying a few words to the people they greeted. Then he broke away from her and made for the bar. He started drinking heavily. Nobody told him he couldn't. Maud saw him ordering straight liquor. She nursed her second champagne, feeling sorry for him. He was clearly unhappy.

After a while, the piano music ceased and Paolo's grandfather stood up, called Paolo to his side, held him there with one hand on his shoulder, and made a speech. It was long and boring, all about family tradition and coming of age and things that made Maud fidget the way she used to fidget in church. Paolo caught her eye and winked.

"And to continue a venerable and sacred tradition, Maud of the family McBride will now bless Paolo on the eve of his eighteenth birthday."

Maud got up, blushing that all eyes were on her, and came forward to where Paolo and his grandfather stood. Helena handed Maud a bronze chalice filled with deep red wine that smelled of pomegranates. Maud held it in both hands, the way Aunt Helena had shown her. She spoke the words in Scottish Gaelic the way Helena had taught her.

"*Slàinte mhòr agus a h-uile beannachd duibh.*"

Then she gave her blessing. "May you live a long and happy life, and bring pride and prosperity to the family of MacDonald." She took a sip, then handed the chalice to Paolo.

"Is that why you're here? To bless me and make me like *them*? Well, here's what I think of family tradition and here's what I think of your blessing, you stupid bitch."

He threw the wine in her face. It splashed over the front of her dress and dripped to the floor in little red patters. She sputtered and wiped her hands over her face.

With a drunken flourish, he dropped the empty chalice on the floor. It thudded like a muffled bell against the carpet. "How's that little crush coming along now, Maud Caldecote?"

Laughter rose up around her, some nervous, some malicious.

Francesca MacDonald applauded. "Well done, Paolo. It's high time this family broke with superstitious nonsense. I'm proud of you."

"Trust me, Mother, I didn't do it for you."

Don't cry. Whatever you do. Do. Not. Cry. Maud had no thought of her mother's beautiful dress ruined. She couldn't get over the shock of having wine thrown in her face, the shock of his malice directed at her. And all she had done was bless him. All she had done was wish him well on his birthday. She'd thought he was flirting with her, but he was mocking her, exactly as Lionel Pipping used to mock her. No. This was worse. He'd convinced her that he really meant it. How could she have been so stupid? Now people were laughing at her, laughing at what he had done to her. Her hurt rose up as rage. Her focus narrowed to his drunken, contemptuous face. She didn't perceive the self-loathing in the contempt, or the beginnings of remorse.

She didn't see her horrified aunt. She didn't see Paolo's grandfather, who was at his side castigating him. She just saw him.

Her arms were stiff at her side, just as if briars entwined her.

In a voice that wasn't hers (was it hers?), she said "I curse you, Paolo MacDonald. I curse you to love me whom you've so unjustly wronged and mocked—to love *nobody* but me—to love me *desperately*. And I swear by everything under the sun and everything under the moon that I will never love you in return. I swear that I will loathe you and everything about you for the rest of my days. I swear that every word you speak to me will only make me scorn you more than I scorn you right now."

"Maud!" Helena cried. "Stop it at once!"

"Didn't you see?" Maud cried. "Didn't you see what he did to me?"

"Come on. We're leaving. Now, Maud."

"Oh! And just look at Mama's dress!"

"Walk, Maudie. Just walk. Keep going. That's a good girl. What was he thinking? Oh heavens, what was he thinking?"

Nobody followed them. Nobody tried to stop them.

The fever seeped into Maud in the cab back to Aunt Helena's. She could barely get up the stairs to Helena's front door, could barely take off Mama's gown. She crawled into bed still sticky with wine. It was in her hair, on her face and neck and hands. Helena came in with a warm washcloth and wiped her skin. But her skin felt too sensitive. The washcloth hurt. And so Helena left her and went to call her doctor.

And that was how it came to pass that Maud spent three days in a fever. And when the fever broke, she had no memory of the party, or of Paolo, or of her curse.

Mama drove all the way to the city to get her. Maud, still exhausted, sat on the bed while Mama packed her things.

"I'm sorry I threw up on your dress," she said, weeping

"Don't you worry about that," Mama said. "That doesn't matter one little bit. All that matters is you getting all better again."

"Maudie, why don't we keep your daydream rock and your tarot cards here for now, and I'll teach you to read on your next visit. All right?"

"Okay," Maud said. She cried harder, feeling in an indistinct way that she was being punished for getting sick. "Can I at least keep the makeup and perfume?"

"Yes, of course," said Helena.

"Sophie is going to have a fit," Mama warned. "I may have to keep it aside for your eighteenth birthday, unless you promise me to only wear it at home."

"I promise," Maud said.

It was bitter, too bitter, to have to leave her gifts behind. But the most bitter thing of all was having missed Paolo's birthday party and having ruined Mama's dress.

She spent the rest of the summer in a listless mood, wandering from room to room at home, or hiding under the cedar tree near the dirt road. She didn't want to read. She didn't want to go to the movies. She gave up on the idea of writing a musical version of *Grafinia*. She felt like a failure.

Lightning, hearing that she was down in the dumps, stopped by one afternoon with a half-gallon of Neapolitan ice cream, having ascertained that it was her favorite. She sat down at the kitchen table and ate it out of the carton with a serving spoon, much to Sophie's disgust and the little kids' dismay. Then she went out back and threw up.

Strangely, it was news of real trouble that snapped her out of it. One night, a week before school started, Mama sat all the kids down after supper.

"I've got some bad news about Aunt Helena," she said. "When she came to see us this July, she'd just found out she has lung cancer. She's chosen not to seek treatment."

"Does that mean she's going to die?" Sophie asked, sounding both angry and frightened.

"Yes," Mama said. "That means she's going to die. This is her choice, kids, and we have to respect it. Treatment can be brutal, and Aunt Helena is an old woman."

"Who's going to take care of her?" Maud asked, her voice trembling.

"She'll have people from home health care helping her, and people from hospice, but I am going to stay with her. Sophie, I'll come out with you when you go to college. I'll stay with Helena during the week and take the train home on weekends. Maud, I'm going to rely on you to get the kids ready for school and to get dinner on the table. Do you think you can handle that?"

"Yes. Oh, Mama, and she didn't even tell me!"

"She didn't want to ruin your visit," Mama said. "And you two had a good time together, didn't you?"

"Yes," Maud said, and broke down crying.

Maud rose to the occasion. She learned to cook, starting with all the exotic-sounding dishes she could find in her mother's cookbooks, then settling down, once bored with soufflés and chicken liver piroshki, to the old favorites on her mother's stained recipe cards. Cole took care of feeding and watering the horses, and he kept the family supplied with cookies and cakes. Aida Kay, naturally motherly, got Gabriel ready for school each day. Dandy took care of the cats and dogs. Everybody took turns with the dishes and took desultory stabs at house cleaning. Papa did all the grocery shopping and laundry and shuttled the kids to their various activities.

However, Maud's grades suffered. She found she didn't much care. She was depressed. She missed Mama. She missed Sophie. She worried about Helena. Despite what Mama had said, she couldn't quite allow herself to understand that this cancer was a death sentence. She persisted in hoping that Helena would somehow get better. Even when Mama stopped coming home for weekends, she hoped. And so, when Mama called up the day after Thanksgiving and said that Helena had died, Maud could scarcely believe it.

"I don't want you children at the funeral," Mama said over the phone. "Helena knew that you loved her, and she would understand."

"Not even me, Mama? I really can't go?" Maud said.

"Honey, my parents are going to be there," Mama said. "It will be tense enough for me to attend. I don't want to subject you kids to that kind of stress."

And Maud understood. Her McBride grandparents had cut off all relations with Mama when she married Papa. They had never acknowledged, by word or deed, the existence of their six grandchildren.

"I've got some things to take care of here at the house," Mama said. "But in a few weeks, I'll come home for good. I'll definitely be home for Christmas. I am so grateful to you, Maud. You've taken such good care of everything. It's been a relief to me to know that you've been in charge."

Maud could not have expressed how much her mother's praise meant to her. As soon as she handed the phone off to Cole, she looked around the house and saw how untidy it was. She would have the house looking spotless by the time Mama got home. She would make sure her praise was well-earned.

Aunt Helena left her house to Mama, who couldn't bring herself to put it on the market yet. She left a ring to each of her great-nieces, and the rest of her jewelry to Mama. Mama put it all in a safe deposit box and said the girls could have their rings when they were old enough. Helena had set up a trust fund for each of the children and one for Mama and Papa.

"She was very generous to this family," Papa said. "You kids will have a great deal of help paying for college."

Papa had gone to pick Mama up in the city. They came back with keepsakes from the house, and three cardboard boxes, taped shut, labeled "For Maud, when she's ready." Mama wouldn't let Maud open the boxes, and she stored them in her own clothes closet.

"But what's in them?" Maud asked.

"Things from her consulting room," Mama said. "When you've grown up a bit more, I'll let you have them."

One day when the rest of the family was out of the house, Maud went into her parents' room, just to have a peek at what was in the boxes. But Mama had moved them from her closet, and Maud couldn't find them. And by and by, she forgot about them.

Papa had taught Maud how to drive while Mama was away. In January, she got her driver's license after three tries at the driving test. To celebrate, she borrowed Mama's van and drove Aida Kay, Dandy, and Gabriel down to the drug store for ice creams. That was when she saw the "Help Wanted" sign on the door of the Sky Cafe. Papa had said it was time for Maud to think about getting a part-time job and starting to save for college. Maud wasn't so sure about the college part, but Papa had said she only had to save half of what she made and could spend the other half any way she wanted. That was tempting. She thought of the chocolate, books, and clothes she could buy, all the movies she could see.

Ms. Avery ("You can call me Robin.") gave Maud a job application to fill out and let her sit at one of the tables. Then she joined her and glanced over the application.

"I'd start you bussing and dishwashing," Robin said. "See about promoting you to waitress after a few months. We're busiest from noon to 1:00 and from 5:00 to 6:00, when the trains stop. I'd want you to work from noon to 9:00 on weekends. Could you do that?"

"Yes," Maud said, excited.

"All right. Can you start this weekend?"

"Yes!"

"Consider yourself hired," Robin said, and shook her hand.

It wasn't long before Robin figured out that Maud was wasted in the kitchen. She had a gregarious charm when bussing tables that made people, strangers and regulars, ask about her. Robin heard "Who is that tall little girl?" so much that she joked about having business cards made for Maud. Maud didn't mind the attention, though she did deeply mind the "little girl" part. She was a sophisticate, after all, or so she imagined. And she was genuinely curious about the train travelers—who they were, where they were going, and why. In school she had grown used to the daily rhythms of the trains, passenger and freight. Now those rhythms became personal, the comings and goings of passengers and railroad workers made concrete.

Eddy Avery, Robin's extremely good-looking nephew, came in one afternoon for coffee and pie and congratulated Maud on her promotion. "Hey, Shorty! I see Auntie has got you waiting tables now. How's that working out for you?"

"Hey, Ugly!" Maud said. "I love it! How are you?"

"Doing all right. How's your sister?" he asked. He'd long had a crush on Sophie and had actually got her to go to their senior prom with him, but Sophie was not at all interested in romance.

"She's good. She loves college. She hardly wanted to come home for Christmas."

"I'm sorry I missed her. Hey, I'm moving to the city pretty soon, and I wondered if you'd sit for me. I'll need somebody to draw to get me settled. Come up and model for me, okay? And no makeup!"

"You sound like my mother," Maud said.

Eddy's personal studio was upstairs, next to his apartment. His family owned the Avery Photography Studio. Generations of Averys had photographed the people of Sky and the surrounding valley since the 1880s. Their photographs filled the Tribal Cultural Center and the Historical Society. As a high schooler, Eddy had fallen in love with the tintypes on display and had unearthed and restored the old equipment. He taught himself the wet plate collodion process (without blowing up the shed his father allowed him to use) and began photographing his friends and teachers. A multi-disciplined artist, he took tintypes of his subjects and then drew enlarged, photorealistic portraits from them. Some of his drawings hung up in the Sky Cafe, including one of Mama dressed in old calico. It was stunning, painstaking work, virtually indistinguishable from the jewel-like originals. Maud was flattered and honored that he now wanted her for a subject, his last subject from Sky before moving.

At Eddy's suggestion, Mama came with her the day she sat for him. He'd asked her to wear a top she could pull off her shoulders, so she wore a peasant top Mama had sewed for her. "I want your shoulders and your clavicle," he said, "You've got an excellent clavicle."

"Gee, thanks," Maud said.

"She gets it from me," Mama joked.

Eddy's girlfriend Lucy Li, who'd taken the train in from the city just for this sitting, parted Maud's long hair and arranged it in Victorian looped braids. Eddy prepared his wet plate in his darkroom, then posed Maud in front of a panel of brocade fabric.

"Turn your face to the left. That's good. Now look down and think of your one true love."

"I don't have a one true love," Maud laughed.

"No laughing! If you don't have a one true love, make one up and think about him."

Unbidden, Lightning's image came to her mind. He had been in the cafe the other day, had asked about her and her family. It had been months since she'd last seen him, when he'd brought her the ice cream. Their fingers had briefly touched when he paid his tab. Maud thought of the touch and blushed.

"That's perfect. Beautiful."

Eddy took one exposure, taking the lens cap off and leaving it off for several seconds. Then he went to his darkroom to develop the plate. When she got to see the developed tintype, she was stunned. Was this pensive, antique young lady really her?

"Thanks for sitting for me. I'm going to enjoy drawing that clavicle."

It wasn't but a few weeks after that that Eddy moved to the city to join Lucy. His art attracted attention quickly. Six months after moving, he sent her a postcard for his first exhibit, "Forgotten Faces," at a bar called the Rendezvous. Her portrait was on the front of the postcard. She later heard from Robin that her portrait was one of two that Eddy had sold. She didn't know what to think of her image hanging on a stranger's wall.

"Me and my famous clavicle," she joked.

For a while, life was placid for Maud. Though she still hated school and still did poorly (by Sophie's standards, bringing home Cs on her report cards where Sophie, and now Cole and Aida Kay, brought home As), she enjoyed her work at the Sky Cafe. She kept a tally of where her train customers came from and hung a map in her room, sticking a pin in each new location.

Then, one busy August Sunday, a strange, surly-looking young man came into the cafe from the train. He was a few inches shorter than Maud, and skinny, with a shaved head scabbed with nicks and red with old scars, and a lean face likewise nicked and scarred. He was dressed in a gray tank undershirt, faded khaki pants that hung low on his hips, and a pair of busted high tops. He carried a stuffed backpack patched with duct tape. He ordered nothing but coffee and responded to Maud's friendliness with a sour expression and monosyllabic replies. She didn't think much of it. They did get an odd bird every once in a while. Despite the backpack, he didn't look like a hiker to her. For all she knew, he had all his worldly possessions in that backpack.

As the cafe emptied out, Maud brought him his bill. "You'd better hurry," she said. "The train's going to leave pretty quick."

"I'm not getting on the train," he said. "I'm here to see Robin about a job."

"Oh." Maud looked him over, really taking him in, and thought that there was no chance in hell Robin would hire somebody who looked like an escaped convict. "I'll let her know."

Much to her astonishment, Robin took the young man back to her office to interview him. She was even more thunderstruck when they came back out and Robin introduced him to Maud as Low McElvy, the new dishwasher.

"How could you have hired him? He's a tramp! You don't know anything about him! I mean, *look* at him! He's got 'killer maniac' written all over him!"

"Believe it. He's going to work here, and he's going to rent the upstairs."

"He's going to rent the upstairs? You're letting him stay in *Eddy's* place?"

"He's a friend of Eddy's, Maud."

"I don't believe it. A murderer-looking thing says he's a friend of Eddy's, and you just—"

"Maud, he has ears, you know. He can hear you."

"What?" Maud asked scornfully. "Is he going to strangle me in my sleep?"

"No, Maud. He is not going to strangle you in your sleep. Have some manners, for pity's sake."

But Maud, without pity, found that impossible to do.

Robin figured out that Low was wasted on dishwashing and bussing so she promoted him to her prep cook. Maud, despite loathing him, couldn't help but notice the dexterity of his hands and fingers as he chopped the vegetables and herbs, the movements of his muscles under the skin. She'd never noticed a man like this. Not since Lightning. She chalked up her fascination to revulsion.

When Robin found out Low had a gift for baking, she added that to his duties, and he went full-time.

"I don't want to keep baker's hours, Low. I'm too old for that." She was, for the record, forty-five.

"No machines," he said. "I do this by hand, or I don't do it at all." With his wiry strength, he invested the breads and desserts with his energy.

He mostly ignored Maud, which suited her. But sometimes he would make up his mind to try to engage her.

"Hey, Cowboy Girl…what's Irish and sits in your back yard?"

"I'm sure I don't know and I'm sure I don't care."

"Paddy O'Furniture."

Maud clapped her hands over her mouth and ran to the ladies' room to have her laugh. She didn't want to give Low the satisfaction. Not that it mattered. When she came back in, he cast her a sidelong glance, an embryonic smile of triumph.

She got used to that smile. He'd bake a new loaf or come up with a new frosting for the chocolate cake, and slide a bit to her on a plate, a spoon. It was always good. She had a hard time disguising her enjoyment. And then he'd smile that smile. It infuriated her. She felt as if he were somehow getting at her, getting *into* her, when she didn't want anything to do with him.

In April, he planted a container garden on the roof so that Robin could pick fresh herbs as she needed them. He set out a deck chair and would sit in the sun, stripped down to his baggy, nothing-colored pants, an arrow of hair rising from the band of his boxer shorts, cigarette stuck on his lower lip. Though he was skinny, what meat he had was all muscle.

Maud came up one afternoon to gather some rosemary for Robin, and Low caught her looking.

"Whadda you want?"

"Nothing. You need a belt."

"He ought to wear a shirt up there. Why does he want to get a tan, anyway? Like anybody wants to look at his skinny arms and chest," Maud said to Robin.

Low wasn't much of a conversationalist. He might talk to a few choice people—Robin and Lightning—but he mostly clammed up when Maud was around, unless it was to fire an infuriating shot at her.

"He's a troll," she said once to Robin. "He *looks* like a troll."

Low overheard, as he was meant to overhear. "Yeah, I'm a troll, and I'm living under your bridge." He made it sound indecent. She replayed it in her head that night, and many nights afterwards, pretending that she imagined Lightning saying it. But, of course, Lightning hadn't said it. He wouldn't. Lightning wasn't a troll. She always felt ashamed afterwards. She didn't know what was wrong with her. She must be some kind of pervert. And she did it again and again.

Word got out, as it does in a small town, that every day Low walked the two-mile trail around Foreign Lake and stopped at the marshy bit to feed the red-winged blackbirds. Folks said he would whistle to them, arms outstretched, and they would fly to him and alight on his fingers and peck the seeds from his palms. Maud once watched him do it from the road. She allowed as he might have a gift for animals, or at least red-winged blackbirds, so he might not be completely despicable.

Something about his stance reminded her of Aunt Helena's statue of Cernunnos. And that comparison made her blush to the roots of her hair and quickly hurry away.

Eventually, in spite of herself, Maud was set to graduate from high school. She began to receive cards and little congratulatory gifts from her cafe regulars. Lightning stopped by one afternoon with a little cardboard box. Inside was a sterling silver pendant, hung on a delicate silver chain, of a begowned Art Nouveau lady reclining on a crescent moon.

"I saw this at a street fair in the city, and it reminded me of you." he said.

She'd never seen anything like it. She thanked him and immediately put it on and went to look at her reflection in the foyer mirror. She loved it. It made her feel magical.

That was the beginning of her great blushing crisis. She would think about Lightning and blush. She would simply think his *name* and blush. It was crippling, infuriating. She was thankful that he didn't come in to the cafe for a while— off, she presumed, on a job out of town. But she wore the necklace every day, and she wondered what it was about it that made him think of her.

Low, sneering at it, said, "Congratulations on not flunking out or going to jail."

"I assume you've done both," Maud snapped back.

Low just smiled his embryonic smile.

That summer, Maud started working at the cafe full-time. Unlike most of her friends, she hadn't applied to any colleges and had no plans to go. This was a bit of a sore spot with her parents, who valued education for their children. Her grades were too poor for her to get into a four-year college or university, but she could always start with a two-year degree at a community college.

She didn't want to think about that. Fresh out of hated school, the last thing she wanted was more education. Though she faithfully saved half of everything she earned, she had no particular aspirations except to someday travel.

July came, and summer ripened. It would soon be Maud's eighteenth birthday, a milestone she looked forward to with excitement. She'd finally be an adult. For her birthday, Mama was sewing her a little black dress, her very first, from a pattern with a distinct 1930s flavor—bias-cut, mid-calf length, with short flutter sleeves. Maud bought a pair of kitten-heeled black sandals to go with it. It would be too dressy to wear to work. She wondered where she could wear it so that Lightning could see her in it, and she blushed and hid her mouth.

"Are you sunburned?" Aida Kay asked.

"Just overheated," Maud said, mortified.

The morning of her birthday, she woke up electrified with excitement. "Something's going to happen!" she said to herself. "Something's going to happen!"

She was scheduled to work that day. She didn't mind. There was a chance that Lightning would come in. And if he came in, there was a chance…a chance…that he'd just been waiting for her to turn eighteen to kiss her.

She put on her lady in the moon necklace, that had reminded Lightning of her. Mama brought her the makeup Aunt Helena had bought her in the city, two long years ago. "I guess you're old enough to wear this now." Feeling as if she were performing a magical ritual, Maud put on the blood-red lipstick and blotted her lips on a tissue. Her mouth looked glamorous and kissable.

"I am Maud of Sky," she said to her reflection, "and something amazing is going to happen today."

Yellow Silk Blues

"I dreamed last night," said Fortune, "that I learned to read palms from an old white Englishwoman I met on the road. She'd come into a cafe and set up, and folks would give her five dollars, or maybe only one if it was a poor town. She'd read for a while. Then she'd get one person, she'd look at their palm, close her lips tight, shake her head, close that person's fingers, get up, and leave without saying a word. I wondered if it was just a trick, you know, showmanship. But she said, no, there was always somebody who had too much trouble written on their palm. It was bad luck to read a hand like that and better to just get up and leave. I said I felt so sorry for those people with troubled hands. Lord only knows what they thought.

"That woman said to me. 'They know what they've got on their hands. The money they just gave me, that was payment in advance to keep their secrets.' But I couldn't believe it was so. There was one girl, she was young like us, a pretty, cool-blonde woman, big wide blue eyes, damned smart looking, but not like she was hiding a thing. I said, 'What about her? What's a girl like her got to hide?' And that palm-reading woman pushed her forefinger against my lips. I got such a burning there, where she'd touched, that I kept checking the mirror this morning to make sure I hadn't blistered across my mouth."

"Do you think that's a real memory?" Maud asked. "Do you think it might have really happened that way?"

"I don't know. It sure felt real."

Traveling with Maud for nearly two months, sleeping next to Maud in their tent, seemed to amplify the detail and intensity of her dreams. Or maybe it was simply that Maud snored (she did) and awoke Fortune more frequently, so that she remembered more.

Maud was taking a turn driving Fortune's '56 Bel Air. Their road rose and fell gently in a series of low hills, curved gently along the lines of a small river, before spanning out in a faded gray satin ribbon between fields and farms. They had a fine, mid-September day, warm enough that they had the windows rolled down but not so hot that a peach or a thermos cup of cool water couldn't refresh them.

Gradually, the fields gave way to evergreen woods, and the road began to rise. Maud turned off the highway onto a two-lane blacktop road. Here the speed limit dropped from 50 to 45 mph, lower in stretches where the road twisted. Fortune's ears popped as they gained elevation. The sun spattered and flashed through the boughs of Douglas Fir and Western Red Cedar. Fortune studied the map. The road signs gave them miles to bigger towns. The nearest was thirty miles away from Dareton.

They passed a sign instructing them to reduce their speed, and another giving word of a stop sign ahead. The road was marred with dirt, sand, and gravel here, tire-furrowed formations of dried mud, and larger bits of debris, all run through and marked by the tires of trucks. Fortune loosened her focus, as if she might be able to divine from the patterns. She blinked and focused again as Maud braked at a four-way stop.

Just after she braked, a red semi-truck without a trailer pulled up at the stop sign on the left. Maud went through the intersection and continued down the road. The semi made a left turn and followed.

"Hey!" Maud said indignantly. "He's right on my tail!"

She accelerated. Fortune glanced back. The rig was still uncomfortably close.

"What's the speed limit?" Maud said tensely.

"45."

"Damn, I'm going 50."

"Slow down, then."

"I can't. He'll run us over."

Fortune made her voice calm. "He's not going to run us over, Maud."

"He's pushed me up to 60 now—"

"Calm down," Fortune said. "Calm down and slow down and just pull over."

"I can't! There's barely a shoulder."

They rounded a slight curve, and the road straightened before them. The rig pulled out to pass and roared by them. It stayed in the oncoming lane long past the point of necessity before finally pulling back. Only a few moments, and it was far out of sight.

"He was showing us," Maud said angrily. She let up on the accelerator. Her shoulders trembled, and her face and neck were shiny with sweat.

"Pull over," Fortune said. "I'll drive."

"Thank you," said Maud. "That scared me to death."

Maud pulled over, and the two swapped places. With Fortune at the wheel, Maud had a chance to calm down. If she were wise, she would have done so. Instead she nursed her fear until it turned to anger.

"He wasn't trying to kill us," Fortune said. "Honestly."

"If I'd had to brake suddenly, we'd be dead."

"Well, so would he, probably. He was just being a jackass. You're taking this way too personally."

"I can't help it. When somebody's trying to kill us—"

"Listen to me, Maud. He wasn't trying to kill us."

In the end, Fortune just had to sigh and keep her peace. Maud was on a tear. And when Maud was on a tear, you just had to wait it out like any other kind of storm.

They came into Dareton a little bit before noon, passing the sizable lumber mill that was the town's primary employer. Maud was still shaky, so Fortune suggested they splurge on lunch at the local sit-down burger joint. It was the type of thing that ordinary people took for granted. But for Fortune, black, pretty, dressed in a 1918-vintage dress and boots, and with what Maud called "complicated hair," eating in a small-town diner was always fraught.

Her micro-braids were complicated enough on their own. But since she had awoken at a crossroads more than a year ago with nothing but a guitar and a '56 Bel Air to her (forgotten) name, and no memories of her past, Fortune had woven in something from every place she went, and her hair was an ever-evolving shrine to memorabilia. She had learned to dance away from grasping hands, to evade, to protect, and with the rude and entitled, to outright block. At times she felt her hair a heavy burden and longed to cut it off, to be blank of a year's experiences, to start over again without stories, talismans, reminders. But she wasn't ready to risk it. A year's memories were all she had.

Fortune tensed when the waitress, a white woman in her mid-sixties, came to take their order. She held the menu up to her face protectively, ready to swat grabby hands. But the waitress took their order without incident, except to lean close to Maud and say "Honey, you've got lipstick on your teeth."

"Oh. Thanks." It was an occupational hazard for Maud, who wore red lipstick at all times and had a bit of an overbite. However often it happened, it still embarrassed her.

But Maud soon forgot about it when a red semi-truck—
the red semi-truck—pulled into the parking lot and a
red-headed white man got out of the cab.

"It's him," she hissed. "The guy who tried to kill us. He's
coming in."

"Maud, please don't—"

But Maud had already gotten up and stalked to the door
to meet the man. Fortune could tell just from his body language and his affect that he was trouble. He was like a walking middle finger. Fortune reckoned he was perhaps forty
years old, perhaps ten years younger and aging badly. He
was also a good four inches shorter than Maud's six-foot-
two-in-cowboy-boots. This was going to go great.

"Hey!" Maud said. "You just tried to run us off the road."

He gave her a dismissive glance but stood up as straight
and tall as he could. "What?"

"You tried to run us off the road. Red and black Bel
Air...remember?"

"Don't cut off a big rig next time," he said.

"I didn't cut you off!"

"Maud, come on. Sit down."

"You could have killed us."

"Don't cut off a big rig," he repeated. "Now get out of
my face."

"Maud! Let it go."

"But—"

"Let. It. Go."

Maud sat down, red in the face and trembling with
anger. The truck driver seated himself at the counter and
would, from time to time, look back at them with a hu-
morless smirk. The waitress spoke to him deferentially. She
apparently knew him well and didn't like him. He ate his
burger, drank his coffee and left, and the waitress came to
their table.

"That's Jeff," she said. "Jeff MacKinnon. He's the meanest man I've ever met, and I've been alive for sixty-five years. It's best to just stay out of his way. There's nothing else you can do about him."

"Thanks," Fortune said.

"I don't doubt he tried to run you off the road. He hates women. Absolutely hates 'em. Everybody was shocked when Venitia Purcelle went and married him. She was a pretty little African American girl like you," she said to Fortune. "She could have married just about anybody, but she went and married him. She disappeared five, six years ago and nobody's convinced he didn't have something to do with it. I'm sorry you had a run-in with him. But you're a brave girl to stand up to him," she added to Maud. "I wanted to cheer, but I've got to live in this town."

When the waitress left, Fortune leaned in and said quietly, "You really need to calm down, Maud. You're going to make yourself sick if you don't."

"I *can't*."

"Sure you can." Fortune put down her burger, pulled her guitar into her lap, and sang "Dying Crapshooter's Blues." She could see Maud relaxing. When she got to the line about dancing the Charleston, Maud laughed out loud.

"Say, you can play that guitar and sing," the waitress said in admiration.

"Thanks," said Fortune. "Maud sings, too. Any place in town where we can play for a bit of coin?"

The waitress blew out her breath. "Money is tight around here these days. The mill has gone down to one shift a day, and one of the two grocery stores had to close. You could ask at Randy's Tavern. At least they get hikers coming through at the end of the day."

"Thanks." Fortune and Maud finished their burgers and left a generous tip, as folks who know what it's like to be tight on money tend to do, and went out to find Randy's Tavern.

It was a grim, smoky place with dark wood paneling and a pull-tab machine, the usual lighted signs for cheap brands of beer, wood-veneer table tops ringed and sometimes carved and gouged. Loud country music played for the benefit of the bartender and the four old men already drinking.

"I don't serve minors," Randy (they assumed) said when they came up to the bar.

"We're the band," Fortune said, smiling persuasively and brandishing her guitar.

"We don't do live music. We don't have nothing to pay musicians."

"What if we play for tips?" Fortune said.

Randy laughed. "Tips? Nobody's got money for tips."

"What if we play for fun?" Fortune said. "Just let us play you a couple of tunes, see what you think. If you don't like us we'll stop pestering you."

"Let 'em play," said an old man at the bar. "Nothing else going on around here."

Randy gave a brief nod. They sat down at a table.

"Are you ready?" Fortune asked Maud.

"Of course," Maud said.

They sang "Pretty Polly." Fortune, whose voice was sweet and clear, marveled anew that a sheltered rural white girl like Maud could have such a husky, sex-and-sulphur voice. The marriage of their two voices never failed to raise goosebumps on her arms.

They were applauded, so they followed up with "Down in the Willow Garden."

"I like that one," Randy said. "The Everly Brothers did that one. If you want to come tonight after seven, I guess I'll let you play if you want. You might get a quarter or two for your trouble. No drinking."

"We wouldn't dream of drinking," Fortune said.

With time to kill, they went out to explore the town. There wasn't much of it—a gas station and convenience store, the grocery store that hadn't closed down, a hardware store, a couple of cafes, an espresso shack, a Baptist church, a couple of schools, and the ranger station. They passed the cemetery on the way to the campground.

"Look at that!" Maud said.

"What is *that* doing *here*?"

Fortune pulled into the cemetery and parked in front of the mausoleum. It stood two stories high, the size of a small chapel, the upper story topped with a spiked steeple and pierced with trefoil windows. At each of the four corners, an angel stood facing the corner, hands up to their bowed faces. A barred glass door showed the Tiffany stained glass window at the back of the mausoleum. There were six individual crypts inside. A bronze vase full of fake lilies sat as if forgotten on the marble-tiled floor. An American flag leaned against the wall.

The name inscribed above the doorway was Dare.

"The Dares of Dareton," said Maud. "They clearly think highly of themselves."

Fortune, glancing around at the modest headstones all around, agreed. "Particularly in comparison to their neighbors." She peered through the mausoleum door. "Look at this, Maud. The crypts are hinged like cabinets. That's not a little bit creepy. I wonder if that's so the family can take their corpses out for a nice drive on Sundays."

She stepped back. Then she started. There was a young black woman standing inside who hadn't been inside the moment before. Fortune blinked. It was just her own reflection. But in that fragment of a moment she'd been certain that a woman was within, and that she was dressed all in yellow.

At the campground, as they set up their tent, Fortune chanted:

> Cinderella dressed in yella,
> went upstairs to kiss a fella.
> Made a mistake and kissed a snake.
> How many doctors did it take?

"What brought that on?" Maud asked.

"Good evening, ladies and gentlemen. We're Damned Pretty Things, and this is 'Where Did You Sleep Last Night?'"

Fortune played, and their voices twined and rose to the rafters. Conversation had ceased when they began to sing. The people of Dareton were in the mood for distraction and novelty. Whether they intended to heckle the girls or contribute to the camp sink on the floor, only time would tell. Fortune didn't mind. She played because she loved it. She played because she had to.

They sang "Barbara Allen." They sang "Darlin' Corey."

A wit in the audience yelled "Free Bird!" at them, and everybody laughed.

"How about 'John Hardy' instead?"

"How about you bitches shut up?"

The room fell silent. Jeff MacKinnon stood at the bar, a bottle of beer in his hand.

"Oh, swell," Fortune said under her breath.

"How about you make us?" Maud said, standing.

"Now, Jeff, don't be bothering these girls," said Randy. "They're not doing anybody any harm."

"They're doing my eardrums harm," Jeff said. "I never heard such a caterwauling in my life."

"If you don't like it, you can leave."

All murmuring ceased. The new voice belonged to a middle-aged white man dressed far better than anybody else they'd seen in Dareton. He was a superficial sort of handsome, tanned, his hair smooth and silver white, and he had an air of easy authority. He was somebody who was certain he was liked and certain he would be obeyed. Even as he spoke, his eyes crinkled with an almost self-deprecating smile.

"Oh, the big boss is here," said Jeff, waving his hands in the air. "Better do what the big boss says."

"Shut up, Jeff," shouted a woman.

"Sit down, Jeff!"

"Ladies, don't mind him. Please continue," said the middle-aged man, with an unnecessarily gracious nod of his head.

Maud slowly sat back down. Fortune reached over and patted her arm. "Let me solo on this one." And she sang "I Want to Be Evil" to general laughter and enjoyment.

The people of Dareton wouldn't let the camp sink stay empty. With the exception of Jeff MacKinnon, everybody put in at least a quarter. At the end of their set, when they stood and stretched, the well-to-do man came up to them. He pressed a hundred-dollar bill into Fortune's hand. The movement was nearly a caress.

"That's much too much," Fortune said, trying to give the bill back.

"Nonsense. That was pure pleasure, and worth every penny," he said. "We don't get much live music here. Where are you girls from?"

"Oh, nowhere you've ever heard of," Maud said, instinct instructing her to be evasive. "We're just traveling around for a while."

"And your traveling around was good enough to bring you to Dareton. I'm Matthew Dare, by the way."

"Maud Caldecote."

"Fortune."

"Fortune. I've heard of you. You're the girl who weaves memories into her hair, am I right?"

"Mm-hm." To stave off any possible attempts to grab her hair, she changed the subject. "We're on our way to the city, just decided to stop and have a look around."

Mr. Dare laughed. "There's not much to see here. If you hadn't stopped, you'd be in the city by now."

"We're taking the slow way," Fortune said.

"I like that. No need to rush when you're young. Take it nice and slow."

The way he smiled at Fortune made Maud uncomfortable. "The mausoleum in the cemetery," she said abruptly. "Is that your family, Mr. Dare?"

"I hope you didn't try to go in there," he replied, turning on her quickly.

"Of course not," Maud said. "Why would we?"

"Never mind. I keep it locked, anyway. It's what you'd call an attractive nuisance. Local kids used to go there to drink and indulge in other adult activities, if you know what I mean."

He turned to Fortune, and his face and tone were a good deal friendlier. "My family's mausoleum is a bit of an anomaly in this part of the world. The Angel House...that's what they call it here in town. You might not have noticed but the crypts are hinged."

"No, are they?" Fortune said innocently. "Why is that?"

"My family is originally from Pittsburgh. That's why the mausoleum looks the way it does. It's pure Pittsburgh cemetery gothic. My grandfather made his first fortune in mining. He was down one of his mines during a cave-in. It took hours to get him out. Because of that he developed a terror of enclosed places and a phobia about premature burial. He designed those crypts to open from the inside by means of a brass lever. Pretty ingenious for the early 20th century, don't you think?"

"Hmm!" Fortune said.

"As you might have guessed, my family founded this town. The lumber mill is mine. This recession has all but shut me down. We've gone from three shifts to one. Of course, the whole town suffers when my lumber mill suffers. But at least I don't have to worry about premature burial."

"I hope business picks up for you soon," said Fortune. "If you like, I'll read your palm and tell you your prospects."

"That's very kind of you, Miss Fortune. Ha! That didn't sound right, did it? But until the economy recovers and developers start building again, I'm afraid we'll stay in this particular pickle, no matter what you might read in my palm. Speaking of staying, where are you two ladies staying tonight?"

"Out at the campground," Maud said.

"Oh, no, no. That won't do for a couple of young ladies such as yourselves! Especially not in September, when the nights are getting cold. Tell you what...I've got a nice big house—"

"Here," Fortune said abruptly, and put the hundred-dollar bill in Mr. Dare's hand. "I don't know what you think you were paying for. Maud, would you get the camp sink? Let's go."

"Ladies, ladies, I meant no disrespect."

"Good night, Mr. Dare," Fortune said firmly.

Outside, Randy caught up to them and handed them twenty dollars. "You helped me sell a lot of beer tonight," he said. "Come back again tomorrow night, if you're still in town. By the way, I saw you give that money back to Dare. That was smart of you. He has a thing for girls like you. Jeff MacKinnon's wife Venitia…yeah, Dare paid a lot of attention to that woman. People used to say they wouldn't blame her for having an affair, seeing as how her husband is, but talk about being between a rock and a hard place."

"Mr. Dare is a charming man," Fortune said sarcastically, as they drove back to the campsite.

"Terribly charming," said Maud. "I always think slick people like that are hiding something dreadful."

"Such as?"

"Bodies in the basement," said Maud.

"Why does your mind always go to bodies in the basement? Why not bodies in the attic? Why not bodies in the ingenious Angel House?"

"You laugh, but just wait and see. I'll bet we read about him and his basement in the papers someday."

"We'd be more likely to read about your boyfriend Jeff. He's the one I'd put my money on for bodies in the basement."

"He wouldn't bother to hide his bodies. He'd just leave them lying around in the open and dare you to say anything about them."

"I was afraid you were going to get into a fistfight with him tonight."

"I was, too, and I've never been in a fistfight before, so I'd have lost."

The night had grown chilly. At the campsite they locked the car and crawled into their tent, where their sleeping

154

bags looked snug and inviting. The various male denizens of Dareton forgotten, they soon fell asleep.

The moon woke Fortune. It was bright and full, and its light shone through the nylon tent as if it were made of cellophane. Wide awake and conscious of her bladder, she unzipped the door on her side and scrambled out. She put on her camp shoes and walked to the pit toilet. The moon was so bright she didn't need her flashlight.

On her way back she thought she saw a woman standing by the tent. She squinted, but the outline was evasive, despite the bright moonlight. She blinked rapidly, trying to focus.

"Hello?" she called.

Then she turned her head slightly. Out of the corner of her eye she could see the figure more clearly. It was a young black woman, her straightened hair brushed back from her face and held with a ribbon. She wore a dress that fell to her knees. Both ribbon and dress were clearly, vibrantly yellow.

Fortune tried to look at her straight on. The woman faded and blurred.

It was like looking at a comet, she realized. You could see more clearly through your peripheral vision. It also occurred to her that this was very strange.

"Can I help you?" Fortune asked.

The woman brushed both hands down the front of her dress, then touched the ribbon holding back her hair. She took three steps toward Fortune, then stopped.

Feeling strange and foolish at once for entertaining a newly formed suspicion, Fortune said tentatively, "Venitia, is that you?"

Instantly and completely, the woman vanished as if she'd never been there.

Fortune scrambled back into the tent and shook Maud by the shoulder. "Maud! Maud, wake up. I think I just saw a ghost."

"A what?"

"A ghost. I think I saw a ghost."

Unimpressed, Maud rolled over on her other side. "I told you that man had bodies in his basement."

To Fortune's surprise, Maud fell back asleep almost instantly (if she had, in fact, been fully awake to begin with). While Maud slept, snoring intermittently as she did, Fortune lay awake, thinking about the woman (or ghost) she'd seen, the way she'd disappeared when Fortune spoke Venitia's name. And she thought about the brief flash of a moment, there at the Dare mausoleum, where she'd thought she'd seen a woman standing within, dressed all in yellow.

She dreamed that she returned to her house in the city. She knew it was hers, though she'd never seen it before. She had been away for a year and was afraid she'd been evicted during that time, her possessions cleaned out and perhaps sold.

She climbed the stairs. She gathered a year's worth of mail from her mailbox. Her key still worked in the front door.

It wasn't until she opened the door and stepped inside that she remembered her cat. Who had been looking after her cat while she was gone? Who had been feeding her and watering her?

The answer, of course, was no one. The cat lay curled in an open dresser drawer, just where it had died.

"The ghost was wearing a yellow silk dress," Fortune said that morning. She picked out a bluesy tune on her guitar while Maud made oatmeal for breakfast.

"How could you tell it was silk?"

"Because of the sound it made when she walked. It swashed just like silk."

"And you think it was Venitia MacKinnon?"

"Yes."

"I *am* sorry," Maud said. "I was hoping she'd just left town. Do you think her husband murdered her?"

"I don't know."

Then she sang, to the bluesy tune she picked:

> Meet me in the graveyard
> where all my old folks lie in bed.
> I said, meet me in the graveyard
> where all my old folks lie in bed.
> I got you a yellow dress,
> a yellow ribbon for your head.

"I like that," said Maud. "Did you just write it?"

Fortune shook her head. "I don't know. I suppose I must have."

"Maybe Mr. Dare was having an affair with her. He'd have the money to buy a silk dress, don't you think?"

"This is very creepy, Maud."

"I thought you were used to strange things happening."

"Not ghosts. There have never been ghosts before. Or ghost lyrics, for that matter."

"So do you want to stay? Should we go and sing again tonight?"

Fortune sighed. "I keep thinking about that hundred-dollar bill. Maybe he was just being flashy and meant nothing by it."

"Maybe we should give him another chance," Maud said, smiling.

"Maybe he'll double it from remorse."

"Or maybe he'll give you a yellow silk dress."

They went back to the cemetery. Fortune was drawn to the Angel House with a strange combination of curiosity and dread. When she touched the locked door, she felt queasy. She leaned her forehead against the glass and counted ten breaths.

"Venitia," she said softly. "Venitia. Nitia."

She saw her out of the corner of her eye. "Maud. She's here. Can you see her?"

"No," Maud said, sounding far away.

Venitia was dressed in jeans and a T-shirt, but she held the yellow silk dress up to herself and swished this way and that, as if in front of a mirror, or in front of an admirer. Somebody else was there, tall, silver-haired, dressed in neat chinos and a button-down shirt. Venitia let the dress slip from her hands as they kissed. Then they pulled apart, alert and listening as a pair of startled rabbits. He pulled open one of the crypts and urged her inside. She hesitated. He insisted. She bent her head and shoulders and climbed in. He threw the yellow silk dress in after her and closed the crypt. The crypt door didn't shut all the way, so he slammed against it. Then he left, passing out of Fortune's vision like a shadow. Then her vision dimmed, darkened, until all she could see was black. Her skin grew slick with cold sweat.

"Maud," she said. "Take my hands. Please."

She felt Maud grip her hands through the fingerless gloves she wore.

"I need to sit down. Help me. I can't see anything."

"Here." Maud gently helped her to sit on the mausoleum steps. She leaned against Maud, stealing her warmth. She heard intermittent gunshots in the distance, a chainsaw, birds, an angry squirrel.

"Okay?" Maud asked.

"In a minute. Have you ever blacked out without losing consciousness?"

"Yeah, once, when I was dehydrated. Let me get you some water."

"No. Stay here. Please." She kept her eyes closed. The pervasive blackness was less dreadful that way. She listened to her heartbeat and to Maud's tense breathing. At last the spell passed and she opened her eyes.

"Okay," she said. "Let's get out of here."

Word had spread about Damned Pretty Things. Randy's Tavern was more crowded that night, and the atmosphere was almost festive. Jeff MacKinnon sat in one corner like a specter at the feast. Matthew Dare leaned against the bar and surveyed the room with a benign, proprietary smile. He came over quickly when Fortune and Maud arrived.

"I want to apologize for last night," he said. "I honestly meant no offense. My intentions were honorable."

"As they were toward Nitia MacKinnon?" Fortune asked.

Mr. Dare had admirable control over his face. If he was surprised, he didn't show it. "I see gossip is alive and well in Dareton. Poor Mrs. MacKinnon. I would have done anything in my power to help her leave her abusive husband. I pray almost every night that she's safe and far away from him."

"Is that possible?"

He shrugged. "If I were the keeper of her secrets, I wouldn't be likely to tell, would I?"

"I suppose not."

"You offered last night to read my palm. If you read it tonight, how much could I give you to keep *my* secrets?"

"Don't show them to me," Fortune said. "I don't want them."

159

He laughed. "I guess I don't have many you haven't already heard from the town gossips, anyway. I guess I don't have any secrets from anybody."

"That would be impossible," said Fortune. "If you'll excuse me…."

Fortune joined Maud on the makeshift stage. The crowd grew quiet with expectation.

"Good evening, ladies and gentlemen," said Fortune. "We're Damned Pretty Things, and this is a song called 'Murder in the First Degree.'"

They had played three songs when the queasiness came upon Fortune. She briefly bowed her head over her guitar and breathed deeply, slowly.

"All right?" Maud whispered.

Fortune shook her head. "I think I need some water."

Maud went to fetch it, and Fortune felt the blackness fall over her vision. She drank thirstily when Maud returned but instantly regretted it when a new wave of nausea swept over her.

"I have to do this," she said rapidly. "I've got to do this. Let me do this."

"Fortune?"

She raised her head. She couldn't see a thing. Her fingers picked out the bluesy music she'd played that morning. The words came to her as if dictated to her, and she sang them obediently.

> Meet me in the graveyard
>> where all my old folks lie in bed.
> I said, meet me in the graveyard
>> where all my old folks lie in bed.
> I got you a yellow dress,
>> a yellow ribbon for your head.

Well, she met him in the graveyard
where the Dares lie asleep.
Yes, she met him in the graveyard
where all those Dares lie asleep.
Inside that big cold house
where all the angels weep.

Well, her husband came a'lookin,
and Dare pushed her in the grave.
Her husband came a'lookin,
and Dare, he pushed her in the grave.
Said, wait here just a little bit.
I got my own skin to save.

The slab closed over Nitia,
and she could not get out.
That slab closed over Nitia,
 and that girl could not get out.
Nobody heard little Nitia
when she start to scream and shout—

"Stop! Stop it!"

Fortune's fingers stilled on the strings. She lowered her head, and when she looked back up her vision was clear, and Mr. Dare stood before her, breathing hard but smiling a strained, too bright smile.

"Stop," he said. "No more."

"That's all I know," Fortune said. "There is no more."

"*How* do you know it? How can you possibly know?"

Fortune's mouth trembled at the corners. "Nitia showed me."

"Nitia," he said, as if choking on the dryness of his mouth. "You've seen Nitia. She's alive. My yellow beauty. My canary diamond. I knew she got out."

Jeff MacKinnon pushed through the crowd and grasped Mr. Dare by the collar. "Yours? She wasn't yours. She wasn't mine, either. She ran out on both of us. She made fools of both of us."

"She didn't run," Fortune said, her voice void of emotion.

"What do you know about it?" Jeff demanded.

She said to Mr. Dare, very clearly, "She didn't get out."

Mr. Dare spoke to her almost dreamily. "You know, from the moment I saw you last night. I felt drawn to you. From the moment I heard your voice, and your fingers on those strings. I had some inkling that you'd be my undoing. You're the midwife of my guilt, and I'm almost grateful to you for it.

"I told her to wait five minutes. Just five minutes, and then pull the lever and hurry on home. I thought she had. Then MacKinnon came into my office the next day, demanding to know what I'd done with his wife. I thought she must have gotten up the courage to leave him. To leave me. I didn't go back to the Angel House for three months. Then, on Memorial Day, I went back and found this hanging outside the crypt."

He pulled out of his breast pocket a discolored scrap of yellow silk.

"The mechanism was jammed. I couldn't get the crypt open. I always hoped—"

"But you were too much of a coward to find out for certain," Fortune said, her voice devoid of emotion.

"The girl who weaves her memories into her hair. I've heard you braid in something from every place you've been. Maybe you can braid this in to remind you of Dareton, and Nitia, and me."

Fortune took the scrap. It had been laundered, but it was stained nonetheless. She couldn't stand to look at it too closely.

"Does she wait for me, Fortune? Does she love me? Does she miss me?"

"No," Fortune said. "She just wants to go to sleep under her own name."

He looked at her, and swallowed, and briefly bowed his head.

"Ladies and gentlemen," he said, his voice loud and steady. "May I suggest that we adjourn to the Angel House?"

"She died in that little dark box, all alone. God knows how long it took her to die. How many days. How many hours. Was her voice hoarse from screaming? Did her fingers bleed from clawing at the granite? And nobody came. Nobody came."

Maud drove, silent, listening. Fortune leaned against the passenger door, cooling her cheek on the window.

"Now all I want is all she wants—we want out."

Maud nodded, and calmly drove, and soon Dareton was less than a speck in the rearview mirror.

The Love Song of Long Maud and Low

I.

After they left Dareton, Fortune and Maud spent the night in a motel a few towns over and drove back toward Sky the next day. Maud did the driving. Fortune seemed so hurt; there was really no question. She leaned her face against the passenger-seat window and didn't speak. Sometimes she cried, soundlessly, the tears sliding down her face almost as if she weren't aware of them until they pattered on her skirt, beaded, then sank and spread into the black fabric.

An hour away from Sky, she suddenly said, "To hell with this. I need a drink." She unsnapped her seatbelt and climbed awkwardly over the back of the seat. Maud knew that she kept a bottle of vodka in the back. "For celebrations and medical emergencies," Fortune had said once. When she found the bottle, she climbed back over and put on her seatbelt. She unscrewed the top and took a quick swig.

She shuddered. "Oh, that's awful! Why do people drink this stuff?" She took another swig.

"Hope it helps," Maud said gently. She felt as if she should almost whisper to Fortune right now. There was something of the sick kid about her, vodka notwithstanding.

"At least I'll get a placebo effect," Fortune said grimly. She took a third swig. This time, she didn't shudder. "Either that or I'll puke. Puking has a way of taking one's mind off other things."

"Yes, it has," Maud agreed. "Just let me know when to pull over. I'll hold back your hair."

"Thank you."

But it didn't come to that. Fortune screwed the lid back on the bottle and stuffed it into the glove box. She slumped against the door, her face against the window, and sighed deeply. "Wonder if it's made the news yet?"

"Papa can call some newspaper people he knows in the city and see if the Associated Press ran the story."

"You have got a very useful father."

"Thank you."

"You're welcome. Oh, Maud. Sometimes I hate the world so much I can scarcely breathe. Do you think I *want* to hate it? No. I do not. I want to love the world, and I want the world to love me back. Is that so much to ask?"

"*I* love you," Maud said simply.

"Do you?" Fortune straightened up and looked at Maud curiously.

"Yes," Maud said. "You're my best friend. You're the best friend I ever had."

"Wow! I don't know if I've ever been anybody's best friend before. You know what, Maud? I love you, too. I think you're a swell kid."

Maud laughed. "I think that must be some swell vodka."

"Want some?" Fortune opened the glove box, then shut it again. "Oh. Probably better not. Since you're driving and everything."

By the time they reached the red bridge to Sky, Fortune was singing, her words only slightly slurred, and Maud listened, instinctively knowing that Fortune needed to sing it out on her own.

"Almost home," she said.

"I'm sorry we didn't get all the way to the city this time," Fortune said.

"Oh, we'll get there one of these days."

When Fortune saw Lightning's truck on Main Street, parked in front of the Sky Cafe, she said, "Pull over. Lightning's here. I need to talk to him about something. You take the car and go on home. I'll have him give me a ride."

"What's up?" Maud asked. She parked, turned off the engine, and got out. She stretched with a groan.

"Tell you later," Fortune said, and walked, a bit unsteadily, into the cafe.

Maud stretched again. It had been a long drive, and she could do with something cool to drink. She wondered what Fortune could possibly have to discuss with Lightning, especially in her current tipsy state. She walked into the cafe, the bell on the door chiming a greeting.

Fortune stood on tip-toes, her high heels a good inch above the floor, with her arms around Lightning's neck. Lightning bent, his hands framing Fortune's face. They kissed each other, then they drew away from each other and smiled.

"I think the bees approve," said Fortune, her voice clear.

Maud took a few steps back. She blinked rapidly and put one hand over her mouth, as was her habit when she didn't want to give her emotions away. She didn't know if there was anybody to give herself away to. All she could see was Fortune and Lightning, and all they could see was each other.

Maud turned and walked out. She glanced at the car. She thought about what she'd seen. She looked at the Blue Mouse Theatre and walked quickly.

She had to hold it together.

"The show's already been running an hour, Maud," said Mr. Dougal Avery, who was sitting in the box office reading a newspaper.

"That's okay." She put her money down and got her ticket. She went in. It took awhile for her eyes to adjust to the dark theater. She sat in the back row, all by herself. She had no idea what was playing out on the screen. All she could see was Lightning kissing Fortune, Fortune kissing Lightning. Her breath came in sharp bursts. Her chest felt tight as a fist. She started crying, silently, seismically, bent double as if she were about to be sick.

She knew him from his high tops when Low came in and sat down beside her. She couldn't raise herself. She couldn't face him. She didn't care. Let him think what he wanted.

She expected really anything from him than what she got—a gentle hand resting on her back, barely there. She sat doubled over for a good ten minutes, calming herself under that hand. Her tears stopped, and her breath steadied. She sat up. Low was watching the movie, paying her no attention. When she sat up, his hand slid off her back onto his lap.

"This movie sucks," he said after a minute.

And then, a few minutes later, "Who you crying over? Him, or her?"

Her breath caught. She didn't know. Either. Both. She hadn't stopped to wonder. She'd just stood outside, alone, shut out and looking in.

"Leave me alone." He terrified her because he knew why she was crying.

"Doesn't matter. I bet I can make you stop crying."

"I'm not crying."

"You were. And you will again. I bet I can make you stop. I bet I can make you forget all about both of them."

"Why, because I'd be puking too hard?" *Puking has a way of taking one's mind off other things.*

His eyes narrowed. "Okay. You go ahead and have your heart broken for you. You go ahead and cry. Welcome to not-good-enough, Maud. I hope your stay is a long one." He got up and left, and Maud broke down again from fear and anger as much as from heartache.

She cried until the closing credits, and then she left under cover of darkness. She began the two-mile walk home. She still had the keys to Fortune's Bel Air. She didn't give a damn. Lightning could give Fortune a ride home. (Would he take Fortune home with him?) Every once in a while a car would approach, bright headlights blazing, and pass her. She was afraid somebody would recognize her and stop. She couldn't face anybody. Not now. Not yet.

When she got home, Fortune was in Maud's bed, and delirious.

"What's wrong with her?" Maud asked. She had blown her nose and washed her face and hoped that it didn't look as if she'd been crying for the better part of two hours.

Mama, who dabbed Fortune's forehead with a cool, wet washcloth, whispered, "She's burning up with fever. She could barely stand up when Lightning brought her in."

"She didn't have *that* much vodka," Maud said. She felt spiteful saying it. Mama didn't need to know that Fortune had had a few drinks. But Fortune had kissed Lightning, and Low knew that Maud cared about it, so why should Maud be the only one exposed?

"She isn't sick from vodka. Though it might have sped things up. What happened out there?"

"Mama, yesterday was awful." Maud told her about Dareton, about Venitia MacKinnon being shut up alive in an empty crypt, and about Fortune seeing her ghost, singing about her death, and exposing Matthew Dare's guilt.

"Hmm." Mama looked at Fortune consideringly. "This happens sometimes, Maud, to people who have brushed against strangeness. They get physically ill afterwards. The stress is just too much."

"Or she might have just got it from kissing Lightning."

Mama took her by the shoulder and gave her a shake. "I don't like that tone. What does it matter if she kissed Lightning or not? Fortune is your friend, and she's a very sick girl. Have some sympathy."

"Got to take Maud," Fortune said.

"Where do you have to take me?" Maud asked, her voice kinder. "What is it, Fortune?"

"Got to take Maud to the city."

"It's okay. We'll get there by and by. Right now you have to rest and get better."

"No. Got to take Maud to the city. Got to take Maud to the rich old man."

"What rich old man?"

Fortune struck the bedcovers and cried out, exasperated. "Magnus MacDonald."

Mama started at the name. "Magnus MacDonald?" She leaned closer to Fortune. "Why do you have to take Maud to see Magnus MacDonald?"

But Fortune just shook her head on the pillow, over and over again. "Got to take Maud to the city."

"Isn't he the man Aunt Helena used to work for?" Maud whispered.

Mama looked at her, her expression cold, almost angry. "Aunt Helena didn't *work for* him. She was *associated* with him."

"Well, okay," Maud said, abashed. "Associated with. Sorry. But how would Fortune know him? And what would he want with me?"

"You'll have to ask Fortune that once she's better," Mama said, turning that hard expression on the sick girl. She shook her head, then sighed, and her expression softened. "I wondered what brought her here, but I didn't question it too deeply."

Fortune was feverish for two days, getting up only to use the bathroom and to take the chicken broth and the willow bark and feverfew tea that Mama made for her. On the morning of the third day her fever broke, and she felt strong enough to take a shower while Mama changed the damp sheets. Freshly showered, in fresh pajamas and a freshly-made bed, she looked much better. She was hungry, so Mama made her egg-on-toast.

Maud had spent a great deal of those three days in her room with Fortune, playing game after game of solitaire. When she lost a game, it meant that Fortune and Lightning were in love with each other. The few times she won a game, it meant that the kiss was simply an expression of friendship. And who was she kidding? She'd never kissed a friend like that. She'd never kissed anybody like that.

She'd spent most of the rest of her time sitting under the cedar tree, hidden from the world. She chastised herself for taking it this way. Hadn't she told Fortune her own self that she was no longer interested in Lightning? Maybe she was wrong about that. Maybe she'd thought she was going to travel with Fortune for a while and then come back to Lightning. But if Fortune and Lightning were in love, that would mean the end of both dreams. They had shut her out of both their lives the moment they'd kissed.

And she wondered about Magnus MacDonald, and why Fortune seemed convinced she had to take Maud to see him. But that didn't feel as important as the kiss did. Especially not when Lightning stopped by every morning on his way to work to ask how Fortune was doing. Maud always left the kitchen when he came by. She didn't want to see him or have to talk to him, have to pretend that she hadn't seen the kiss, have to pretend she didn't care. For all she knew, Low had been bastard enough to tell Lightning she'd been crying about it in the movie theater.

"So how are you?" Maud asked, as Fortune ate her egg-on-toast.

"Much better now that I'm eating this. That's the sickest I've been since…well, since who knows when. I kept dreaming that you wanted me to count all the flowers in your wallpaper. I don't know why, but you made it sound as if it was the most important thing in the world."

"You talked a lot in your sleep," Maud said.

"What did I say?"

"You talked about Magnus MacDonald." Maud watched Fortune's face closely. Fortune blinked, then gazed steadily back at Maud.

"Did I, now?"

"You kept saying you had to take me to him."

"Huh." Fortune cut another piece of egg-on-toast but left it on the plate. "That's weird."

"How do *you* know Magnus MacDonald?"

"How do *you?*" Fortune demanded. She shoved the tray away. "Look. *He* approached *me*, not the other way around. I'm just an innocent bystander in your little family feud. He asked me to find you and bring you to him. I decided to let him twist in the wind. There's no need to get all pissy with me about it. It's not like I betrayed you or anything."

"Whoa!" Maud said, taken aback by Fortune's vehemence. "Did I say anything about you betraying me?"

"Then why the interrogation?" Fortune said. She breathed hard. "I'm not exactly in great shape right now, Maud. I feel like I got hit by a truck."

"I'm sorry," Maud said, not really feeling sorry. "But can you blame me for being curious about it?"

"There's such a thing as waiting for the right time."

"Which is when *you* say it is?"

"God, will you get out? Just get out and leave me alone."

"Sure," Maud said, getting up. "I'll get out of *my* room and leave you alone. No problem."

She left, slamming the door behind her, and ran into Lightning.

"Sorry, Maud," he said, steadying her by her upper arms. "Is Fortune awake?"

Maud sighed in exasperation and shook her head. "No. I slammed the door because she was fast asleep, and I'm just that kind of jerk. Please, feel free to go into *my* room and talk to her. Don't mind me one little bit."

She stormed out of the house and up to the top of the pasture, to her sanctuary cedar tree, and crawled beneath its lowest boughs. There she cried, more from anger than heartache. But she looked at her watch, and she noted that Lightning spent nearly an hour at the house, in her room, by Fortune's side. She didn't leave her cedar tree until Lightning drove away. And then she climbed onto Mab's back and let the grazing horse carry her around the pasture. She leaned against Mab's neck and wondered what on earth she was going to do.

Finally, she slid off Mab's back and returned to the house. She went downstairs to her room and knocked on the door.

"Come in," Fortune called.

She opened the door, came in, and sat down on the bed. Fortune had been crying, too. Maud took her hand and said, "I'm sorry."

Fortune nodded. "I'm sorry, too."

"Can I get you anything? Juice? Broth? Tea?"

Fortune shook her head. "I asked Lightning to let me stay at the Mansion so that I'd be out of your way."

"What did he say?"

"Well, he left without me, didn't he?"

"You don't have to go."

"You have to understand, I can't do anything on my own without my car, and Lightning says that's in town."

"I'm sorry about that. I went to the movies and forgot about it."

"You forgot about my car and walked two miles home?"

"It was that kind of movie," Maud said.

Fortune smiled, barely. "You are crazy."

"I really am sorry," Maud said. "I don't know what's wrong with me."

"Just be gentle with me. Between Dareton and getting sick as a dog, I'm really not in terrific shape. I'll tell you all about the rich old man. Just—not today, all right? Is that all right?"

"Yes."

"Can we be friends again? Please?"

"Yes. I'd like that more than anything."

"All right. Friends."

"Friends."

Fortune fell asleep soon after that. Maud sat down and shuffled her deck of cards mechanically, not really interested in playing solitaire or doing anything else. The cards couldn't tell her whether or not Fortune and Lightning were in love with each other—certainly not more accurately than Lightning coming to see Fortune, Fortune asking him to take her with him. Relieved that she and Fortune had made up, Maud was nonetheless uneasy in herself. She was ashamed of her strong reactions. She was ashamed of her anger and her pettiness. Hadn't she just told Fortune that she loved her? Didn't she mean it?

"'Love is patient and kind,'" she recited morosely. "'Love is not jealous. It is not irritable or resentful.'" What had she been but jealous, irritable, and resentful nonstop for the past three days? In a rare moment of clarity, she acknowledged that she had a lot of growing up to do.

She looked at Fortune, whose ornamented braids were splayed out across the pillow. Fortune's chest rose and fell gently, regularly, with her breathing, and her eyelids fluttered with dreams.

"Don't count the flowers," Maud whispered. "It doesn't matter at all."

The next day, Fortune showered and dressed and came upstairs to eat breakfast. When Lightning came by to see how Fortune was doing, Maud got up to leave.

"Where are you going?" Fortune asked.

"Just giving you some privacy."

"That's hardly necessary."

"Well, anyway." Maud went down to her room to hide. There, the warm, indistinct rumble of Lightning's voice still reached her. She shuffled the cards, over and over, and tried not to hear. Fortune and Lightning laughed. For one hateful moment, Maud wondered if they were laughing at her.

"Oh, come *on*!" she said. "You are so paranoid it's not even funny."

She heard him drive away. The kitchen was silent. She came upstairs to find Mama knitting in the living room.

"Where's Fortune?"

"Lightning took her into town so she could get her car."

"Is she talking about leaving again?" Maud asked anxiously.

"You'll have to ask her that when she gets back. Maud, I think we need to have a talk with her."

"About Magnus MacDonald? I tried. She told me she was too sick to talk about it."

"If she's well enough to get her car, she's well enough to talk." Again, Mama's expression was uncharacteristically cold and hard. Maud feared for Fortune. It wasn't a good idea to go up against her mother, who could be McBride enough when angry. "She has enjoyed our hospitality. The least she can do is be honest with us about why she's here."

"But she said—"

"I don't want to hear it from you, Maud. I want to hear it from her."

"Okay. Just don't be too hard on her."

"No worries," Mama said, in a tone that indicated just the opposite.

When Fortune returned, Maud was outside singing to Nut. Fortune came and found her.

"You look tired," Maud said.

"I am."

"Mama wants to talk."

Fortune smiled. "I had a feeling she might. Before we do, you might want to unload your stuff from the car. I may have to beat a hasty retreat."

"Is that really necessary?"

"Yeah," she said. "I think it is. I'm really sorry, Maud."

Fortune went inside, and Maud unloaded her duffle bag, sleeping bag, and sleeping pad. The trunk looked lonely without her things in it. She carried everything inside and found Fortune in the living room, sitting on the couch with her hands folded in her lap. Mama still knit, her eyes on her work, but they both glanced up when Maud came in.

Fortune began without preamble. Maud listened, astonished, to Fortune's story of meeting Magnus MacDonald in a mountain cafe. She listened, astonished, when Fortune sang the ballad of Long Maud.

"Somebody wrote a song about me? About *me*? But it *can't* be me, because I never went to that party. I told you that I got sick, remember? Mama, isn't this the craziest thing you ever heard?"

Mama glanced from Maud to Fortune and back again. "Wait here."

She left the room and came back a few minutes later with a one-dram amber glass vial with a black stopper. It was the same kind of vial she used for her herbal tinctures. This one was labeled "For Maud." Mama handed it to her and sat down.

"What is this?" Maud asked.

"This is something from your Aunt Helena. Open it."

Maud unstopped the vial and raised it to her nose. She inhaled. She jerked back, fumbling the vial. Its contents spilled, blood red, over the front of her white T-shirt and onto her lap. The smell of alcohol and pomegranates filled the room.

Fortune exclaimed and got up to bring some paper towels. Mama stayed where she was, watching Maud closely. Maud shook her head, over and over again, as if trying to shake something out of, or into, place. She held her hand to her forehead. It felt hot to the touch. She closed her eyes.

"How could I have forgotten?" Maud cried. "Oh my God."

"What is it?" Fortune asked, sounding genuinely frightened.

"The song got it wrong," Maud said. "I didn't have a lily *crown*. It was just one lily blossom. Just one. Right here." She touched behind her left ear.

Fortune stopped scrubbing Maud's T-shirt. "You were there."

"Yes. I was there. Paolo MacDonald humiliated me. He threw wine in my face, so I threw a curse on him. I'm glad it worked. I'm glad he's suffering."

"Maud," Mama said gently.

"Everybody laughed at me, Mama. Fortune, everybody laughed at me. I blessed him, just the way Aunt Helena taught me, and he called me a stupid bitch and threw wine in my face. And now his grandfather wants me to break the curse? Big fat hairy chance!"

"Maud, it's been two years."

"No, it's not. I've only just remembered it. So as far as I'm concerned, it happened just yesterday."

"What I mean to say is, that boy has been suffering for two years."

"Good. Let him suffer. I hope he's a bum in the streets. I hope he sleeps in a pool of his own puke every single night." Now Maud cried. She had taken the paper towels from Fortune and scrubbed the front of her shirt over and over.

"Maud, you're going to make yourself sick."

"I'm sorry," Fortune said, to Mama, to Maud. "I'm so sorry. The old man lied to me about you. He said it was an accident. I don't even know what to say. I should never have come here."

"Hush, child," Mama said to her. "You came where you were needed, and you came when you were needed. Oh, now, I can't have *both* of you crying. Shh, shh, girls. Let's all settle down. It's all right. It's going to be all right."

But it wasn't all right. Nothing was all right. And there was still the question of Low. Was he going to tell everybody that she'd been crying in the movie theater? Was he going to expose her shame?

That night she had had a dream that she was in a gallery lit entirely by beeswax candles. The only painting in the gallery was created of colored river sand on the floor, in the bottom of a frame of clear, still water. She knelt to look at it, and then found she couldn't stand back up again. She called on the wind to help her up, but the wind couldn't lift her. Maud had to resign herself to walking on her knees the whole rest of her life, and considered the implications of this, and how it would alter her life.

Then the dream shifted. She knelt on the banks of the creek at the red bridge, in sunlight so bright she could barely keep her eyes open. "I'm on my knees to you, Sweet Honey. I need your help. If you exist, if you're real, please help me. Please, please help me."

"What you want from me, Long Maud?"

Blinding in sequins, Sweet Honey hurt Maud's eyes. She had to shut them tight and cover her eyelids with her hands.

"I want Lightning," she said.

"Fortune's got him. You can't have him."

"But—I—"

"Don't you dare say 'I saw him first.'"

"Oh. No. I mean, I always thought that he and I were— that we were destined to be together. He gave me this necklace. He said it reminded him of me. And every time I twisted an apple stem—"

"It landed on 'L.' I know that. Lots of 'L's in this world, Long Maud. Doesn't have to stand for Lightning."

"*Please* help me."

"I can't. You already used up your love spell that night you cursed that boy to love you. You used it all up. You walked into that party already in love. And that boy hurt you and humiliated you because he was weak in front of his family, and you cursed him to love you. Listen to me, Long Maud, and listen well. What I am saying is, if you want love, I guess you'd better find that boy. You might find him if you look hard enough."

"I don't want some boy who I hate. I want Lightning."

"Child, you are not now, nor will you ever be, woman enough to handle Lightning."

"You only say that because you're on *her* side."

"What are we, you and I, Long Maud? What do we do? We help. We facilitate. We move the story along. You brought those two together. That's your role in their story."

"I want my own story."

"Everybody wants their own story. Everybody *gets* their own story. Their *own*, not somebody else's. You are just a part of their story, of Fortune's and Lightning's, and if you don't want to cry, you'd better learn it quick."

"Where is *my* story?"

"Find that boy. He's your story. Break the curse you put on him, and break the curse you put on you. You need to learn a little humility."

Maud awoke. Impulsively, she got up, got dressed, drove Mama's van into town and parked behind the cafe. She went up the outside stairs and knocked on Low's door. When he answered it, he looked her up and down.

"What the hell?"

"Do you believe in curses?" she asked.

"Uh, you want to come in?"

"Do you believe *I* could curse somebody?"

"Or you could stand out there."

"Does learning humility *have* to mean being humiliated?"

"What, are you a cat? In or out, Maud."

She came inside. He shut the door behind her.

"You think *I* could humiliate you?" he asked. "You've always had me wrapped around your finger."

"What?" She was surprised.

"Looks like I'm not getting any sleep tonight. I'm gonna make coffee. You want some?"

"You're offering me *coffee*?"

"Okay. No coffee for Maud. Please excuse me while I help myself?"

Maud was cognizant of the fact that this was the single longest conversation she'd ever had with Low. This struck her as actually rather terrifying. She sank down on his bed and broke down crying. She clutched her arms around her ribcage, her forehead almost touching her knees. Her tears hit the bare floorboards.

"Aw, no. Don't do that." Low sat down beside her. "Stop that. Maud, I said stop it. You're gonna flood the restaurant. Robin'll kill me dead, she finds her restaurant flooded. 'Low, why is my restaurant flooded?' she'll ask me, and I'll have to say, 'On account of me making Maud cry last night.' Oh. Huh. Maybe I'd better not say that. That wouldn't sound so good. That means I'll have to lie. 'On account of me crying over Maud,' I'll have to say. You don't want me to lie for you, do you, Maud? Lie, and go to hell, just on account of you making like Little Sky Falls, huh? Huh, Maud?"

She looked up and laughed, and Low appeared to relax. "Don't blow your nose on my sheets," he said.

She made a face. "I had no intention—"

"Here." He handed her a box of tissues.

"Why are you being kind to me?" she asked, and blew her nose.

"Am I?" He scratched the back of his neck.

"Yes."

"I guess it's because you're on my bed," he said. He glanced away and moistened his lips with his tongue. His shoulders looked tense. "Rules of hospitality."

He turned and faced her again, and some of his usual sullenness had returned. "You look terrible when you cry. Don't ever cry thinking it'll make some guy's heart get all soft, because it won't."

Anger made her stop crying. "I'll keep that in mind."

"That's better," he said. "Be your usual hateful self."

"Why are you here?" she demanded. "People come here to heal. That's what Mama always said. They come, they get well, and sometimes they stay, but most of the time they go back into their own world and their own lives. Why are *you* here? Outsiders come here for a reason. What's your reason?"

"You are," he said. "I came here for you."

"That's not funny."

"Get out, Maud."

"Well, you can't expect me to believe—"

"Get out!"

"You really are a bastard."

"So you say. What if I'm not, huh? What's it gonna kill in you to maybe be wrong about me?"

"I'm wrong about everything. I'm sick of being wrong."

"So you'd rather be right than be my—"

"Don't say it!"

"—friend."

"I thought you were going to make coffee," Maud said peevishly.

"What, you changed your mind?"

"About what?"

"About coffee."

"What *about* coffee?"

"You do this on purpose?" he demanded. "You think it's funny?"

"You aren't making any sense at all, Low."

"I'm not? Fine. Go home. Go to bed. Get right in that warm place where you're almost asleep, and you don't even think about it anymore. Then I'll come banging on your door and blow my snot all over your bedroom and see how much sense you make."

"I just want to know," Maud said, crying again, "If you intend. To humiliate me. In public."

He stared at her for a long while. Then he said, "You know how many times I've thought about this? About having you up here like this? And having knowledge I could use as a tool for persuasion? And you just hand it to me, like you were giving me a cup of coffee. Like it means nothing to you at all. Are you really that innocent?"

"Coffee again. I don't even know what you're talking about."

He stared into her eyes until her color mounted and she had to look away. Her breath came quickly and she felt hot all over.

"You do now."

She didn't say anything.

"What do you think? You came up here with the intention of offering me something to keep me quiet. How about it, Maud? I'll be your villain. I'll be all the villain you could possibly wish for. Your virtue for my silence."

"I hate that word used that way."

Grinning, he said, "What? Silence?"

"Now who's being stupid?"

His face grew expressionless. He just stared at her. Then he covered her eyes with his hand.

"What color are my eyes, Maud?"

She found the warmth of his skin on her hot, wet eyes soothing. (He, feeling the wet eyelashes under his skin, the movement of her eyes under their lids, the faint tremors of the lids, themselves, was anything but soothed.)

"I don't know."

He dropped his hand. "Go home, Maud."

She did. She went home, and she sat up all night shuffling the deck of cards and playing solitaire over and over again, wondering about the color of Low's eyes and the feel of his hand on her face.

The next day, Fortune suggested that they go to town and hang out at the Sky Cafe. Maud was reluctant. There was a chance Lightning might be there. If he and Fortune acted like lovers in front of her, Maud wasn't sure how she would handle it. Also, Low would definitely be there. She didn't know if he could be trusted to keep his mouth shut. But Fortune prevailed at last, and they drove down into town.

The cafe was nearly empty when they got there. Regina took their order and brought them coffee and lunch. Low ignored them. He didn't even give Maud a knowing glance and acted just as if she hadn't gone to his apartment the night before.

"Here's the thing," Fortune said. "When he first approached me to find you, the rich old man promised me my memories, or enough money not to miss them, if I brought you to him. That's it. Doesn't mean you have to break the curse, if you're not inclined to. Naturally, I'm curious to know if he can deliver on his offer."

"Naturally," Maud agreed cautiously.

"If it's money he gives me, we can split it and go where our fancies take us without having to worry about making coin. We can still sing, just when and where we want. And we can stay in hotels! With real beds, Maud!"

"And if he gets your memories back for you?"

"Well, then, that's a whole other story, isn't it?"

"Sleeping Beauty goes back to her castle."

"Maybe. Or maybe Sleeping Beauty, if that's really who I am, goes right back to sleep because she likes her dreams better than her reality. Either way, I need to find out."

Maud played with her food and thought about what Fortune said. It occurred to her that either way, it didn't sound like Fortune was planning to stay in Sky and have a relationship with Lightning. Despite her dream of Sweet Honey, Maud clung to the idea that the kiss was just a one-off, and that Fortune wasn't the type of person to be tied down to a man. She touched the lady-in-the-moon pendant that Lightning had given her and took hope.

"What do you think, Maud? Should we tell him to go to hell? Or should we go see him, and see what he really can do for me?"

"Why didn't you just tell me about this in the first place?" Maud asked.

"Because I think he's a dangerous man," Fortune said.

Maud laughed. "I'm not afraid of him."

"You haven't met him."

"Oh, but I did...at the party. Aunt Helena introduced me. He was polite."

"Yeah. Before you cursed his grandson. Think about it." She got up and intercepted Low as he headed out for a smoke break. "Hey, Low...skip the cigarette. You promised to teach me how to tango, remember?"

"Fine, but you gotta hum 'La Cumparsita' for me," Low said.

"I'll do my best to fake it," Fortune said, grinning.

The idea that Fortune had had one or more actual private conversations with Low struck Maud as utterly bizarre... every bit as bizarre as the idea that Low knew how, and apparently loved, to dance. Maud watched them with a nagging sense of envy and admiration. Low was a good teacher, Fortune a quick and graceful pupil. They moved beautifully together. She was sick of finding beautiful things in Low, brought out by other people (or creatures, in the case of the blackbirds). She doubted she could bring out anything beautiful in him. That suited her. They could hate each other for the rest of their lives, and that would suit her fine.

When her lesson was finished and Low escaped for his cigarette, Fortune came back to the table and sat down. She took a drink of water and looked at Maud expectantly.

"So what do you think about going to the city?"

Maud reached across the table and took Fortune's hand in her own.

"I'd better put my sleeping bag back in the Bel Air," she said.

Fortune got out the DeLorme atlas, and she and Maud studied it at the kitchen table. Mama gave her recommendation for the route least likely to have heavy traffic, while Papa, coming home from work, advised the fastest and most direct route.

"Girls, I think I should take you," Mama said. "I don't like the idea of your meeting Magnus MacDonald on your own. He's a very powerful man."

"I'm not afraid of him," Maud said again. But she began to wonder if maybe she ought to be.

"Think of it this way," Mama said, smiling. "It would give me a good excuse to visit Sophie at college."

"I think we'll be all right," Fortune said. "I appreciate the offer. Don't think I don't. But—"

"But I know how to throw a curse," Maud said.

"That doesn't make me feel any better," Mama said.

Fortune and Maud went to bed early that night. They got up at six the next morning. Maud put on her little black dress and her black sandals and sprayed on some L'Heuer Bleue. She left the lady-in-the-moon necklace on the dresser.

"You look nice," Fortune said.

"Do I look like I mean business?"

"Definitely."

Mama cooked them a big breakfast and also packed them a sizable lunch. She made each of them take a twenty-dollar bill for expenses.

"You call me when you get into the city," she said. "Call me collect. I don't care how much it costs. I just want to know that you're all right. And call Sophie while you're at it. The more people who know where you are, the better. And if Magnus MacDonald makes you feel the least bit uncomfortable, I want you to leave right away. Don't worry about being polite. And drive carefully. City drivers have no concept of life or death. Are you sure you wouldn't like me to come with you?"

"We're positive, Mama," said Maud, as she and Fortune rushed to the door.

Fortune drove up the driveway and turned on to the dirt road. Maud looked back, half expecting to see Mama in a hiking headlamp, chasing after them with more instructions and advice.

"I really sort of adore your mother," Fortune said.

"So do I," said Maud, with a touch of pride.

The road trip, unlike their other road trips, was focused on reaching the city without tantalizing detours to hike to a waterfall, or to sing in a strange town. Fortune turned on the radio, which faded in and out as mountains blocked the radio waves. They sang snippets of songs and pointed out things they saw…a herd of deer, a roadside cascade, a patch of mountainside afire with vine maple and huckleberry. At the pass, Maud said abruptly, "Teach me the Long Maud song."

"Are you sure?" Fortune asked. "Won't it be traumatic for you?"

"I'm sure," said Maud.

Fortune sang the ballad, her voice sweet and pure.

"Who wrote it?" Maud asked, feeling the curious mixed sensations of anxiety and flattery.

"No idea," said Fortune. "I don't suppose you noticed any folk singers at the party?"

"I can barely remember the party at all. I remember flirting with Paolo, and him calling me a bitch and throwing wine on me. Oh, and his mother was rude about my height. Nobody expects you to be shy and sensitive if you're a tall girl. They expect you to throw furniture."

"They do not, Maud."

"Paolo's mother did. She practically called me Godzilla, except she probably doesn't know who that is. Nobody can tell from looking at me that I'm really a fair and fragile flower. It's not my fault my father is from Texas."

"I know you're a fair and fragile flower."

"Thank you."

"But you do have a temper."

"Well, yeah."

"And apparently you're a witch."

Maud thought for a moment. "I guess I am. Or was. I don't know how he expects me to pull off the curse, when I couldn't even say how I threw it in the first place. I wish Aunt Helena was still alive. Sing me the song again. I want to learn it. I think we should perform it."

They sang. Their ears popped as they lost elevation. Fortune pulled over at a ranger's station, and they demolished their plentiful lunch under a canopy of big leaf maple. Maud consulted the map.

"We're about 50 miles from the city," she said.

Gradually, the forest gave way to farmlands and small towns. The small towns gave way to larger towns, to suburbs, shopping centers, strip malls, big box stores. They merged onto the freeway, where traffic moved slowly. Fortune, her knuckles pale, kept her eyes on the lane. Maud watched the exit signs. At the other end of a broad bend in the freeway, the cityscape rose up, towers of glass and steel glittering in the mid-September sunlight. A helicopter dipped like a dragonfly. The broad bay, fiery as if with sequins, glinted through the gaps in the highrise canyons.

"They cut the city in half with this freeway," Maud said disapprovingly. "Look...up on the hill, all the churches and apartment buildings, and down there toward the water, all the skyscrapers."

"Where should they have put the freeway, then?"

"I don't know. Not here. Stay right. Ours is the next exit."

Fortune took the exit with a grateful sigh. Maud read the directions to his house that the rich old man had given Fortune. They passed a hospital, a private college (not Sophie's public college), and eventually found themselves in a neighborhood with stately houses of stone and brick, and impeccably but impersonally landscaped yards. Magnus MacDonald's house was fronted by a stone wall. Fortune pulled into the semi-circular drive and parked behind a late model Lincoln Continental The air outside was warm. Juncos and chickadees scattered to the shrubs.

"All right?" Fortune asked Maud.

"Yes. You?"

"I guess."

They walked up the steps to the front door. Maud rang the doorbell.

An elderly man answered the door. He stared at Maud, then Fortune.

"Well done," he said to Fortune, unsmiling. "Come in, both of you."

Maud got the impression, as she and Fortune followed Mr. MacDonald into a small study, of a house of costly austerity. The color palette was muted and cold, the ornamentation sparse, the furniture luxurious and forbidding. There was nothing to indicate that Mr. MacDonald traveled, very little to show that he read, and nothing of music to be seen or heard. At least, she told herself with a grim smile, he was not likely to murder her. Blood would show too stark on the ice-blue carpet.

He sat down behind a desk and gestured for the girls to take the couple of chairs on the other side. "Please, sit." They did, and snuck glances at each other before turning their attention back to him.

To Maud, he said, "I suppose she told you why I wanted to see you."

"That's why I'm here," Maud said. "You want me to break the curse I threw on Paolo."

"That is correct."

"I'll be happy to discuss that with you," Maud said, surprising herself, "as soon as you've given Fortune what you promised her."

"She told you that, too, eh? Discretion isn't one of your virtues, is it?"

"Not much," Fortune admitted. "After a while, it seemed like honesty was the best policy. I don't see why it would make a difference to you, one way or another."

"I prefer that things be done my way," he said.

"Everybody prefers that," said Fortune.

"Here." Mr. MacDonald took a thick, legal-sized manila envelope out of a desk drawer and shoved it across the desk to Fortune. "Take your pay and go wait in the car."

"Excuse me?" Maud said, angry. "Why should she?"

"Because her job is done," Mr. MacDonald said. "I have no more need of her. And I would prefer to speak to you in private."

"It's fine, Maud," Fortune said, getting up. "I don't mind. Unless you're afraid?"

"I'm not afraid," she said, glaring at Mr. MacDonald. "I just don't like the way he dismissed you. You see, Fortune is my friend. I'm sure even you have had at least one friend in your life."

Magnus MacDonald actually smiled at this. "At least one," he admitted. "For many, many years, your great-aunt Helena was my good friend. Forgive me for dismissing yours."

"Tell it to Fortune," Maud said.

"I beg your pardon," Mr. MacDonald said to Fortune. "I hope you'll understand that I wish to speak to Maud alone."

"No problem," Fortune said. She took the envelope. To Maud, she said, "I'll just be in the car if you need me. All right?"

Maud nodded, and Fortune left. After the sound of the front door shutting, Mr. MacDonald, who'd been watching Fortune, turned his attention to Maud.

"Stand up and turn around. I want to have a look at you."

Maud did as she was told.

"Your dress is wrinkled, front and back," he said. "Your great-aunt's clothing was never wrinkled."

"I was in the car for a long—"

"Not much to your breasts, is there? You're far too tall and skinny. Not that Paolo is much to look at. He never was a handsome boy. Sit down."

Mortified and angry again, Maud sat.

"I won't waste your time or mine with any chitchat. You know why you're here. Presumably you remember cursing my grandson. You didn't for a while, according to your great-aunt."

"I remember."

"Are you going to break the curse?"

"Of course not. He humiliated me. He deserved to be cursed."

"Two years is long enough for petty revenge. You lower yourself by continuing to hold a grudge. Do the right thing and lift the curse. I will ask you one more time."

"I have no idea how to do that, and I don't see why I should care."

"Just as I thought. Your mother married trash, and you're trash, too. Here." He reached into his desk and drew out another fat manila envelope. He threw it at her. She looked inside. It was full of hundred-dollar bills.

"Go ahead and count it. I know you want to. More when you bring Paolo back home."

Maud tossed the envelope back on the desk. It landed with a heavy smack.

"What? Not enough? I had a feeling. Why else did you curse him to love you, if not to rob us blind?"

"I don't know who you think I am, but I don't want your money," Maud said. She was so angry she was on the verge of tears. "I don't want anything to do with your money. Anyway, if Paolo were really in love with me, wouldn't he try and find me?"

"He did. He calls himself Low McElvy these days."

"*Low?*" She felt ill. "*Low* is Paolo?"

"Yes."

Maud laughed. She laughed until tears came to her eyes. Catching her breath, she said, "I'll tell you flat, the curse didn't work. Low does not love me. And if he did…ah, I think I'm going to throw up."

"If you don't want him to love you, then break the curse."

"I don't know how! Do I just say it? I break the curse. Oh God, do I have to say it to *him*?"

"Break the curse and send him home. Do it for your great-aunt's legacy, if not for Low's sake."

"What does my great-aunt have to do with it?"

"You destroyed her reputation. She brought you to Paolo's party, and you ruined my family. Helena died in utter disgrace."

"How dare you say that about her? You seem to be forgetting that Paolo threw wine in my face! I blessed him and he humiliated me."

"He was drunk," Mr. MacDonald said grudgingly. "I understand, and mind you, I keep tabs on Paolo through various sources, that he hasn't touched a drop since that night. Surely that signals remorse?"

"If he were remorseful, he'd apologize, instead of pretending to be somebody else."

"Perhaps he's tried. Perhaps he's not physically able. 'I swear that every word you speak to me will only make me scorn you more than I scorn you right now.' That was a part of your curse. You left him without a means to defend himself or make amends."

"I—did I say that?"

"Yes."

Angry though she was, Maud had to admit to herself that that wasn't fair. Everybody should have the ability to apologize for doing wrong. Not that she would accept Low's apology if he made one...

"Do the right thing, by your aunt and your own sense of honor. Break the curse and send Paolo back home where he belongs."

Yes. Send Low back home, away from Sky, where there would be no chance of him spreading tales about her. Send him out of her life.

"I'll do my best," she said. "That's all I can do."

Mr. MacDonald smiled. It wasn't a nice smile. "There's a good girl."

Fortune was sitting on the hood of the car, eyes closed, face turned up to the mid-September sunlight, when Maud left Magnus MacDonald's house. She opened her eyes at the sound of the front door closing and smiled at Maud.

"You're alive," she said.

"Barely," said Maud.

Fortune hopped down. She and Maud got into the car, and she started the engine.

"Let's get out of here," Maud said.

"Don't you want to count the loot?" Fortune asked. "There's quite a lot of it."

"I don't want any of it," Maud said. "Let's find a pay phone and call Mama, and then let's go see Sophie. God, Fortune. Low is Paolo MacDonald."

Fortune said, "I had a feeling he might be."

"You *did*? Why didn't you say anything?"

"Because I didn't know," Fortune said. "And would it have made a difference anyway?"

II.

I knew a young McBride girl was going to be at my party. Grandfather spent some time haranguing me on the importance of being polite to her. "You don't know...she may be to you what Helena McBride is to me. If this family is successful, it's in no small part due to the McBride influence." That was enough to predispose me against her. I liked Helena McBride. I really did. But I gave not a single damn about the success of our family.

It was a symbiotic relationship, that between the Mac-Donalds and the McBrides. My father thought it was bullshit. My mother thought it was vulgar. But my grandfather was a true believer in Helena McBride's power, and he wanted me to be a true believer, too.

The thing I remember about Helena was that she was kind to me. She paid attention to me in ways that nobody else did—not my grandfather and certainly not my parents. She listened to me, and because of that, I actually spoke to her.

I was bullied at school, bullied at home, dictated to, told who and what I would be, how I would carry the family into the next century, how it was my duty. I wasn't arrogant. They tore me down too much for me to be arrogant. At least, I wasn't *personally* arrogant. I wasn't smart enough or good looking enough or athletic enough for that. But I was a Mac-Donald, and that made me a cut above. That entitled me to be arrogant.

"Don't forget you're a MacDonald," they would say to me. How could I forget it?

The semester I brought home all As except for a B in physical education, all I heard was "Too bad about the B in PE." No word about the As. Perfection was the bar.

Then one semester I ended up taking home ec, one of the very few boys who did, and found that if I followed instructions, I would always get good results. Cooking and baking were little miracles to me. After school I took over the kitchen at home and cooked for fun, all under the watchful eye of our chef. Mother allowed it as a whimsy. But when I mentioned wanting to study the culinary arts in school, well, that brought on a storm of anger, accusations, and wailing of how could I do this to them, after all they had done for me.

When I drunkenly threw the wine in her face, I didn't see *Maud*. I didn't see a human being. I just saw a tool of my family, a means of humiliating me and keeping me in line.

Which is not to say that I didn't earn that curse.

The day after my eighteenth birthday party, my grandfather took me around to Helena's house. He accused Helena of collusion.

"Couldn't you have seen this coming? You must have seen this coming!"

"I swear to you, Magnus, I didn't. If I had, do you actually believe I would have brought her?"

"Well, do something about it."

"I can't."

"What do you mean, you can't?"

"Just that. Only Maud can break the curse."

"Then get her out here."

"I can't. She's very sick."

"Well, call me the instant she gets better."

"I'll see what I can do."

"You'd better."

My parents didn't believe in the curse. They took me to neurologists, psychiatrists, and a number of other-ists in an effort to find out what was wrong with me—why I bit the inside of my mouth until it bled, why my words slurred, why I would claw at myself until it looked as if I had been thrown into a sack with a dozen angry cats. I once heard my mother weeping that she'd given birth to an idiot. An idiot. How's that for maternal love? My father, not to be outdone, collared me and assured me it was not too late for him to have another son. I asked him if he intended to get another wife first, since Mother was getting up there in years. He slapped me.

Of course, these physical manifestations had nothing to do with the substance of Maud's curse. She'd just cursed me to love her, with the promise that the love would be requited by hatred. Maybe I was punishing myself for humiliating her. Maybe I was punishing myself for being a MacDonald, with the typical MacDonald arrogance and typical MacDonald disregard for the feelings of other human beings.

After all, I'd learned that from the masters of arrogance and disregard.

I thought about Maud constantly. I dreamed about her. I doodled her name in the margins of my books. I wondered where she was and when I could see her again. I didn't care if she hated me. I just wanted to see her, apologize to her, ask her forgiveness.

I went to see Helena McBride a couple of months before she died of lung cancer. It was on a Saturday, when Maud's mother wasn't there, just the caregiver from home health. Helena was a little thinner, a little paler, a little weaker, but she surprised me. She didn't cough or wheeze. Her grip was strong when she took my hand. She didn't look the way I imagined a dying person would. She just looked tired.

"Paolo," she said, "I'm so sorry." She touched my cheek where I'd clawed it, and ran her hand over my roughly shaven head. "I had no idea she was so powerful. I had no idea."

"It was my fault," I mumbled. "I deserved it."

"No," she said. "You did wrong, but you don't deserve this curse, and neither does Maud. She cursed herself too, you know."

"To hate me? Some curse."

"Hatred is a terrible burden. It hurts nobody but the person doing the hating."

"I'm leaving home," I said abruptly.

"Oh. That's good. That's good, Paolo. I'm glad you're leaving. What are you going to do?"

"Get a job somewhere. See if anybody will hire me. City Southern Community College has got a culinary arts program and a baking and pastry program. See about doing those."

"I'm so glad," Helena said.

"About Maud," I said. "Can I see her? Can I apologize to her and ask her to break the curse?"

"Paolo, she doesn't even know she cursed you. She has no memory whatsoever of the party or anything that happened that night."

"Then how can she hate me? Does she even remember meeting me?"

"No. I wish there was something I could do, but I'm awfully weak."

"That's okay," I said. It wasn't okay. She knew it, too.

When I left to study culinary arts at City Southern, my parents cut me off without a penny. However, it's amazing how long and well a body can live on the proceeds from selling a Ferrari. Fortunately, the title was in my name, which was my father's mistake. I studied culinary arts during the day and got a job as a dishwasher at night. That was how I met Eddy Avery. He bussed tables at my restaurant. We got to be friends...at least, as much friends as I was used to having. Though I kept my skin-clawing to a minimum, people didn't really like the looks of me or want to be around me. The shaved head, with all its nicks, probably had something to do with it.

Eddy was an artist who specialized in photorealistic drawings. That August, he had a small show at a bar called the Rendezvous. He asked me to come see it on opening night. I'd seen photos of his work on his cell phone but hadn't seen any in person.

One of his portraits was of Maud. I recognized her immediately. Her face was turned three quarters, her eyes downcast, her shoulders bare. Her dark hair was parted in the middle and dressed in looped braids. She wore pendant earrings in her ears. They might well have been genuine antiques. The drawing ended, tantalizingly, just below her collar bone. Was she nude beyond the parameters of the drawing? the viewer was invited to wonder.

I smiled when I saw the title: "Maud Is Not Seventeen." Just how many people quoted that bit of Tennyson at her?

I hadn't thought about her much, except in bed at night. I hadn't had time, between going to school and working, to brood upon her. But the drawing brought it all back—the night of the party, the way we flirted, my appalling treatment of her, and her curse. I bought the drawing from Eddy on the spot. The show would run for two weeks. He wouldn't let me take it home until the show was over, so I took a picture of it with my phone. I knew I was going to be gazing upon it tonight while on my date with Mrs. Palm and her five lovely daughters. In the past, I'd had to rely on my memory.

"Tell me about her. Tell me everything about her."

"What do you want to know?"

"Everything. Starting with where she lives"

"She lives in my hometown, Sky. She's, oh, a few years younger than me. I went to school with her sister Sophie. She works part time for my aunt, waitressing at the Sky Cafe. I think she's set to graduate high school this year."

"Does she have a boyfriend?"

"No-o," he said. "Those Caldecote girls have got too much McBride in them to date mere small-town boys. I had a massive crush on Sophie from first grade on. She went to prom with me but only as a friend. Look, Maud's a stunner, but I don't think she's your type."

"What do you know about my type? You ever seen me with a woman?"

Eddy admitted he hadn't.

"You mean I'm not Maud's type," I said. "That's true. I'm not anybody's type."

"Hey, now," said Eddy, who was the handsomest man of my acquaintance and could afford to be generous.

"Tell me more about her. Tell me anything you know."

"I really don't know much. She's from a big family. She's a good kid. She sings all the time. My aunt likes her. Most everybody likes her."

Eddy was no help. But that night I did an Internet search on Sky. And I saw that you could get there by train. And I knew that was what I was going to do. I was going to get on a train and go to Sky.

"Think your aunt will give me a job?" I asked Eddy the next night.

"Oh, man. You're starting to sound like a stalker."

"You should know me better than that. Have you ever seen me creep on a woman?"

Eddy admitted he hadn't.

"Just call your aunt. Just ask her. Do it for a friend, hey?"

Eddy said, "I have to say, Sky is a good place to think things over. The air smells good. It's quiet, and you can go hiking."

"I don't hike," I told him.

"Well, whatever," he said "I'll call her tomorrow. Is tomorrow soon enough for you?"

I told him it was. I knew it would have to be.

I packed what I wanted in a backpack, including the framed drawing of Maud, and left what I didn't want. I took the train to Sky and went right to the Sky Cafe. And there was Maud, waitressing. And I knew I'd made the best decision of my life.

It was one of their busy times. The train stopped in Sky for an hour and brought in a lot of business. I decided to order coffee, and wait, and watch Maud as she went from table to table, bringing food, filling coffee cups, smiling and laughing at things her customers said.

"Now, my lovelies, what can I get for you?" she asked a middle-aged couple at the table next to mine. The way she said it was artless and completely charming. If she'd called me "my lovely," I don't know what I would have done.

When the cafe had mostly emptied out, she brought me my bill. "You'd better hurry. The train's going to leave in a minute or two."

"I'm here to see Robin," I said. Then she really *looked* at me. She gave me the once-over, taking in my drab clothes, my backpack, my busted high tops, my shaved head.

"Is Robin expecting you?" she asked, her voice doubtful.

"I'm here about a job."

Her eyes momentarily flashed wide in apparent alarm. "Excuse me a minute."

She got Robin, who took me back to her office and interviewed me. I got the job because Eddy vouched for me, and because Robin trusted his judgment. It wasn't full-time work, she warned me. There were slow times that I'd have off. She'd hire me as dishwasher and busboy and see how things went. She might have me do some prep cook work when things got busy. She also agreed to rent me Eddy's apartment upstairs while he was gone.

When all that was settled, she introduced me to Maud. Maud didn't remember me, of course, just as her aunt had told me, but she didn't have to. The curse was apparently in full force anyway. She followed Robin around the cafe in a state of outrage. When she failed to convince Robin that I was a dangerous criminal, she turned to me.

"You," Maud said, pointing at me and narrowing her eyes. "You watch your step."

My heart pounded. I wanted to take her in my arms and kiss her. I wanted to take her upstairs and lay her down. I wanted to take her to the Justice of the Peace and marry her. And the curse was in full force. *I swear that every word you speak to me will only make me scorn you more than I scorn you right now.*

"I'd rather watch yours, Cowboy Girl," I mumbled, nodding at her boots. "You look like you could crush a heifer."

We went on as we had begun. Badly.

I learned how best to annoy her. For instance, I'd be working in the kitchen and stop to pop all my joints.

"That's revolting," she said. "Everything you do is revolting."

"I do it just for you, Cowboy Girl," I said.

Maud was always singing in that spooky, scratchy, sexy voice of hers. She sang because she thought nobody was listening. When she wasn't singing, she was humming. My family wasn't musical beyond being on the board of the Civic Light Opera and the Symphony. I wasn't used to people singing just for the hell of it. She had a fondness for folk music and for the songs of Johnny Cash. Maud singing "Folsom Prison" slow like a dirge would set the hairs of my arms standing straight up.

I couldn't figure out what a mostly good-natured (to everybody but me) girl saw in the gloomy music she favored. It might have been her way of coping with fear, the way kids look at pictures of death and disaster online—as a way of knowing the pain life can throw at you. Or it might have been a streak of McBrideism coming out to play. A girl who could throw a curse must have at least a passing acquaintance with darkness.

Lightning was a good guy. I liked him better than I liked most people. But it didn't escape my notice that Maud was interested in him. She pretended she wasn't. She treated him with considerably less respect than she did her other customers. But I could see the way she looked at him when he wasn't watching. I could see her quick primping before going to take his order. I heard her lovesick-high-school-girl sighs. Why *wouldn't* she sigh? He was tall and good looking—two things I wasn't. And the curse ground into me like a broken bottle.

And then Lightning brought Fortune over the red bridge into Sky, the very day of Maud's eighteenth, and my twentieth, birthday, and I could tell right away that the jig was up for Maud's crush. Inwardly, I gloated. I wondered how Maud could be so blind to the obvious chemistry between Fortune and Lightning. She was clearly smitten with Fortune her own self.

It wasn't but a few nights after I'd sat with Maud when she cried in the theater that she came to my apartment again. It was well past midnight. Maud had on a wrinkled black dress and a pair of black sandals. I'd never seen her out of cowboy boots before.

"I just came from the city, and I'm really tired, so don't jerk me around. What is your name? I mean, your *real* name? Be honest."

"My birth name or my legal name?"

"Birth name."

I said, "Paolo MacDonald."

She slapped my face as if throwing her entire life energy into it.

"Cheese and rice!" I yelled. "That freakin' *hurt*!"

"You deserved it. So it really is true," she said. "Could my life possibly be any stupider?"

"What's your problem?" I demanded, rubbing my burning cheek.

She squinted. "Yeah. I can see it now. Throw some hair on you, and a tuxedo. Give you a cup of pomegranate wine to lob at me."

"Oh." She'd finally remembered. "I'm sorry." I meant it. I'd meant it from the moment I flung the wine. And I'd waited two years to say it to her.

Strange girl that she was, she made a sweeping gesture as if my apology wasn't even necessary. "Have you suffered?"

"Yes," I said.

She smiled, showing her teeth. "Good. But listen to me. If you're in love with me, I'm seriously going to vomit my life out. I hereby break the curse. So don't be in love with me."

"Okay," I said.

"Okay. So am I done here?"

"Suits me."

"Good. Now you can go back to your jerk family. Don't send them after me again. If the curse isn't broken now, it never will be."

"I didn't send my jerk family after you. Wait, did you *meet* them?"

"I met your grandfather."

"I'm really sorry to hear that. Do I have to go back right now?"

"I guess you can give Robin two weeks' notice. But don't ever talk to me again."

And she left, just like that.

A few days later, this big guy came in to the Sky Cafe looking for Maud. When I say big, I mean college football player big. He walked with a kind of stiff-legged swagger, arms close to his sides, hands fisted, that I always associated with jocks. He was good-looking in a jock kind of way, or might have been except for the porn 'tache and the hair crisp with product.

He came in during our downtime, when Robin and I were playing double solitaire in the dining room.

"Sit anywhere you like," Robin called. "Menu's on the table."

"Don't you remember me, Ms. Avery?"

Robin squinted at the guy hulking over her. "Lionel? Lionel Pipping?"

"Lionel Pipping?" I mouthed at her. She kicked me under the table. With a name like Lionel Pipping, you almost had to be huge to live it down.

"See, I knew you'd remember me."

"How are you doing?"

"Great. Hey, I heard Maud Caldecote works here. Where is she?" He looked around the empty dining room as if expecting her to suddenly appear.

"That's old news. Maud doesn't work here anymore."

"That's too bad," he said. He grinned. I didn't like it. "She had such a crush on me in high school, she actually kissed a slug just to get my attention. She was a dog then, but I heard she grew up tasty. Guess I'll have to go up to Wolf's House to see if she's worth the climb."

I was up. I'm not sure how I got to my feet so quickly. He towered over me a good six inches, but I got up in his face on the wings of pure jealousy.

"Who the hell are you?" I demanded.

"Who the hell are *you*?"

"That's none of your damned business, and neither is Maud Caldecote."

He laughed. "Don't tell me a mush-mouthed runt like you is her *boyfriend*."

"Cool it, boys," said Robin. But I could tell there was no love lost between her and Lionel.

"I'll cool it when he gets his ugly face out of town," I said.

"No way would she be giving it up to you. I'll have to ask her when I see her."

That was when I threw the first punch. As it turned out, it was my only punch. I woke up in the ER. They'd already X-rayed me and found no obvious fractures. My face hurt like hell, and I couldn't open my right eye. The right side of my nose was running. When Robin handed me a tissue, I blew my nose and felt the skin on the right side of my nose inflate. I didn't blow my nose again.

"Well, you look pretty as a picture," Robin said.

"You should see the other guy," I said.

"The other guy doesn't have a scratch on him. Here's hoping the other guy doesn't press charges."

I stood and found a mirror and then wished I hadn't. "Jesus Christ."

"Amen," said Robin. "I'm going to use the pay phone, ask Mollie Caldecote to bring down some of her calendula oil. You're going to need it."

I got discharged not soon afterwards, and Robin took me home. I lit a cigarette and puffed it cautiously. It hurt.

Somebody knocked on the door. I figured it was either Robin or, much less likely, Mrs. Caldecote.

"Who is it?"

"Maud."

"What do *you* want?"

"Mama sent me. I've got calendula oil for you."

I opened the door, ready to see her disgust. What happened to her face when she saw me made my heart pound. She never was any good at hiding how she felt. She dropped the jar. We both bent down to get it, and she bumped my face. I yelled, she apologized.

Then, decisively, she said, "Sit down." She washed her hands and sat beside me, opened the jar of calendula oil and touched some to my split lip. I winced from the pain.

"Sorry."

"Your hands," I said.

"What about them?"

"They're shaking."

She held them out and looked at them. Sure enough, they trembled.

"What do you expect? It's brutal," she said. "What he did to you. It's the worst thing I've ever seen. It makes me wish I weren't a human being."

"Are you going to throw up?"

"I don't know."

"Breathe." I gave a short, bitter laugh. "Thought you hated me so much, you'd be glad to see it."

She said, "I thought so, too."

"At least you're honest about it."

"Well, I've hated Lionel Pipping longer than I've hated you."

"Always the bridesmaid, never the bride."

"After Mama told me, I went to my room and laughed and laughed. I'm not proud of that. Especially not now that I've seen what he did to you. Here, hold still." She took a deep breath and held my jaw in one hand. She smoothed the oil over my wounds, frowning in concentration, being very careful around my right eye.

"What even made you pick a fight with Lionel Pipping, of all people? He's ginormous."

"I did it for you."

"Yeah, right."

"Okay. I did it for me. He was talking shit about you."

"So what? You could have ignored it."

"Aren't you even curious what he said?"

She yawned hugely. "Not in the least."

She touched my face so tenderly, so gently. She glanced into my eyes and stopped, arrested, as if seeing *me* for the first time, seeing the humanity in me for the first time. Her thumb rested lightly on my jaw, right over my pulse point.

"I hated him especially because every time I twisted my apple stem to see who I'd marry, I always ended up on L, and he was the only L I knew."

"Low begins with L."

She blinked, lowered her hands, screwed the lid on the hex jar, took my hand, put the jar into it.

This was the first kind thing she had ever done for me. The first time she had ever touched me—a gesture that began in pity and ended in something else, or so I wished. She made to stand, but I held her wrist fast. I couldn't just let her go.

Find my humanity, Maud. Bring it out. Coax it out. To be this close to her, to feel her breath warm and steady, the touch of her, the scent of her. She could respond to me like she'd respond to any hurt animal. And it was a measure of my hunger that I'd let her tend me that way.

But what I said was "Robin don't want me working for a while. She's maybe afraid stuff'll drip onto the food."

"Eeew!"

And quickly I said, "Come to me tomorrow."

She caught her breath, surprised.

"Come to me every night, just like you did tonight, until my face is healed up."

She nodded. She hummed assent. She would come. She would be here again tomorrow night.

"Stop shaving your head," she said. "This cut needs to heal. And don't scratch!"

I wanted to loosen her hair. Loosen her hair, feel it against my face. Mary Magdalen with her jar of balm.

"Whatever," I mumbled.

She came to me, then, every night, to treat me with her mother's oil, and to talk about Lightning. Sometimes she'd forget where I was, and lean close to me, so that I could feel the warmth radiating from her. Her hair would brush my bare shoulder. Her breath would tease my ear.

"He's happy," she said. "And she's happy. They're both happy, without me."

And I understood what she meant. Their happiness had nothing to do with her presence or her absence. She was a null set. I understood. And she'd understand, eventually, how somebody who meant so much to her could care so little about her. She'd understand.

She'd live.

And so would I.

"Love breaks me, and breaks me, and breaks me. I can't think of a single pleasant thing associated with love."

"You're not thinking hard enough," I said. "How about that thrill you get when you think about him? What about that time when you think it's possible?"

"It's not possible. Maybe it was never possible."

"He's a man. He's got eyes."

She brightened at that. "Do you think he ever thought of me that way?"

"I repeat: he's a man. He's got eyes."

"Then why didn't he do anything about it?"

"Maybe because he knew it wouldn't work out. You can want somebody and not *want* them."

But this was the wrong thing to say. Maud started weeping again. "What's wrong with me that nobody *wants* me?"

What I wanted to say was "I want you." What I did say was "Maybe if you weren't such a crybaby."

"God, I hate you!" she said.

The third night we fought over Eddy's photography studio.

"You don't go in there, do you?" Maud demanded, suspicious and unexplainably insecure. "That's Eddy's studio."

"You sound pretty protective of Eddy."

"Well, it's his studio."

"So? You think I'm gonna wreck it?"

"You simply existing in there wrecks it."

"Go home, Maud."

The fourth night I was caught by surprise how soft she became with me, her wounded animal. She touched me gently, examined my face to see how my bruises and cuts were fading, healing. Every night, it seemed like she saw a little bit more of me, like she was discovering the rooms in a condemned house.

The fifth night, I asked her to sing for me.

"Sing what?"

"I don't know. Something sad."

She sang me "Barbara Allen." When her voice broke, and her face dropped against my bare shoulder and she started to cry, I made myself be still. I was learning patience again, for the thousandth time. Patience, patience, always patience. Otherwise, the bird spooks and flies away, and you're left alone on the shore with a handful of bird seed. One of her tears rolled down my shoulder blade. She didn't make a lot of noise. It was her sort of helpless, baffled grief that got to me. Which of us was the dumb animal now?

"Don't blow your nose on me."

"I wasn't going to. I don't need to, anyway. I can smell you, see?" And she sniffed loudly. A moment passed. "You smell nice."

She shifted, and a hank of her hair slid down my back.

"Maud."

"What?"

Move. Don't move. Back off. Don't budge. Get the hell out of here. Don't ever leave.

"You wanna cup of coffee?"

She pulled away and looked at me skeptically. "It's past midnight."

"Yeah, so?"

"I don't want to be up all night."

"Go home, then."

"Are you okay?"

I just wanted to reach for her and pull her to me, and hold her against me hard, and just hold her and hold her and hold her until my arms gave out.

"I love you." Maybe I didn't say it loud enough for her to understand. Maybe I did. She looked scared.

"What did you say?" she said.

"I'm fine. Go home. Go to bed."

She nodded at me, not losing that fretful crease between her eyebrows.

"Any old time, Maud. I have to get some sleep, too."

"Okay."

She didn't get up.

"Maud…"

She gazed at me in silence. Then she said, as if from a dream, "What happens if I kiss you?"

"What do you mean?"

210

"Do you turn into something else, or do I?"

"Try it and find out," I said.

"I'd rather not," she said, getting up to go. "If it's all the same to you."

On the sixth night, there wasn't any balm on her finger-tips when she touched me, and her eyes were soft, slightly unfocused. Her hand rested against my face and she said, half-consciously, "Your face."

"What about it?"

"It's yours. It's your face again." She shook herself out of her reverie. "You look different with hair."

"Better?"

She rolled her eyes. "Like that's even possible." But she was blushing.

Now my blood was rushing to all the wrong places. Wrong, in this context. Exquisite torture, as it had been from Day One, teased out to an almost unbearable pitch. I couldn't seduce her. All I wanted to do was seduce her.

"Kiss me." I said it hard, my voice flat. She looked astonished, drew back, blushed deeper.

"I don't know how," she stammered.

I wondered if what she really meant was, she was expecting *me* to kiss *her*.

She could work for it, if she wanted it.

"Good night, Maud."

"I've never kissed anybody before—" She sounded apologetic.

"Good night, Maud."

"Low, I—"

"Good night, Maud."

She got up. She backed toward the door. She turned. She opened the door. "Good night." She went out. She shut the door. She was gone.

The next night, after she knocked, I just opened the door and stared at her.

"May I come in please?" she asked.

I stood aside. She came in. I shut the door, and turned the lock. She sat down on the bed. I leaned against the door and watched her. She looked at her hands. Then she looked up, and her face was determined. She got up and came to me, and I said, "Take off the hat."

"Oh." Flustered, she took off her hat. She bent toward me and her lips brushed, just brushed, against mine.

"Did I do it right?"

I shook my head.

"Oh." She bent forward, pressed her mouth to mine, drew back.

Again, I shook my head. Suddenly, the old Maud was back, irate,

"Well, you could help me, you know. Like I've ever kissed anybody before. Like I've even had time to prepare in my mind. I mean, just all of a sudden, you expect me to kiss you, just like that—"

"Did you need a 24-hour waiting period?"

"I need *something*! I mean, kissing…you don't suppose I've gone my whole life without kissing any man because I was just waiting around for you—"

I unlocked the door and opened it for her. "Good night, Maud." I didn't know whether she looked more hurt or angry. "Goodbye. Your wounded rat is all better now. He doesn't need you anymore."

"Go to hell, you bastard!"

"'Now, gods, stand up for bastards!'"

She slammed out, pounded down the stairs, stopped, stomped back up and pounded on the door.

I opened it.

"My hat," she said.

I pulled her inside. This time, I shut the door and backed her against it. She made a little startled sound. *What big eyes you have.* I felt like a villain. *How about it, Maud? I'll be your villain. I'll be all the villain you could possibly wish for.*

"You do it like this," I told her. I pulled her head down toward mine.

And I kissed her.

I really kissed her.

When I let her go and drew away, her face was dazed. Just for a moment. Her eyes were black, unfocused. And she sighed. Then a tremor ran through her body, as if she was shaking something off, and she shoved me away. Fury. She opened the door, stormed out, without even a parting imprecation. I had rendered her speechless with rage.

It was finished. I was alone. These past seven nights were wiped away. It was only guilt and pity, after all. I wished to hell I'd never come here, never sought her out.

She'd forgotten her hat again. I didn't think she'd come back for it.

I got out her portrait. There was her face, her eyes cast down. There, her bare shoulders. I wanted to take a knife to the portrait, or throw something at it, or set it on fire and watch it burn. I wanted to yell every bad name I knew at her image, every foul name I'd ever heard, but I didn't. I couldn't. She was none of those things. All she was, was Maud, and all the layers of meaning in her name.

And I was just a mush-mouthed mutt and meant as much to her as any stray trying to hump her leg.

"It's not fair," she said, leaning in the doorway. I just about yelped, seeing her there. Caught with my hand in the cookie jar. Her eyes were steady, her voice steady. "You don't give me any time to get used to change at all. I can't move as quickly as you. I'm not stupid. Don't think I'm saying that. It's just…some people need longer to think things over."

"Take as long as you want," I said.

She nodded toward the picture. "I always wondered what happened to that."

"Now you know."

"What's she like?" She sat down on the bed next to me. "The Maud in the drawing?"

I watched her for a long time, barely blinking. A tiny muscle near my mouth twitched. I swallowed. "Want me to show you?"

She nodded.

I curved my hand around her cheek, under her chin. Ever so gently, I drew her face toward mine. I kissed her, slowly, lusciously. I slowly, slowly drew away.

My voice quiet, I said, "She's just like that. Just exactly like that."

Maud didn't go home that night.

III.

The next morning, he made a picnic breakfast for them and they went down to the red bridge together. They stepped from rock to rock until they reached the biggest boulder. His pants kept trying to slide off his hips. She loved watching him hitch them up, an absent-minded gesture nevertheless invested with a brusque grace. They ate, and then he lay down, his head on her lap, and lit a cigarette.

"You should quit," she said, taking it from his lips and dragging on it. She handed it back and blew out a thin stream of smoke.

"Okay. I gotta obey my Cowboy Girl." He tossed the cigarette into the creek.

"*Your* Cowboy Girl? What makes me *your* Cowboy Girl?"

"Anybody else call you that? No? Didn't think so."

"So naming me makes me yours?"

"Sure. Just like calling me a bastard makes me yours."

"I'm not going to do that anymore," Maud said.

"What are you going to call me?"

She ran her hand over the week's dark stubble that grew on his head. "My demon lover."

Low laughed. "I can see it now. You go home today. Your mom says 'Maud, where you been all the night long?' 'With my demon lover, Ma,' you say. 'Well, I hope he is worth the loss of your immortal soul, daughter.' 'Believe me, Ma, he is.'"

"I would never say that," Maud said, laughing. "I call her Mama, not Ma."

Low was silent for a long time. "You going to tell her? About last night? About us?"

Maud sighed. "How can I? Caldecote girls don't spend the night with boys they're not married to."

"You should stop pretending to be a Caldecote girl. Be proud to be a McBride girl. Be proud to be *my* McBride girl. You're a witch, for crying out loud. Embrace your witchiness. Or, if you prefer, go away and moon over Lightning and don't visit me again."

"I don't know what to do."

"Just be who you are, Maud."

"Oh? And who am I?" she asked, her eyebrows arched.

"A hot-blooded girl with more libido than sense."

"I *really* hate you."

"See? More libido than sense."

"And I have to keep on hating you," she said. "Especially now."

"Why especially now?"

"Because if I stop hating you, if I—if I do something crazy like fall in love with you, you'll truly be free of the curse and you won't want me anymore."

He nodded. "That's a distinct possibility. But at least then you'll be crying over me instead of Lightning. I like the sound of that."

"Don't stop wanting me," she said. "Please."

"I can think of a way," he said, "to keep me by your side *and* redeem you from your fallen woman status."

"What's that?"

"Marry me."

"You are so hilarious."

"I'm serious, Maud. Marry me."

She gazed at him, troubled. He *was* serious.

"I want you in my bed, and I want you in my life."

"Forever?" she said.

"Forever."

"I've never seriously thought about marriage," she said slowly.

"Then think about it frivolously. Come play with me, Maud. Come play with me for the rest of our lives."

She smiled, then covered her mouth with one hand.

"You know you want to," he said in a persuasive tone.

"We can't do it here," she said. "There's a three-day waiting period after you get your marriage license. It would be all over town within a half hour."

"Ah, so you want to get married in secret."

"You did ask me to come play with you," she said. "What's more playful than a secret marriage?"

"You don't want a wedding?"

"No," she said. "And I really don't want Papa and Mama to talk me out of it. I know they would. At least they'd try. They'd say I was too young to get married."

"And they'd be right. You're too young, and I'm too young, but let's do it anyway," said Low. "I'll see if I can borrow Robin's station wagon and we can get our license the next county over."

Later, Maud went into the cafe, "Just to hang out," she said. Wanting to be useful, she put up a stack of plates and glanced at him with only her eyes visible over her raised arms. He winked at her. She lowered her arms slowly, smiling as if daydreaming.

"Come here."

He had been blending spices into a garam masala. Now he rubbed some across her lips. She licked it off, held his hand fast and sucked it off his finger. But when Robin came in, they completely ignored each other.

Robin was sharp. She noticed their secret smiles. She took Maud aside. "Is something going on that would make your mother cry?"

"No. Absolutely not."

"I feel a certain responsibility toward you."

"Everything is as it should be," Maud said.

That night he taught her how to waltz. She loved the feel of his hand on her waist, loved her hand on the muscles of his shoulder. They waltzed under the gaze of the portraits. Maud complained about being clumsy, but Low just laughed.

"You're tall, you're pretty, you've got a voice like nothing else, you've got a big family that loves you, and you're whining just because you're kind of a clumsy dancer. Maybe you should fill out a complaint form and send it to God, huh? Maybe you should take heaven to court because you're not perfect. Listen, I can teach you to move if you wanna learn it. Nobody's gonna teach me how to be tall and handsome, and nobody's gonna teach me how to make my family give a good goddamn about me."

"Well, I wasn't trying to turn it into a contest."

The argument ended upstairs in bed. And Maud snuck back home before midnight.

It was three days later that they took their marriage license in to the Justice of the Peace and got married. They went straight to Maud's house afterwards. Low waited outside while Maud broke the news to her family.

"You married Low," Mrs. Caldecote said faintly. "Low. Of all people. And Judge Burnett let you. When I get my hands on that man—"

"When I told you to be nice to Low, I didn't mean for you to be *that* nice," Mr. Caldecote said.

"How could you do that to Lionel Pipping?" Cole asked dryly.

"How could you do that to *you?*" demanded Aida Kay.

Fortune just gazed at Maud with a troubled look on her face.

"I hope he's prepared to support you," Mr. Caldecote said. "You'll be moving into his apartment, of course. He's not living here."

"Just—how could you marry somebody you hate? I just don't understand it," said Mrs. Caldecote.

"I don't hate him all that much anymore," Maud said. She was still more than halfway convinced that if she confessed her love for him, he'd stop loving her and leave her.

"Lord have mercy," Mrs. Caldecote moaned.

Low knocked on the kitchen door and came in without waiting for an invitation. "I can tell by your expressions that Maud has broken the good news."

Mr. Caldecote stood up. He put a hand on Low's shoulder and said, without a trace of a smile, "I've got no objections to children marrying, and there's nothing I could do about it if I did. But I do object to children having children. Do you hear me, Low? Maud?"

"We had no plans," Low said, and Maud shook her head earnestly.

"Don't leave it to chance," Mr. Caldecote said.

"No, sir. I won't."

"Do you love Maud?" Mrs. Caldecote demanded.

Low stepped toward her and crouched down at her feet. "I love Maud so much I think I'm going crazy. I love Maud so much the only thing that keeps it from hurting like hell is having her by my side."

Mrs. Caldecote laid a gentle hand on his head. "Love is a verb, Low. Just don't forget that."

"Yes, ma'am."

"Maud, don't you forget, either."

"Oh, don't worry," she said airily. "I don't love him, and I don't think I'm in any danger of loving him."

"Maud, you got to get over that," Low said.

"And risk you leaving me? No way. I'll hate you until the day I die."

"Fine. You do that. Now let's go pack up your stuff."

"I suppose this is the end of Damned Pretty Things," Fortune said, as Low took a box to load into the van.

"Why should it be?" Maud asked. The two sat on the floor of Maud's room, packing up her things.

"Well, you're married."

"So?"

"Won't Low want you at home most of the time?"

"Oh, probably. But that doesn't mean I have to be."

"I just don't get the impression you're taking this marriage very seriously," Fortune said.

"And I just think there's more than one way to be married. Hey! We can add this to our set now." Maud sang "Single Girl, Married Girl."

Fortune laughed. "No rocking cradles or babies on knees. Remember what your father said."

"He's one to talk. He was twenty-three when Sophie was born."

"I think he was referring to our maturity level," Low said, coming in for another box.

"What do you think, Low...is this the end of Damned Pretty Things?" Fortune asked.

"I don't know why it should be," he said.

"See?" Maud said, poking Fortune in the ribs. "What did I tell you?"

Mama wandered in and sank down on the bed with a heavy sigh. "I just can't get over this, Maud. I want to be angry, but I don't know what good that would do. I'd cry but it's all so absurd. It's hard for me to think of a less likely circumstance than you and Low being married."

"There's something I haven't told you yet," Maud said. "Low is Paolo MacDonald."

"Good Lord." Mama covered her face with her hands. "Maud, I don't even know any more."

"Does that make a difference?" Maud asked anxiously. "In how you'll treat him, I mean?"

"You know that the last straw between my parents and me was my marriage. They cut all communications with me when I married Jordan. I would never do that to any of you. I love you with a heart and a half, and I believe in unconditional love. And so I want for Low what I'd wanted for Jordan. As long as he's good to you, Low will always be welcome in this house and in this family."

Maud sat down next to Mama and hugged her. "Thank you, Mama. That means so much to me."

Mama laughed. "I wonder what on earth Magnus Mac-Donald will have to say about this?"

Low, coming back into the room, said, "He'll say 'You married a *McBride*? Good God, boy, we don't *marry* them!' Now, if you were my mistress, like Helena was Grandfather's—"

"What?" Maud exclaimed. "She was his *what*?"

"She was his mistress for years…decades. You really didn't know?"

"Mama?"

"It was an open secret," Mama said. "Not something to discuss in front of you children. That reminds me." Mama got up and left the room. Low sat down where she'd been and put an arm around Maud.

"Your mother is one in a million, you know that?"

"Low…was I supposed to be *your* mistress?"

He tugged a lock of her hair. "Oh, probably. But I was supposed to be the heir to the MacDonald family glory and majesty, and look what happened there. Nothing to do with your curse."

Mama came back in with one of the boxes labeled "For Maud" that had come from Aunt Helena's house. Maud had forgotten all about them until that moment.

"There are two more," Mama said. "Low, come and help me."

Maud opened the box. At the very top were the notebook and pen, the unopened box of tarot cards, and the daydream rock.

"That's a damned pretty thing," Fortune said, when Maud took the daydream rock out of the box.

"You're supposed to be packing, not unpacking!" Mama called as she and Low took the other two boxes up to the van.

Maud put the daydream rock back in the box and closed the lid. She looked around her room, cleared of everything but the furniture. "All right," she said. "I think we're done."

"How long do you suppose we'll live here?" Maud asked, once they'd taken all her belongings up to Eddy's apartment. Low didn't have many possessions, and Eddy had left little behind. Mama promised to take Maud and Low shopping for household goods once Maud had settled in. She also said firmly that she would sew Maud a trousseau. "You may have done me out of a wedding, but you'll have everything else I can give you."

"Unpack your things," he said. "Otherwise it looks like you're hedging your bets."

Out of curiosity, she began with the boxes from Aunt Helena's house. She put the pack of tarot cards, in their embroidered silk bag, under her pillow, the daydream rock and the notebook and pen on her bedside table. She unfolded the Hermes scarf and put it on top of the dresser. She found the statues of Saint Brigid and Cernunnos, and placed them on the Hermes scarf, along with Aunt Helena's crystal ball and stand.

"I remember these things," said Low. "I *really* remember *him*."

"He reminds me of you," Maud said, smiling.

"I can see why."

"Oh!" Maud drew out the bronze chalice. Packed with it was a bottle labeled "pomegranate wine."

"Better put that away," Low said. "That's dangerous stuff."

"No." Maud shook her head. "We're going to do this right." She opened the bottle and poured wine into the chalice. Holding the chalice in both hands, she briefly bowed her head over it. Then she looked up, looked into Low's apprehensive eyes, and smiled.

"*Slàinte mhòr agus a h-uile beannachd duibh.* May you live a long and happy life. May you forever love your wife, and may your wife forever love you."

She took a sip of the wine, then held the chalice out to Low. Not breaking eye contact, he took it with both hands and drank, and handed it back to Maud empty. He kissed her.

"Forever," he said.

The Museum of Mystery and Industry

When Fortune and Maud returned to town after the incident at Dareton, the mid-September sky was already dark. A single bright star shone. Fortune remembered the child-rhyme that Maud and Sophie had chanted. Under her breath, she said "Star light, star bright, the first star I see tonight, I wish I may, I wish I might, have the wish I wish tonight." Then she saw Lightning's truck parked in front of the Sky Cafe and knew her wish had been granted.

She asked Maud to pull over. Alone, she went into the cafe, stopping a moment to glance herself over in the huge mirror opposite the doors. She looked all right. She looked good enough. Her face burning, woozy and lightheaded, but emboldened by the vodka she'd drunk in the car, she walked up to Lightning, who drank coffee and read a well-worn copy of Knut Hamsun's *Pan*. Fortune tapped him on the shoulder. He looked up, then broke into a smile.

Without preamble, she said, "Kiss me."

"I beg your pardon?"

"Kiss me. Now. Pretty please."

He put down his book and got up. He tilted his head to the side and smiled questioningly.

"What about the bees?"

"I'll take my chances."

Lightning put his hands to the sides of her face, bent, and kissed her gently on the lips. No bee stung her. She stood on tiptoes, linked her fingers at the base of his neck, and kissed him back, just to make sure. She sighed, relieved, and rested her head against his chest, suddenly exhausted. His heartbeat was strong as a drum.

"Now what?" he said, his voice low and gentle.

"I think the bees approve," she said. "And when you kiss me, I hear bells ringing."

"That was Maud leaving," he said, and kissed her again.

"No, it happened again."

"That was Low leaving."

"Why are you paying attention to their comings and goings when I am standing right here?"

"How much did you have to drink before you came in here?" he asked, amused.

Fortune clapped her hands over her mouth. "Oh, no! How could you tell?"

"The taste of vodka is distinct but pleasant on your sweet lips. What prompted all this, anyway? Is it just tipsiness?"

"I needed to know that it's not all abusive husbands and premature burial," Fortune explained.

Lightning put a hand on her forehead. "I don't think this is just the vodka talking. You're burning up. I think I'd better take you home."

She hopped. "Yippee!"

"Not *my* home."

"But I'm burning up with *love*."

"I think it's more likely the flu."

"Now you listen to me, David Lightning Levain. The bees approve of you. That means one thing, and one thing only."

"And what is that?"

"You are *my* man now."

"If you say so."

"I do say so. You are *my* man. And furthermore, you are not to kiss any other girls who aren't me."

"I promise you I won't."

"Swear it on a stack of Bibles?"

"How about if I just pinky promise, instead?"

"Oh my word, you are so adorable!"

"Actually, I think you're the adorable one."

Robin came in. "Hey, Fortune. How's it going?"

"Robin, this is Lightning. He kissed me, so he is *my* man."

"Congratulations. Didn't see that coming from a mile away."

Lightning went to pay. Donita Chance was working that afternoon. While she and Lightning chatted briefly, Fortune picked up his book where he had laid it down, and read, "Then it was evening again, and Dundas was gone. Something golden thrilling through me. I stood before the glass, and two eyes all alight with love looked out at me; I felt something moving in me at my own glance, and always that something thrilling and thrilling round my heart. Dear God! I had never seen myself with those eyes before, and I kissed my own lips, all love and desire, in the glass..."

She put the book down again, abashed by the sensuality of the prose.

"Ready?" He picked up his book and, unexpectedly, offered her his arm. She bit her lower lip, still warm from the kisses, and smiled, and took his arm.

They left the cafe. The Bel Air was still parked out front. Maud had probably ducked into the Blue Mouse Theatre, which was currently showing a movie called *Inframan*. Maud and her movies.

They were silent for most of the drive, lost in their separate mazes of apprehension and desire.

At the Caldecotes', Mollie rested her hand against Fortune's head and said, "That's a fever, all right. Thank you for bringing her home, Lightning. Fortune, get into bed, and I'll make you some willow bark tea."

Tucked up into Maud's bed, Fortune couldn't stay awake long enough to finish her tea. The next thing she knew, Maud was crouched on her chest, smiling down at her.

"Get off, Maud. You're too heavy."

"I'll get off once you've counted all the flowers," Maud said. She raised a hand. Her fingernails were long and orange, like her livid, orange-flowered wallpaper. "Count all the flowers on the wall."

Fortune tried. She really tried. But there were just too many of them. She wept from frustration, at the futility of the task, and from Maud's crushing weight.

"Please get off," she said.

"Not until you've counted all the flowers."

She should have taken Maud to the rich old man. If she'd only done what she was commissioned to do, Maud wouldn't be so heavy on her chest right now and asking for the impossible.

"We have to go to the city," she said. "We have to see the rich old man."

The rich old man would take care of Maud. Then Fortune would be free.

"Which rich old man?" Maud asked, running her fingernails lightly down the sides of Fortune's face.

"Magnus MacDonald!" Fortune cried, shaking her head back and forth to shake off Maud's fingernails.

In one corner of the room, Mab, showing the whites of her eyes, whinnied shrilly.

For two days, Fortune drifted in and out of fever dreams, getting out of bed only to use the bathroom, reluctantly sitting up to take the broth and teas Mollie Caldecote made for her. Maud continued to appear in her dreams, crouching on her chest, demanding that she count the flowers.

Once, Sweet Honey appeared at her bedside dressed in a nurse's uniform from the 1910s.

"Well, aren't you in a state, little girl," she said. "All fevered and shaking and dreaming terrible things. That's what happens when you speak for the dead. Don't worry. It'll get easier next time, and easier still the time after that."

"I don't want there to be a next time," Fortune said. Her teeth chattered. Sweet Honey's nurse's whites were so bright they hurt her eyes.

"There will be as long as you travel with Miss Windy's personal property."

"I don't know what you mean."

"Long Maud, that's who I mean. She's a child of that hot-headed graveyard lady. She can't see spirits herself, but she makes it so you can see them. A lens, that's what she is. Venitia MacKinnon isn't even the first spirit, but she's the first you spoke for. But don't you worry. I got a little something for you, take the edge off. Open wide like the pretty little bird you are."

Fortune opened her mouth, and Sweet Honey poured a spoonful of honey over her tongue. And then she was gone.

The morning of the third day, the fever broke, and Fortune dragged herself weakly to the shower to wash off the sweat that had grown cold on her skin. Mollie had a freshly made bed and fresh pajamas waiting for her when she came back.

"Thank you," Fortune said. "I honestly couldn't tell you the last time I was this sick."

Mollie was kind. Maud, not. She and Fortune fought, and she slammed out of the room. Almost immediately after, there came a knock on the door.

"What?" Fortune yelled.

"It's me," said Lightning. "May I come in?"

"Oh, God. Yes, come in. I thought you were another Caldecote coming in to pester me."

"That doesn't sound good." Lightning sat down on the bed and patted her hand.

"What's going on, lil' sick girl?"

A thought suddenly occurred to Fortune. "Did Maud happen to see you kissing me?"

"She might have done," he said. "Why are you worried about that?"

Fortune sighed and linked her fingers together. That might explain some things. "I don't know that she's over you."

"Why does that matter? I don't mean to sound callous, but if she's not over me, that's her problem. I never declared myself to her by word or deed. Like I said before, I've never seen her as anything but a kid. And I'm not responsible for how she might see me."

"Yes. But it's going to be awkward," Fortune said. "When I tell her…what am I going to tell her?"

"That you're seeing me," Lightning said. "That we're an item."

Fortune smiled, satisfied and somewhat relieved, and leaned into him. "Good."

"At least until your husband shows up and shoots me for kissing his wife."

"What are you playing at, giving me a husband I don't have?"

"A husband you don't *know* you have. There's a difference."

"I'm not married." Fortune held up her left hand, her fingers splayed. (She'd removed her fingerless gloves only to shower and had put them back on again from habit.) "No ring."

"You might have taken it off."

"I am not married," she said decisively.

"But you're something to somebody. You're a daughter, or a sister. Maybe a lover. How can you say 'yes' to me unless you know what you're saying 'no' to?"

"Too late," she said. "I already said 'yes' to you."

"There's a difference between 'yes, I'd like a bite of cake' and 'yes, I'd like to marry the baker.'"

"Marry? My word, you move fast! Is that why they call you Lightning?"

"Your bees took one look at me, said, 'Now *that's* the man for Fortune,' and here we are. We can't disregard the bees, can we?"

"Be serious."

"All right. I would really like to spend time with you. A lot of time. But don't you have any pity for the life you don't remember? Don't you wonder about your name or your family?"

"Of course I do. All the time. But what if there's nobody?"

"If you find out there's nobody, then you come right back here. You come back to me, and to Maud, and to Robin, and to the Caldecotes. You come back to Sky."

"I could have gone back to the city any time. But I haven't. Maybe there are things so bad I don't *want* to remember them."

"Maybe there are."

"Would you have me face them anyway?"

"Fortune, if I were a worse man than I am, I'd do everything in my power to persuade you to stay."

"One time, Maud said to me, 'What if you're Sleeping Beauty and you're just dreaming all of us?'"

"That sounds like Maud."

"But what if it's true? What if I'm a lost princess, dreaming and weaving dream fragments into my hair? What if the king and queen are waiting for my return? What if I decide I would rather live in the dream, rather be a poor wandering musician, than be a princess?"

"At the risk of sounding like a broken record, don't you think you ought to find out?"

Abruptly, Fortune made up her mind to confess. "Have you heard of Magnus MacDonald?"

"Who hasn't?" said Lightning.

"Well." Fortune drew a deep breath. "He's the reason I came to Sky in the first place. He commissioned me to come here. He commissioned me to find Maud."

Lightning looked surprised. "What does Magnus Mac-Donald want with Maud Caldecote?"

"He says that she cursed his grandson, and that his grandson has gone to hell in a handbasket ever since."

"Um...."

"It's crazy, isn't it? Do you think Maud has the power to throw a curse?"

He laughed. "If she did, I think she would have cursed me two years ago for making her work at the Mansion."

"This supposedly happened at the grandson's eighteenth birthday party, but Maud told me she never went to that party."

"That sounds about right. I think she got pretty sick in the city. So Maud knows Magnus MacDonald is looking for her?"

"Well...I didn't exactly *tell* her. But I guess I said something about it when I was delirious, so the cat's out of the bag now."

Lightning said, "Wait...you didn't tell her, but you were going to take her to him anyway?"

"That was the plan." Fortune didn't quite squirm under his gaze, but her face grew clammy and she questioned the wisdom of telling him at all. She had a feeling that she was now on the outside, and that Lightning, perhaps rightly so, was siding with the girl from Sky. "I wanted to give her a taste of life on the road first."

"What do you get in return for bringing Maud to Mac-Donald? Thirty pieces of silver?"

"My memories—enough money to buy them back. Or enough money not to miss them."

"I see. When I first met you, I wondered if you might be running a con. I just didn't know what kind."

"Look, I *want* to be a good person. That's why I'm telling you all this. And that's why I haven't taken her yet. I'm trying to figure this out."

"If you want to do right by Maud, then tell her everything and give her a choice to go or not go."

"Do you think she'll hate me for it?"

"On the contrary. I think she'll be over the moon. Such intrigue! Such mystery!"

"Do *you* hate me for it?"

"I'm your man, remember? How could I possibly hate you?"

She asked Lightning to take her home with him. She figured her days in the Caldecote household were numbered. But Lightning kissed her and told her no, that she needed to stay where she was and clear up her business with Maud. Otherwise, he said, she'd be running away.

"And I want you running toward."

He left shortly afterwards with the promise to come visit the next day and the mostly unnecessary admonition to get some rest. Fortune didn't think there was anything else she could do. She felt so frustrated and helpless and lonely after he left that she broke down crying.

Maud came back down not long afterwards, smelling of horse and looking contrite. Her eyes and nose were red. She glanced at Fortune's uneaten breakfast. "Can I make you some fresh?"

"No, thanks. I'm not hungry right now."

They apologized to each other. The apologies felt complete and healing. Not long after, Fortune fell into a deep, exhausted sleep. And, blessedly, she did not dream.

The next morning, Fortune felt good enough to get dressed and come upstairs to eat breakfast. When Lightning stopped by and Maud disappeared, "To give you two some privacy," Fortune was even more convinced that Maud had seen the kiss and was hurt by it. She tried to feel sympathy for the younger woman, but that didn't change her conviction that Lightning was her man.

"Let's go get my car," Fortune said. "I feel stranded without it."

"You sure you're up to it?"

"Up to driving a couple of miles? I think so."

In Lightning's truck, he said, "What about talking to Maud? Are you up to that, too?"

"I guess I'd better be," she said grimly. "I'm serious, Lightning...if I'm no longer welcome at the Caldecotes', I'll need to stay in your spare room."

"And you *will* stay in my spare room. But I don't think you're giving the Caldecotes enough credit. I especially don't think you're giving Maud enough credit. You'll be giving her a chance to be a knight in shining armor to your damsel in distress. I think she'll eat it up."

"If I sell it like that, won't I be running a con?"

"Not necessarily. Don't worry about selling it. Just be honest. Your honesty will see you right."

"My honesty." Fortune laughed. "Okay."

When Fortune returned with the Bel Air, she went to meet Maud, who was up at the pasture gate, stroking Nut's nose and singing to her about the joys of being a horse named Nut. Fortune suddenly realized how much she admired Maud's love of volume. When Maud sang, she sang with her whole body, loudly, without the faintest trace of self-consciousness. She would do the same in a pasture, or in a grocery, or in the Louvre, if she ever found herself there. She even hummed vigorously. There was nothing shy about her voice.

> Nut has a nose
> as sweet as a rose,
> and where her nose goes,
> goes Nut, God knows.

Fortune climbed up the bank, past Mrs. Caldecote's spicy pinks, and negotiated her way around various dog deposits until she stood by Maud's side.

"Hey," she said.

Maud turned and smiled, but her smile looked strained. "Hey."

"Where's Mab?"

"Cole's riding her down to Foreign Lake. That boy's crazy to go swimming in the fall. You know that water's going to be ice cold. One June we took a trip up to the Mountain. There was snow everywhere. Cole stripped down to his shorts and rolled in it. I don't know what he was thinking."

"He probably wasn't thinking about anything except being Cole."

Abruptly, Maud said, "Mama wants to talk."

Fortune's heart sank, but she made herself smile. "I had a feeling she might. Before we do, you might want to unload your stuff from the car. I may have to beat a hasty retreat."

"What, to the Mansion? Is that really necessary?"

"Yeah," she said. "I think it is. I'm really sorry, Maud." And she was—sorry for not telling her before about the rich old man, sorry about Maud's obvious heartache about Lightning, and sorry that, if she understood Mollie Caldecote's character aright, Fortune was about to lose her borrowed family.

Fortune went straight to the living room, where Mollie sat knitting. Mollie glanced up when Fortune sat down and simply nodded. That didn't bode well. Fortune stared at her hands in her lap and waited for Maud to finish unloading her things.

"I'm sorry," she said to Mollie.

Mollie kept her eyes on her knitting, but her mouth tightened. "You need to save that for Maud."

When Maud came in, Fortune and Mollie glanced up expectantly.

"Tell me everything," Maud said.

So Fortune did.

Lightning stopped by again on his way home from work.

"How are you feeling? Any better?"

"Yeah. A lot." She couldn't keep the weariness from her voice. She sounded sarcastic without meaning to.

Lightning picked up on it. "Do you need the spare room at the Mansion?"

She shook her head. "I'll have to meet the famous Mansion some other time."

"Why not tonight?" he said. "Why not come up for dinner? Finally see the place? Can you eat stew?"

"It's not Bambi stew, is it?"

"No. It's Ferdinand the Bull stew."

"Poor Ferdinand."

"He was so busy smelling the flowers that he didn't know what hit him. At least, that's what they told me at the butcher shop."

Fortune laughed. "They would say that, wouldn't they?"

Fortune made her excuses to Mollie and left with Lightning.

After climbing to an ear-popping height, the road leveled off and passed a radio tower. A quarter mile further through the woods, the road ended at the 1920s stone cottage the people of Sky called the Mansion. Fortune thought it was as enchanting as its grandiose nickname.

"Here we are," said Lightning, putting the truck into park.

They got out and walked up to the front door, which was lacquered bright red. Lightning fitted a key into the ornate lock and opened the door.

"After you."

The cottage was dim, cool light filtering through white linen curtains. The scent of beef and onions warmed the air, as did the ghost of wood smoke from the big stone fireplace. A blue pottery jug of sunflowers sat on the kitchen table. The dishcloths were red and black buffalo check. A copper kettle shone on the stove. Next to the couch, on an end table, a nearly-full bottle of Tullamore Dew sat next to a shot glass and a mica-shade lamp.

"This is beautiful," Fortune said.

"Thank you. I want it to be everything it didn't get the chance to be before. My grandmother wouldn't consent to live here, not even on weekends or for holidays, so it's got to catch up on eighty years of neglect. She loved my grandfather, but he was never quite fancy enough for her. I sometimes wonder how she allowed him to build this house in the first place."

"Was he from Sky?"

"No. He was on the train once when it stopped here. He got off and decided to stay for a few days. He hiked Wolf's House and fell in love with it and decided to buy the whole summit. He could only get thirty acres of it.

"He took me up here when I was about eight. We hiked up. I'll never forget how intrigued I was by the boarded-up house. My grandfather said, 'I'll tell you what. Some day you can have it and you can take the boards off. It can be your house.' And sure enough, he left it to me when he died.

"I loved my grandfather, and he loved me. He was my one person. I hope everybody has at least one person. I hope you do. Did you talk to Maud about Magnus MacDonald?"

"I did. Lightning, she really was there at the party. She just got so sick afterwards that she forgot."

Fortune described the conversation.

"So now it's up to her whether she comes to meet Magnus MacDonald or not," she said.

The stew, slow-cooked in a cast-iron Dutch oven, was perfectly done by the time they sat down to eat. Lightning made cornbread in a cast-iron skillet to go with it.

They talked about ghosts and gigs and people they'd met on their separate travels. "And now I'm back," said Fortune. "I *needed* to come back here. This may be the only peaceful place I've ever known."

"That's why I come back. I need to know that a place like this is possible."

"Why not just stay?"

"I get restless."

"Just like me."

"Maybe just exactly like you."

"Can two restless people find happiness together?" Fortune asked.

Lightning smiled. "Tune in and find out," he said.

Fortune was tired after dinner, so Lightning took her back to the Caldecotes. She thanked him for dinner, kissed him goodnight, went straight to bed, and slept, again without dreaming.

The next morning, she persuaded Maud to come into town and hang out at the Sky Cafe. She wanted a chance to talk to her about going to see Magnus MacDonald without the possibility of Mollie convincing her not to go.

When Low slouched out of the kitchen, heading for the sidewalk and his smoke break, Fortune intercepted him. "Never mind the cigarette. Teach me to tango."

Low was amenable. "Left hand on my shoulder," he said. "Follow me. Slow. Slow. Quick, quick, slow. No, you're good. Slow. Slow. Quick, quick, slow."

Then, in a lower voice, he said, "Congratulations on making your move. Lightning's a good guy."

"My word! Next you're going to ask me if I remembered to buy milk."

"Huh?"

"By the way, you don't have to keep glancing over there," Fortune said. "She's watching every move you make. She may be sullen, but she's attentive."

His hands briefly twitched.

"You're in love with her, aren't you?"

Low danced in silence.

"By any chance, is Low short for Paolo?"

He stopped abruptly. "That's enough for today."

He left her to go have his cigarette. She went and sat down next to Maud and had a sip of water.

"What on earth possessed you to dance with that thing?" Maud asked, wrinkling her nose.

"He's an excellent dancer," Fortune said. "I know you can't stand him, but you should give him credit where it's due."

"I'd rather not, if it's all the same to you."

"So…what do you think about going to the city?"

238

Maud reached across the table and took Fortune's hand in her own.

"I'd better put my sleeping bag back in the Bel Air," she said.

Fortune smiled and breathed a sigh of relief. "Attagirl," she said. "Let's show Magnus MacDonald what we're made of."

She went to the pay phone and called him. He answered on the third ring.

"Who is this?"

"Fortune."

"Yes."

"We're coming. Tomorrow."

"I'll be ready for you," he said.

They went to bed early that night, but Fortune found it difficult to fall asleep. She lay in bed, fingering the objects in her hair one after the other, in the order she'd acquired them. It was almost like reciting a rosary, naming each place, each town where she'd found or been given the object. The lock of Maud's hair, slippery at first, had begun to mat in its braid. The scrap of Venitia MacKinnon's yellow silk dress was smooth and cool to the touch.

How powerful was the rich old man? Was he actually capable of getting her soul and her memories back for her? Or was he running a con? Money could do a lot, but it did have its limits. She fretted that she wouldn't reclaim herself, and she fretted that she would.

She dreamed that she was about to embark on a journey by train. She had her ticket and half an hour to get to the train station. But all around her were objects she still needed to pack—books, journals, jewelry, knick-knacks, record albums. She knew they would never all fit into her luggage, and that she wouldn't be capable of taking it all, but she couldn't bear to leave any of it behind.

When Maud awoke her the next morning, it felt as if she'd hardly slept at all.

Mostly recovered from her illness, Fortune announced she'd do all the driving. She needed it to take her out of her thoughts, out of the sense of panic and futility her dream had left her with. If she concentrated on the road, she couldn't ruminate about it, or about the question of re-gaining her memories.

Maud, dressed in the black dress her mother sewed her for her eighteenth birthday, seemed to shoot off sparks of ex-citement. She asked Fortune to teach her the song about Long Maud, and Fortune did, touched by Maud's naive vanity.

"I think we should perform it," Maud said.

"You sure about that? Doesn't it make you mad?"

"It does," Maud admitted. "But it also makes me under-stand Barbara Allen a lot better. You know, I never thought I could be a heroine of anything. So I guess I'll just be the witch. Imagine, me having the power to throw a curse!"

"I wouldn't suggest using that power," Fortune said. "Not again. Not if it makes you sick."

"Think about this...I threw a curse and got sick. You saw Venitia MacKinnon's ghost and got sick. I wonder if we're building up our spiritual immune systems?"

Fortune was reminded of her visit from Sweet Honey. *That's what happens when you speak for the dead. Don't wor-ry. It'll get easier next time.*

"Why us?" Fortune said.

"Why not?" said Maud.

Why not, indeed?

240

As the freeway pulled them into the city, Fortune's hands tightened on the steering wheel…not because the chaos of city traffic distressed her but because it seemed so familiar. She had always assumed she was an urban girl. If they weren't going to see the rich old man, she wondered where she might drive, where she might end up, where muscle memory might take her.

Maud read out the directions the rich old man had given Fortune. They soon found themselves in a neighborhood that looked elderly and prosperous, full of neatly-trimmed hedges and beautiful houses of rusticated stone and brick.

"Thank goodness he doesn't live in a gated community," Fortune said. "I wouldn't want to try my luck in one of those."

They found his house and pulled into the drive. Fortune recognized the Lincoln parked out front. She put the car into park and turned off the engine. Her hands trembled again. She'd have to keep them in her skirt pockets. They got out of the car and went up the front steps. Maud rang the doorbell.

Fortune expected somebody else to answer the door—a maid or a butler, anybody really but Magnus MacDonald himself. And yet there stood the man, looking a good deal older than she remembered him, and a good deal smaller. He was dressed less formally, as well, in wool slacks, a button-down shirt, and a cardigan. He looked Maud up and down, as if offended by her height. Then he turned his gaze to Fortune.

"Well done," he said. "Come in. Both of you."

It struck Fortune, as they followed him inside, that there was something of the mausoleum about his house, so cold and impersonal it felt to her. It was as if he'd already cast away earthly goods to reside in expensive emptiness before being consigned to the greatest emptiness of all. She tried to remember that this was a man facing his own death, and to have compassion for him. But there was nothing sympathetic in his demeanor, nothing vulnerable, and she imagined he would think her compassion an impertinence.

After a brief conversation, the rich old man handed Fortune a thick envelope and decisively dismissed her. That suited her. She didn't want to spend any more time in the rich old man's company than she absolutely had to. She took the envelope and left, gently shutting the front door behind her. Once in the warm mid-September air, she breathed more freely. She shook off a shudder and went to sit on the hood of the Bel Air. Her hands trembled as she opened the envelope.

As she suspected and feared, it was filled with cash—a stack of hundred-dollar bills. Mere money. But when she slid it out to count it, something fell into her lap. It was a brass token about the size of a poker chip, stamped with the words THE MUSEUM OF MYSTERY AND INDUSTRY and ADMIT ONE.

She picked up the token and stared at it, willing it to prove its existence to her. The Museum of Mystery and Industry had been an off-the-cuff utterance in the Sky Cafe the day she met Lightning and Maud, a tiny drop of story (or was it a lie?) that had taken on life with Maud's persistent belief. Now Fortune felt as if she were the butt of a cosmic joke she didn't understand. But who was the jokester? She couldn't quite believe the rich old man to be that fanciful. She remembered their first conversation in the mountain cafe.

If you have such an in with the Devil, why not ask him to bring you this Maud?

I did. And then he told me about you.

She raised the token to her mouth and touched it with her tongue. It tasted of tobacco and rum. She dropped the token. It landed safely in her lap, writing side up.

"They were just stories," she said. "Just stories I told because what else could I do? I never thought, I never believed—"

She thought of Sweet Honey, who had come to her more vividly than a dream—first when she had told the bees of her distress, and again when she lay in a fever.

Still, she couldn't quite believe that she hadn't made it all up. It was all too absurd to be real.

And yet the token lay, perfectly real, in her lap.

A sudden conviction that Maud mustn't know about it made her pick up the token and tuck it down the front of her middy blouse into her bra. It lay cool against her breast, and she knew it was imprinting those words against her skin.

She raised her face to the sun and closed her eyes. She was not a praying woman, and she didn't pray now, but she sent up a wish with her whole heart—*let this be real, and let me be able to handle it.*

She remained in that attitude, wishing that wish, until the front door closed. She opened her eyes and smiled at Maud.

Sophie greeted them with a warmth born of two years living away from home. College had matured her and made her kind. Her dorm room was cluttered with books and hiking gear, including a pair of snowshoes. Her roommate, a petite English major, had gone home to visit family for the weekend.

"You two can flip a coin to see who gets her bed tonight," Sophie said.

"Maud, you take the bed," Fortune said. "You've been sleeping on the floor for days."

"But you've been sick."

They argued back and forth. Finally, Maud won out. She went down to get her sleeping bag out of the trunk of the Bel Air.

"So you two finally made it to the city," Sophie said. "Are you singing somewhere tonight?"

In the car, Fortune and Maud had discussed what to tell Sophie, who was, according to Maud, a realist and not sympathetic to what she called "McBridey stuff."

"We'd probably better just say it's a social visit," Maud had said. "I think any mention of curses would make her eyes roll right out of her head."

"Nope," said Fortune. "Just visiting."

"Let me tell you, I'm glad you were able to pry Maud out of Sky. She needs to see the world outside of that dinky little town. I just couldn't believe she'd rather waitress for Robin than go to college…even community college. Mama always says that Maud goes at her own pace, but it seems to me that if it weren't for you, she'd be standing stock still."

That night they ate at a barbecue joint near Sophie's college. Afterwards, Fortune told Sophie and Maud to go back to the dorm without her.

"I want to take a walk, clear my head," she said. "You two go on; I'll be there in an hour or two."

After a few rounds of *are you sure?*, Maud and Sophie left Fortune to wander on her own. The neighborhood surrounding Sophie's college was predominantly African American, and Fortune felt comfortable walking on her own. She nodded to the people she passed, who nodded back (though some did a double-take at the sight of her ornamented hair). As she passed a row of shops in a one-story brick building, she heard a familiar voice.

"You never did buy that pretty dress, did you?"

Sweet Honey stepped out of the shadows. She was dressed in a gold-on-gold gingham fit and flare dress, gold pumps, and a tiny, frilled gold apron. She held a gold pick in one hand and a gold spray bottle in the other. The shop window had "Champagne Salon" lettered in gold upon it.

Fortune took two steps toward her, then hesitated. "Are you real?"

"Why are you always asking that? Your imagination isn't that vivid, Miss Mess. I'm more real than you are. And to prove it to you, I'm going to fix that hair of yours."

Fortune's hands went up to her head. "What's wrong with my hair?"

"Nothing, if you don't mind looking like the Great Pacific Garbage Patch. Get in here. It's too cool to stand outside talking."

Fortune followed Sweet Honey inside. She was surprised to find the place otherwise empty, and immediately missed the congenial conversation of a salon, the busyness and the individual transformations. All the scents of the salon swept over her—the pressed-clothes smell of the hot iron, the ammonia tang of hair relaxer, the sweetness of lotions and shampoos—and she felt a deep, aching nostalgia. She sat where Sweet Honey gestured her to sit, and looked at her reflection in the big mirror. She looked anxious, her eyes tired. And she saw her hair as Sweet Honey doubtless saw it, as full of burdensome junk.

Sweet Honey swathed Fortune in a gold nylon cape. "Ready to get rid of this weight?"

"What happens if I do?" Fortune asked. "Will I forget everything again?"

"Doubt it," said Sweet Honey. "You might even remember better."

"Lightning might not like me as well if I look different."

"If that's true, I'd say he's not worth the worry. Now you just relax and let Sweet Honey do her magic. Take out this scrap of yellow silk. Take out this lock of Long Maud's hair. Take out this, and this, and this. Starting to feel better already, aren't you? Such a shame to clutter up this pretty hair with so much junk."

Quickly, gently, Sweet Honey's fingers unraveled what mere human fingers couldn't, what mere human fingers would have had to cut out and cast away. And as she loosened and unraveled Fortune's braids, the low-level ache in her head, one so persistent that she had learned to ignore it, gently ebbed away.

One by one, the objects in Fortune's hair hit the trash can. Each time, she flinched. But each flinch left her more relaxed than before.

"That's right," Sweet Honey said soothingly. "Loosen all this up. Get rid of all that tightness. Get rid of that ache."

After a while, there was only one braid left—the one that bore Sweet Honey's bee skep charm.

"Been thinking about asking for this back," she said. She unraveled the braid and removed the charm. Fortune sighed deeply, completely relaxed in the chair. Sweet Honey fastened the charm to her charm bracelet. The other charms jingled in greeting.

Sweet Honey opened a bottle and passed it under Fortune's nose. "Breathe deeply. That's right." Fortune inhaled, and almost swooned at the mingled scents of rose and jasmine, sandalwood and vetiver. Sweet Honey poured some of the scented oil into her hand and rubbed her palms together. She massaged the oil into Fortune's scalp. Fortune's eyelids dropped closed, and her head moved, relaxed, under Sweet Honey's fingertips.

"Lotions and potions," Sweet Honey crooned. "Lotions and potions. Got to be pretty to face up to that pesky past."

Fortune's eyelids snapped open. Sweet Honey's reflection smiled at her.

"I know what you've got in your bra," she said. "I know what's imprinted on your skin. I know where you're going tonight, and why."

"Where is it?"

"Hush, child. Right now is right now. Close those eyes and relax."

After a while, Sweet Honey took her to a sink, where she washed and conditioned her hair. Then she took her back to the chair and sat her down.

"Braids again, I think," she said. "Only two, done up like a crown around your head. Got to look like a woman not to be trifled with. Got to look like a princess."

Sweet honey smoothed lotion through Fortune's hair, then parted, gently combed, and braided it wet. When Sweet Honey was finished with her, Fortune opened her eyes and gasped. The new hairstyle emphasized the beautiful shape of her eyes and her elfin cheekbones and showed off her delicate ears. The crowning braids made her look regal. Her baby hairs were arranged so artfully they looked as if they'd been airbrushed on.

"Don't you look pretty as a picture?" Sweet Honey asked, pleased by Fortune's reaction. "Pretty and strong and capable as a picture?"

"I look beautiful," Fortune said unselfconsciously. "You made me beautiful. Thank you so much. What do I owe you?"

"Same thing you owe me from before. Buy yourself that pretty dress. I won't ask again."

"I promise I will."

"Do more than promise. Buy it tonight. That rich old man gave you plenty of money. There's a little shop on the way."

"On the way?"

"On the way to where you're going. And before you go, I've got one piece of advice. Don't you let him push you around. He may think he's boss, but in the end he has to make me happy if he wants to be happy. And you are—" She kissed Fortune on the forehead. "—my particular princess. Don't you ever forget it."

Sweet Honey left the shop with Fortune and pointed out her direction. Fortune had walked a block and was in the middle of the crosswalk when a set of footsteps joined hers. She glanced to her left. There walked the Devil, tall, dark, and handsome. He nodded to her, his eyes glowing from beneath the snap brim of his fedora.

"A fine evening, isn't it?" he asked. "Crisp but not too cold. It's the dying breath of Lady Summer as her soul rises up."

Fortune stopped walking. The Devil stopped, as well, and watched Fortune expectantly.

"I can't believe," she said at last, "that you're friends with the rich old man."

The Devil took out a cigarillo, took out a book of matches, struck a match, lit the cigarillo. He shook out the match and let it drop to the sidewalk.

"Oh, now, I wouldn't say *friends*," he replied. "No. I'd never say *friends*. Not like you and me. You and me, we go way back."

"If you say so," Fortune said, irritated. "I really wouldn't know."

"And whose fault would that be?" he asked.

"Again," said Fortune, walking, "I really wouldn't know."

"Hold up, hold up. You're little but you're quick. And you're about to blaze right past that boutique Sweet Honey told you about."

Sure enough, not two doors down was a little vintage dress shop, with three mannequins in the window. The center mannequin wore a peacock blue, gold-beaded silk robe de style. When Fortune saw it, she gasped aloud, as she had when she saw her hair.

The Devil grinned. "I'll just wait out here."

Fortune went in and found the shopkeeper. "That dress in the window...the center one. I'd like to try it on, please."

"It's a beauty, isn't it. And it looks to be your size." The shopkeeper took down the mannequin and slipped the dress off. She handed it carefully to Fortune, who equally carefully carried it to the fitting room. She stripped off her ankle-length black skirt and her middy blouse and slipped the robe de style over her head. It fit perfectly, skimming her slender figure and flaring out at the hips. She looked at the price tag and flinched. But Sweet Honey was right. The rich old man had given her plenty of money. This frock would barely make a dent.

"I'll take it," she said. She couldn't bear to take it off, so she had the shopkeeper bag her skirt and middy blouse and snip off the price tag.

True to his word, the Devil waited outside, smoking contemplatively. When Fortune came out, his eyebrows raised until they disappeared beneath his hat brim.

"Well, well, well," he said. "This look takes me back. You could be on your way to an exclusive jazz club, and I would be proud to squire you."

Fortune reached down the front of her bodice and pulled out the token. "Perhaps you'll squire me here, instead."

He took the token and held it up between thumb and forefinger, turning it so the stamped letters caught the light from the shop window.

"Are you sure you want to do this?" he asked, handing the token back to her. "Once upon a time, not that long ago, you walked away and didn't look back."

"Oh, I looked back," she said. "I look back every day. I look back and wonder who I was, and why I don't remember. They say if you don't miss a thing after a year to just throw it out. It's been more than a year since you took the lines on my palms. I clearly don't need those memories to survive. But I'm curious. Is somebody crying about me? Is somebody looking for me? Does somebody cuss me for disappearing?"

The Devil looked at her skeptically. "The lines in your palms? Those don't mean a damned thing. They're just lines. You think who you are can be reduced to a few dermal wrinkles? What kind of puny, pitiful worldview do you subscribe to?"

"Then why did you want them?"

"I didn't. You wanted to get rid of them. Now I know why, I'm sorry I took 'em off your hands. Hey, that's pretty funny! Did you hear that? I took 'em off your hands."

"Hilarious," said Fortune.

"Next think you'll be telling me I'm the Devil, and I bought your soul."

"Aren't you? Didn't you?"

"Nope. I'm afraid not."

"I really didn't sell my soul?"

"You think you could play the way you play without a soul?"

"Well, then who are you?"

His fiery garnet eyes sparkled. "Well, you could call me Baby but that would make Sweet Honey mad. I suggest you just refer to me as Mister. Tell me this—aren't you tired of toting that old guitar around?"

"No," Fortune said, perhaps more loudly than necessary. Mister winced and wiggled his pinky in one ear. "Absolutely not."

"Fine, fine. Just checking. Not that I have anything to do with you playing, you not having sold your soul to me. Playing the guitar—that's something you've had since childhood. But since you've spent part of this night getting rid of things, I thought I'd offer to take it off your hands. We're here."

"I beg your pardon?" Fortune said.

"I said we're here. We're at the Museum of Mystery and Industry."

"We haven't gone anywhere. We're still in front of the—" Fortune turned. The dress shop was gone. She glanced around. They appeared to be in an empty park. Tall, Art Deco street lamps threw circles of light on the ground. The glittering cityscape below rose from behind box hedges. And there stood a white stone Art Deco building, curving outward, made bright by three illuminated, floor-to-ceiling stained glass windows. Twin Chinese lions flanked the steps. Above the door were carved the words *Museum of Mystery and Industry*.

"It looks like a mausoleum," Fortune said. "A really big mausoleum."

Mister laughed. "It does that. And maybe it is. But you don't need Long Maud to see your dead in there."

Fortune thought of her dream of the abandoned cat. A jolt of panic made her forearms tingle as if with electricity.

As if he'd read her thoughts, Mister said, "Did you think you could walk away and all would be well without you? Did you think you weren't needed? That lives didn't depend on you? What do you think starved to death in your absence?"

"Don't. This is too cruel. It's too much like my dreams."

"Dreams are cruel. Dreams tell you what you need to hear. A cat or a baby or a miniature dragon…they all die from neglect. You have to feed them. You can't leave them to fend for themselves. Not for a year or more."

"I wouldn't have just left them, would I? I would have asked somebody to look after them, wouldn't I?"

"Would you? Did you expect to be gone this long? Sleeping Beauty dreamed while she slept. What else would she have done for 100 years? She lived lives in her dreams. She fought armies. She bore children. She raised nations to greatness. And while she slept, everybody whom she ever knew, everybody whom she ever loved, died and turned to dust."

"I can't go in there," Fortune said, walking away. She didn't know where she was going. Just away.

Mister stayed where he was. "You can't *not* go in there," he called after her. "There's too much on the line. For one thing, there's that man in Sky. That man is waiting on you. You can't disappoint him, can you?"

She stopped and turned around to face him. "I can lie to him," she said. "I'm good at lying. I can tell him there was nothing to see, nothing to learn—that what he sees is what he gets."

"Oh, the nerve of you telling the rich old man that honesty is the best policy. I will tell you one thing, Miss Fortune, and you had best listen. That token has got an expiration date. You use it tonight or you lose it forever. You lose it, and you will spend the whole rest of your life wondering what lay behind these double doors."

"Death," Fortune said. "You already as good as told me."

"Death, yes," he said. "Life, yes. Come on, now, Sleeping Beauty. Time to wake up."

He climbed the steps past the Chinese lions and stood at the doorway. He smiled. He beckoned. The world beyond the Art Deco building melted away. There was only one direction Fortune could walk, and that was up the steps.

At the doorway, Mister held out his hand. "I'll take that token, thank you."

She gave it to him. She squared her shoulders. She pushed open the door and stepped inside.

Inside was pure darkness. She quickly turned to go back out the door, but her outstretched hands touched empty air. Everywhere she turned, they encountered nothing, no resistance. She thought of Venitia MacKinnon, shut up in an empty crypt, and nearly screamed aloud.

"Easy," said Mister. Two garnet pinpoints hovered nearby. They blinked in and out as Mister blinked his eyes. "I should have warned you. You need to give your eyes time to adjust to the dark. Ten minutes for the cones, half an hour for the rods. Here." He took her hand in his and led her a few steps. "Sit down."

She sat, carefully, on a hard bench.

"I'm going to leave you now. Keep your eyes open and give it time. Goodbye, Fortune."

She called out but knew he was already gone. She pressed the gloved palms of her hands against the bench, assuring herself that she wasn't drifting in space. She made herself breathe slowly, deeply. Faint, lighter black illusions, indistinct as migraine auras, played in her field of vision— perhaps her brain making up for the void. She thought of Maud and her love of movies, and laughed out loud.

"Is anybody here?" she called into emptiness. "Anybody but me?"

She sat in the dark and sang, one song, another, another, twenty minutes, half an hour. Then she saw a line of light so faint she wondered if she were imagining it. Getting to her feet, shuffling from fear of tripping, falling, she slowly moved toward the line of light. It resolved into the outline of a rectangle, which meant one thing to her brain: a door.

She reached out and ran her hand up and down the door until she found the doorknob. She turned it and opened the door, and walked through to a chamber so dimly lit she could barely tell that the room wasn't empty. Light glimmered faintly on a glass case. She reached out and touched it, feeling the cool glass on her fingertips. A light within turned on gradually, illuminating the inside of the case.

"Dorothy McGraw!"

Inside lay a light brown cloth doll with dark brown embroidered eyes, long embroidered eyelashes, and springy dark brown yarn curls. The doll wore a yellow gingham dress and yellow felt shoes. She smiled a subdued pink smile.

"Yardley of London in Juliet's Blush!" Fortune cried out. She could see, in her mind's eye, the gold and silver tube, see the beautiful black woman spreading pink lipstick on her mouth, blotting it, then miming putting it on the doll's mouth.

"Me, too!"

"No, honey. You're too young to wear lipstick. Dorothy McGraw and I are grownups."

"Is Dorothy McGraw going to the party, too?"

"No, honey. Dorothy McGraw is staying home with you. You can have a TV dinner tonight."

"Yay! Salisbury Steak?"

"If you like."

Fortune put her hand over her heart. It was beating hard. She felt a little faint, a little queasy. She yearned for the woman in her memory. Her *mother*. She yearned for her *mother*.

"Mama," she said softly. "Oh, Mama, what has become of you?"

Flashes of memories, so quick she couldn't catch them, flickered around the edges of her mind. She had no words with which to frame and thereby retain them.

"Dorothy McGraw, how did you get in this glass case?" she asked. The doll had no answer for her.

"Mister!" she called. "Mister, I need you!"

Silence answered her. He really was gone. She checked around the case, looking for an opening. There was none. Dorothy McGraw was sealed away as securely as if she were a diamond necklace.

But as she checked the case, she noticed another door leading, presumably, to another room. She reluctantly left Dorothy McGraw and went to investigate.

This room was more brightly lit, the source being a Christmas tree diorama behind plate glass. Christmas lights glowed like candies on a fir tree that dripped with tinsel and frosted glass balls. A red, frosted glass spire topped the tree. Beneath it were gaily wrapped packages. Nearby was a decorated felt Christmas stocking spilling candy, and a child-sized guitar.

"I remember!" she said. "Santa brought me a guitar the year I was seven!"

She remembered. A tall, gentle black man sat down next to her on the blue couch. He positioned her fingers on the guitar strings.

"This is the E Minor chord," he said, his voice low and rumbling. "It's the first chord you should learn because it's used in all kinds of songs."

She strummed the strings and music came out!

"Good! Now see if you can do it yourself. Find the strings and press down. That's right!"

Her *father*. He was her *father*!

"Papa, where are you?" she called. She pressed her face against the plate glass window, trying to see beyond the scope of the diorama. As with the memory of her mother, other memories flashed by and were gone, leaving nothing more than a vague flavor of their passing.

Another door to another room. She left the Christmas diorama and entered a crazy installation the size of a house. Drawers stood half-opened, spilling wooden spools, wooden dolls, paintbrushes, whisk brooms. Doors stood open an inch, giving distorted glimpses of flickering black and white films within. Mechanical things, balancing things, crowded haphazard shelves, creaking or whining as they moved. A Fresnel lens magnified a tiny diorama of dollhouse dolls around a table, with miniature glasses in front of them and a pitcher labeled "Goopwater Wine."

"Goopwater wine!" she said. "I remember that!" That was the name her father had given to Kool-Aid, which she had adored. Cherry Kool-Aid. She could almost taste it. Her mouth watered for it.

A door stood next to the Fresnel lens. It had a peephole in it, just the height of Fortune's eyes. Light shone through it. Fortune pressed her right eye to the peephole. A slide-show played within, the color of the slides desaturated with age, distorted as if water-stained. She could see only glimpses of faces, of places and objects. She thought of a beach, of ice cream, of white clover full of bees, of bare feet stepping carefully, of summer.

Where were her parents—those patient teachers, those fond playmates, those infinite comforters?

"My father was a musician," she said suddenly, with conviction. "And my mother was a painter."

My father was. *My mother* was.

She began to cry.

"Mama?" she called, in the voice of a child.

Dead of breast cancer at thirty-nine. I was fourteen when she died.

"Papa?"

Killed by a hit-and-run driver at forty-five. I was twenty when it happened.

She sank down onto the floor and wept. Her voice rose up in a wail. She grieved as if grief would kill her and so end her pain.

And yet she couldn't remember their names.

When, at last, the storm of her grief subsided, she reached into the bag and pulled out a wad of tissue from her skirt pocket. She wiped her eyes and blew her nose, and she got up from the floor. Another doorway lay ahead, glowing with pink light. She walked down four wooden steps, up five, down one, and ducked through the low doorway.

This gallery had a single glass case in the center of the floor. The walls were painted pink, and pink crystal hearts hung from the ceiling, slowly spinning this way and that. Some of the threads had snapped, and pink crystal fragments lay where hearts had shattered on the ground.

Fortune's whole body tensed with anger. She knew, before she got to the glass case, what she'd see inside it...a ring with a pink crystal heart, the gift of a trifling man.

"I don't even want to know," she said. "Whoever you are, you deserve to be forgotten."

She left the gallery as quickly as she'd entered it, her shoes crunching in broken crystal as if it were sugar or ice.

The next gallery was hung with photographs...a funny, triangular house like a slice of cake. An old-fashioned bascule drawbridge with ornate towers. Sailboats going up a canal. And a calico cat yawning on a rumpled bed.

"A. C.!" she cried. "Admirable Cat."

She knew this was her house. The drawbridge was in her neighborhood. And she knew that she and A. C. took walks to the drawbridge to watch the boats sailing up and down the canal between the two lakes.

It looked like a charming life, a peaceful life, a respite from the wrenching loss of her parents and the heartache of a false lover. So why had she chosen to leave it? Why had she chosen to forget? What had happened that was so terrible that she'd walk away from A. C. and her little slice-of-cake house?

She remembered her dream of the cat dead in the drawer. It was just a dream. It wasn't about A. C. at all, but about Venitia MacKinnon.

But A. C. was an old cat, and A. C. did like to sleep in a dresser drawer. Sometimes Fortune would forget and close the drawer. Then she'd hear A. C. yowling to be let out. Fortune was always home to hear her. Fortune was always home to let her out.

Except for the time she wasn't.

Leaving for the hot weekend to go to the mountains with that man. She'd left bowls of water, bowls of food. A. C. couldn't get to them. She was shut up in the drawer. And she died.

In perfect darkness.

Weeping, Fortune groped her way around the perfectly dark space until she found the bench, a bench. Was it the same? Was it the same room? Was the Museum a loop? She sat down and wrapped her arms around her ribcage, weeping for the small life that had depended on her, that she had failed so completely. She wept for twenty minutes, for half an hour. Her brain drew squiggles of dark gray on the blackness.

Then she saw the line of faint light, the lines that outlined a rectangle, which her brain knew meant a door. She got up, her arms outstretched in front of her, until her fingertips touched cool wood. She pushed, and the door swung out. She walked through. She was outside on the steps. Three panels of stained glass, floor to ceiling, blazed with light and color.

Mister waited for her, puffing on his cigarillo.

"I assume you found your answers," he said. "Here... I've been holding these for you. Might as well give 'em back to you now."

He held out a house key and a flat, laminated card. It had a picture of Fortune, looking younger; an outline of the state; and the words Driver's License at the top. Fortune took it.

"Julia Day," she said. "My name is Julia Day. And I'm twenty-five years old."

"And you're an organ donor," Mister said. "Atta-girl."

"Is this real?" Fortune asked.

"As real as the lines on your palms," he said.

Fortune pulled off her fingerless gloves and held her hands, palms up, to the light. They were lined and creased. She couldn't read them. They were, after all, only dermal wrinkles.

"Might as well toss out those ratty gloves, Miss Julia. You don't need them anymore."

"Who says I don't?" Fortune pulled them back on. "I need them even more now. I invented myself for a reason. I made myself up because I didn't like who I was. I gave birth to myself at the crossroads so I could be brand new. Who and what I was doesn't matter anymore. I had nothing and nobody. That's how I could leave. I had nothing left to lose."

"And you're ready to walk away all over again, are you, Miss Julia?"

"My name," she said, "is Fortune. And I am a damned pretty thing."

She found herself alone, in front of the vintage dress shop. She turned and quickly walked away. If she passed

the Champagne Salon, she didn't notice it. She didn't notice anything. Her eyes, her cheeks burned from tears she'd
cried. She didn't cry any more. The clock tower at Sophie's
college said it was nine o'clock. She went into Sophie's dor-
mitory, ran up the three flights of steps to her floor, found
her room, knocked.

"Maud," she said, "Let's go."

"What happened to your hair?" Maud exclaimed.

"I'll tell you in the car."

"And that fabulous dress," Maud said, as if mesmerized
by the changes in Fortune.

"Home, Maud," said Fortune. "Let's go home."

"Tonight?"

"Right now. Sorry, Sophie. I just really need to go home."

"No problem," Sophie said comfortably. "Give my love
to everybody."

But once they were in the car, driving the three hours
back to Sky, Fortune found she couldn't talk at all. It was all
too raw, too painful. What she had thought she was running
away from when she woke up in the crossroads a year ago
had been patient. It had waited for her.

Maud seemed to understand, lost in her own set of rev-
elations. "I guess I'll have to talk to Low," she said. "I'd almost rather eat my own viscera."

"I'll drop you off," Fortune said.

"Don't leave me there!" Maud exclaimed. "Take me
home. I'll borrow Mama's van and go back."

"I'm glad you're doing it tonight."

"I'm *not* glad," said Maud. "But it has to be done."

It was past midnight when they got back to Sky. Fortune
drove up the road to Wolf's House and dropped Maud at the
Caldecotes'.

"I'm going to see Lightning," she said. "I might as well tell you. I don't think I'll be coming back tonight. Lightning and I are—"

"You're a thing," Maud said quickly. "I know. You'll—you'll make a beautiful couple."

"Thank you, honey." Fortune gave Maud a quick hug. "Now scoot. I've got to get up to the Mansion."

Maud scooted, and Fortune drove off. Her ears popped as the road climbed. She hoped Lightning was up. She'd wake him up if he weren't. She didn't care, and she had a feeling he wouldn't mind. She pulled up next to the Mansion and shut off the engine. She was tired, tear-stained, and her dress was rumpled. One of her braids was loose and had slid over the tip of one ear. She blew her nose loudly. She tried to smooth her hair. She got out and smoothed her dress.

"Sleeping Beauty's had a hell of a night," she said.

Lightning opened the door and stood in the warm, lit doorway, looking at her with a welcoming smile on his face.

Author Biography

Holly Wade Matter's short fiction has appeared in *Asimov's Science Fiction*, *Century*, and the Bending the Landscape anthology series. She is a graduate of the University of Washington and of the Clarion West Writers Workshop. She has twice been awarded literary funding from the Seattle Office of Arts and Culture, and in 1998 she received a creative writing fellowship from the National Endowment for the Arts. She lives in Seattle with her husband Brad and two house rabbits.